What the cri... aying

"This bo... f reality, and the love sce... *Sensual Romance Reviews*

Ellora's Cave Publishing, Inc.
PO Box 787
Hudson, OH 44236-0787

ISBN # 1843605597

Swept Off Her Feet, 2003.

Swept Off Her Feet edited by Allie McKnight.
Cover art by Darrell King.

Warning: The following material contains strong sexual content meant for mature readers. *SWEPT OFF HER FEET* has been rated NC-17, erotic, by a minimum of three independent reviewers. We strongly suggest storing this book in a place where young readers not meant to view it are unlikely to happen upon it. That said, enjoy…

SWEPT OFF HER FEET

Written by

CAMILLE ANTHONY

Dedication

All my respect and love to Shadoe—you know why.

And to Allie. When I needed it, you pushed me; you consoled me, cried with me and took away my ellipses. Thank you.

Author's Note

Throughout the text there are a number of Rbquarmli words and phrases. I have included a glossary for your convenience. Enjoy!

Prologue

Planet Rb'qarm, One Fael after the surrender of Rb'nTraq

His world was in chaos.

Sick at heart, young Prince Glendevtorvas exited the prison cell of the high-caste Lord Glentereion, jaw clenched tight against the urge to release his rage and pain. The gloating captive had just confirmed the reality of the threat the prince had received anonymously. After years of grueling, relentless battle, Glendevtorvas and his loyal warriors had finally won the generations-long civil war, but since hearing the information the defeated general had smugly imparted, the victory had chilled to bitter ashes, leaving a nasty taste in Glendevtorvas' mouth.

Lord General Glentereion had been happy to inform the young warrior-prince of the Lord General's brilliantly laid plans. Glendevtorvas had listened in growing horror to the story of how, even as the enemy fell in final defeat, a suicide taskforce had been dispatched to loose a heinous revenge: they'd introduced an insidious poison into the atmospheric cycle of the *Rb'qarmshi* home world. The poison, tasteless and deadly, was even now entering the food chain. Once situated, it would attack one specialized marker on the DNA thread of every *Rb'qarmshi fem*, destroying their ability to flower, thus rendering all *fem*—and their male counterparts—sterile.

Having lost their revolt, the enemy cared not that they condemned themselves as well.

What in the hurdles of *Pythin* could these people have been thinking, targeting *fem* as their victims? Glendevtorvas shook his head in horrified disbelief over the unfairness of his world's fate. Were he and his friends never to have a mate…never to sire children?

He had to remember that throughout his two worlds, males would suffer through this tragic time along with the *fem* in their lives. It was his job to comfort his people, yet in his secret heart the prince doubted his ability to serve his people effectively.

The war that had raged for over two hundred years was finished, but unless a miracle came along, so, too, was the *Rb'qarmshi* race…

Earth, San Francisco, May 10, 2005

The heat of the wreck was horrific. A disjointed, garish jumble of fractured memories coalesced into choppy action upon the screen of Glennora's dreaming mind, and she moaned, seeing herself as a young child thrown from a wrecked conveyance with great force. Nnora winced as she heard, recalled, a whimper of pain escaping bruised lips, saw a tiny thumb popping free of plump baby lips.

"Mama!" Nnora understood her dreaming self to call – the instinctual cry of a hurt, lost child.

While asleep, she always knew and could understand the conversation, though when she awoke, she could never recall the words. Her waking mind erased the experience every morning.

"Get…back! Get…free…child of…mine," groaned a voice, harsh and weak sounding to Nnora's dreaming ears.

She watched helplessly as her younger dream-self ignored the command, falling on unsteady feet as she tried to reach the one who represented comfort and care, wandering perilously close to the raging flames ignited by the spilled fuel.

"Mama!"

A blackened hand reached to push her away, yet the child persisted. Nnora wailed along with her child-self at the ringing slap falling on soft cheeks and echoing in a troubled memory.

Never struck before, her child-self screamed with the grief of betrayal and hurt.

Again, the harsh whisper to leave came.

Her dream-self, the child, could not recognize her mother in the bloody, blackened thing that warned her away with the life-giving sting of rejection. The adult, watching, but unable to comfort, could not impart her understanding. Sobbing aloud, Nnora watched her dream-self back away, still calling piteously for the one who had never before deserted her...

Planet Rb'qarm, Three Fael after the surrender of Rb'nTraq

Thirteen cycles, roughly twenty Earth years, had passed since the ending of the *Rb'nTraq* Rebellion. Both *Rb'nTraq* and *Rb'qarm,* their citizenry decimated by the military actions seen during battle and the introduction of the *Rb'nTraq* Solution, were fighting a desperate war of survival.

The poison, though it had been quickly neutralized upon discovery and isolation, had done its work too well. Search as they might, the coalition of *Rb'qarmshi-Rb'nTraqi* doctors and scientists had not been able to find a single viable *fem.*

An older, grimmer Prince-Regent Glendevtorvas—along with his cabinet and both castes of Lords—strove desperately to find answers to the "solution." He was determined, somehow, to avert the extinction of his people.

To that end, he had accepted the role of Regent from his father so he could ram his aggressive programs of reunification and rebuilding down the throats of both sets of High-Caste Lords and Ladies. Loyal to his father's vision of a peaceful coexistence of *Rb'nTraq* and *Rb'qarm*, he allowed no one to trespass his laws of tolerance and forgiveness.

With that stern, implacable spirit, he had ruthlessly quelled the uprisings of the *Rb'qarmshi* commoners, bent on venting their ire on their innocent *Rb'nTraqi* counterparts. The social programs were in place and functioning, yet still the populace was in turmoil. The suicide rate increased daily. Many among the infected *fem*, confronted with a lifetime of loneliness, had chosen to end their existence, thus adding to the pain and loss of the already emotionally overwhelmed masses. Young men, destined to live their lives alone, turned to mayhem and crime, and kept the warrior caste busy policing their sectors and ensuring the safety of the citizens of the different wards.

Lonely and frustrated, a large portion of his youth bled away in service to his people, Glendevtorvas was often tempted to give up. Then a pleading look, a sobbing father, brother, mate or child would look to him for solace, for answers—and he knew he could not stop until he found a way out of this terrible chaos…

Earth, San Francisco, May 20, 2005

"Nnora, wake up! It's just a dream, Nnora!"

"I'm okay… I'm good. Thanks, Lori. I'm awake now."

"You sure you're okay?"

"I'm fine. Honestly."

Glennora endured the intense study her sister subjected her to, knowing Lori would not leave until she was convinced of her "little" sister's emotional well-being. She slumped in relief when her concerned sibling nodded her satisfaction and left her side to return to her own bed. Nnora continued to suppress her shudders and hold her breath until she heard her foster sister settle down in her bed. She didn't want to disturb Lori's sleep any further.

Her foster sib would be up early, preparing her speech as the keynote speaker at some highbrow biochemical symposium scheduled for eight a.m. Lori's peers and clients put extraordinary demands on her time—she had a grueling schedule that Wonder Woman would have found hard to keep up with. The last thing she needed to be doing was coddling a grown woman with nightmares. Nnora was too proud of Lori's achievements to allow her own dysfunctional needs to interfere with her sister's career.

Glennora sat up amid her tousled bed covers, scrubbing her face free of tears. Drawing an uneven breath, she fought to clear her mind and calm her agitated emotions. It was hard to do. The sights and smells and feelings of the recurring dream were so…overwhelming. The sudden reappearance of the childhood dream had to be due to her upcoming trip to Mars. The journey would mark the first time she'd returned to the world that had been her home as an infant and she was naturally feeling some anxiety.

She was of two minds. She wanted to go—she didn't want to go. Oh, she wanted to see her half-sibs and her father and his wife, again, but she was afraid seeing the palace and the surrounding grounds would bring back memories she couldn't cope with.

Damn. I've finally adjusted to this world! I don't want my life to change!

Nnora straightened her covers, turned, pounded her pillow and threw herself back down. She knew she wouldn't sleep anymore tonight. Once awakened, her body had quickly made its needs known. Her mound felt heavy and tender, her empty vagina throbbed and wept. The plump flesh of her breasts was swollen and achy, and her nipples drew tighter and stiffer as she lay with her hands clasped beneath her head, determined not to touch herself.

She was in heat.

Like a damned cat, she wanted some cock. Tonight. *Now.* Unlike a cat, however, Nnora knew from painful experience that not just any Tom would do. It would take *Rb'qarmshi* cock to ease the growing, insistent ache gnawing at the tender flesh between her clenched thighs.

Why are males so stupid? Why did they have to kill each other off until there were no grown males left? Well, no grown males I can mate with! Father isn't in the mix and his cronies are too damned old. Nnora almost laughed aloud remembering the old wrinkled-up fossil that had propositioned her with talk of lapping up her juices. "Eeuww! Not living…not even when I'm dead," she whispered, spreading her thighs to ease the constriction of her labia.

The problem was, even that decrepit old dinosaur was beginning to look palatable.

She hurt.

With a despairing cry quickly muffled behind her left fist, Nnora slipped her hand between her legs, fingering open her tender folds. The cool air washing over her distended clit caused her to shudder. Her hips jerked upward to meet her teasing fingers.

"Go slow, go slow!" she chanted under her breath, forcing her hand to pause. "Make it last!" But she already knew tonight was going to be a Jumbo night. Reaching to the concealed panel in her headboard, Nnora drew out the pouch that held her favorite lubrication gel and the dildo she had nicknamed Jumbo. Twelve inches long with a circumference of four inches, Jumbo was a state-of-the-art, battery-driven wonder. Made of the newest real-skin material, it was warm and velvety soft on the outside, hard as plasteel on the inside. The piece de resistance was the head section with the accordion action.

Yep, Jumbo had cost her a pretty penny, but it was money well spent. Nnora couldn't help the hungry sigh that slipped past her lips as she rubbed the slick head between her labia and against her clitoris. She positioned the cock at her seeping entrance, canting her hips up as her free hand pressed down on the sensitive swell of her belly. The tension sent a delicious thrill all through her lower body and up into her jutting breasts. A deft thrust sent the dildo surging up into the clasping grip of her needy vagina.

Yeah! Fill my pussy up. Get in there and pump! That's what I like...nice thick cock reaming me! Nnora bit her bottom lip, the slight pain helping her focus, keeping her cries sub-vocal as she pumped her arousal higher with her naughty thoughts and her steady thrusting of Jumbo. A flick of the remote started the head action, and Nnora wedged the pseudo-cock up to its hilt, the pleasure rolling and swelling within as, crossing her ankles to hold the thick cock within her, she undulated against it. She shimmied her hips and torso to intensify the sensations of the dong within her hot, wet sheath while her nipples throbbed and burned, aching with unfulfilled need. She pinched and tugged on them, massaging them with the palms of her hands, frantic to reach the taunting, always retreating finish line of orgasmic completion.

Something was missing…something elusive, just out of her reach…and she didn't know what it was, only knew she needed it desperately.

Her nipples peaked, stabbing toward the ceiling as her legs stiffened and jerked. Her pussy clamped down on the dildo, squeezing in a rhythmic pulsating beat as fire flashed through her nerve endings. Even as she convulsed with the first of a building series of orgasms, a new ache began, tormenting and teasing Nnora with the itching, burning need for more.

She needed more…a partner…a lover. The lifeless cock between her legs mocked her attempt at satisfaction. Without the missing emotional attachment, the orgasms were unsatisfying and unfulfilling. Sobbing as she came, Nnora turned her head to the side and allowed her silent tears to soak into the pillow…

Planet Rb'qarm, Royal Palace, Four Fael after the surrender of Rb'nTraq

The announcement by a diligent archivist of the possibility of a long-forgotten colony of rebels electrified the two planets. It had begun as a rumor. "There was another rebellion...a thousand years back...exiles...whole family groups...enough to start a colony..."

During the thousand years since the exiled renegade group of families had been placed aboard ships and aimed toward a distant star, they must surely have given birth to *fem*...had they not perished in the interim. Those *fem* would be free from the taint of the war.

Actual records of the group of dissenters had been hard to unearth, but a diligent search, led by his father, finally revealed the story of a royal sibling exiled after an abortive attempt to usurp the throne. The lords that had sided with the ousted princess had been banished alongside her and her family. She and her followers had chosen life over death, had opted to board a generation ship—navigational system disabled and aimed toward a cluster of far-away worlds—to make a one-way trip. The dispossessed Princess would have a chance to claim and rule a queendom of her own if her group could survive.

Hope flared in the hearts of the multitudes. Young men trained hard, competing for coveted spots as warriors and crew for the flotilla forming under Prince-Regent Glendevtorvas' command. The flagship would head an armada of twenty satellite ships, jointly crewed by *Rb'qarmshi* and *Rb'nTraqi* crews.

Determined to find and repatriate the long-lost colony, Prince-Regent Glendevtorvas prepared to set forth, armed with marriage contracts and an edict from his father to return home with a royal bride. Such were his intentions. Be she ugly, misshapen and deformed, he would embrace any *fem* capable of holding and nurturing his seed, of softening his *terat*. His *cherzda* rose and hardened in anticipation—he fought a constant battle to conceal his readiness from his entire personal cadre of fifty elite warriors. All of his men would accompany him on this trip, their loyalty through the years having earned them the right—behind himself—of finding brides from among the outcasts.

The night before they set forth, Glendevtorvas met with his father.

"This is the only hope left to our race, my son," the retired *Chyya* commented in his scholarly voice. "You must deal with a rebellious colony of our distant genetic brothers and sisters who might care nothing for our plight. Talk marriage, first. Peace and compromise. Only should those diplomatic overtures fail are you to talk war."

"I hear your counsel, Father, and find wisdom in your words. Truly, I am sick to *Deth* of war and would seek out no new conflict. Yet, more than my tiredness of warfare, I am weary of the constant loneliness my life has been these last twenty years. Diligently hope we find this colony, Father. Hope they are willing to come to our aid. Because I cannot vouchsafe the survival of my honor should they have what we need, and deny us…"

Chapter One

"Of all the days to be late," Glennora muttered under her breath, shifting her packages to fumble in her purse for her keys.

"Gotcha!" she waggled the keys in triumph. "*Damned* chemical spill…and isn't it just my luck getting caught in the worst traffic jam San Francisco's seen in a year. Sure put paid to that long, soaking bath I'd planned."

Conscious of the relentless passage of time, of the countdown to departure-hour, she wrestled the front door open and rushed into her apartment, dumping an armload of shopping and papers onto the coffee table. Toeing off her shoes, she quickly stripped, slinging clothes left and right in a trailing line from living room to bathroom as she rushed towards the shower.

She ducked her head as she whipped past the ornamental hall mirror, deliberately avoiding the disappointing image reflected in the glass—no time to waste bemoaning her looks, something she couldn't change. She hurried on into the bathroom, again averting her eyes, her many full-length reproductions in the mirrored walls, shaking her head and harrumphing as she recalled Lori's oft repeated attempts to make her feel beautiful. Her sister's groove-worn phrase was: "Nnora, you have an otherworldly beauty which defies description."

Yeah, right! she snickered as she gathered her washcloth and towel. Defies description as in, no one can think up a way to describe me without hurting my feelings.

Despite her foster sib's soft-hearted compliments, Nnora knew she was no great exotic beauty. Standing at an even seven feet and tipping the scales at two hundred, thirty-eight pounds, she figured she had a long wait before her prince came along to sweep her off her feet.

The grandfather clock in her living room struck the half hour. She brought her wrist up and glanced at her watch. "Good lord! Look at the time!"

Unlatching the band of her timepiece, she leaned over the sink and popped out her custom-made colored contacts. In her hurry, her clumsy fingers took longer at the task than usual. After rinsing and storing them away in their small carrying case, she tossed them into the back of the medicine cabinet and closed the door with a satisfied dusting of her hands.

Her 20/20 vision did not require assistance and she hated wearing the contacts, whose sole purpose was to make her eyes appear human—normal. To add insult to injury, she had to use the daily wear kind since her eyes could not tolerate the extended wear brand of contacts.

"Yes!" She pumped a fist in the air, exulting over the fact that, as of three hours ago, she had officially begun her summer-long vacation. She gleefully anticipated three months of freedom from the irksome daily contact routine…among other things.

A small zip of excitement ripped through her as she stepped into the glassed-in shower cubicle and adjusted the thermostat with a practiced twist to the sleek, faux gold handles.

Hot water gushed out, cascading down her long black hair, sheeting over her quivering body. She lifted her face into the spray, eyes half-closed against the streaming water and allowed the flow to relax her tension-knotted muscles. After a long sybaritic moment under the pounding spray, she turned and presented her back to the downpour, groaning softly as the water's massage aroused her sensitive nerve-endings.

Methodically squeezing shower gel onto her bath sponge, she lathered vigorously, scrubbing until her skin glowed, all the while trying to ignore her peaking nipples and seeping cunt.

How ironic, she thought, re-soaping her sponge and attacking her legs. Now that I am coming to grips with my life, no longer Jones-ing for what I can't have, I find out I'm more alien than I ever imagined.

As it turned out, not only she was an alien Princess from Mars, she was a Princess in sexual heat. Horny as a she-cat and mad as hell about the situation.

This entire situation went against the grain of what she felt was her nature. Like the foster mom who'd raised her, she prided herself on being pragmatic and down-to-earth. She didn't consider herself to be flighty, a woman easily swept off her feet...romantically or otherwise. So she was not best pleased with the discovery that she would have to go through these cycles of *pava*—the *Rb'qarmshi* version of ovulation the women of her race underwent every one point five Earth years—twice more before she could hope for relief.

She had also learned that while in *pava*, in addition to her breasts and pussy, every inch of her skin—especially her scalp and shoulders—became erotically sensitive areas, responsive to the lightest touch. Having learned the mind-stealing pleasure she gained from masturbation carried a high price, she tried not to stimulate herself too much. Every orgasm wore off more quickly, the unfulfilling pleasure rapidly giving way to the relentless, knife-sharp ache of escalating need. Her father's colony boasted not a single eligible male to assuage her biologically induced lusts, and she'd learned the hard, humiliating way that a human male couldn't assuage her heat. Her unlamented ex-husband, Ronald "the Rocket" Waldon had been the proof of that.

Of course, she'd gained all this information after having suffered ignorantly through her first *pava*. Before entering *pava*, she had felt mild arousal and sexual desire as she matured—after all, watching Arnold Schwarzenegger materialize as a naked cyborg was enough to spark the gonads of any breathing, ovulating female—but she had never experienced anything like the passionate, all-consuming yearnings that flamed hotly under her skin, stoked and fueled by her body's biological imperative to breed, to take a mate.

She'd met Ronald half way through her first year-long cycle. Tortured with the incessant, burning, aching needs of her newly awakened body, Nnora had thought the husky pro basketball player to be the answer to her insecure, romance-starved dreams. Instead, he'd been her monumental marital mistake. Nearing the end of his less than illustrious career, Ron had wooed her with a player's practiced ease, scheming to bolster his failing earnings with her foster-family's money. Unfortunately, she hadn't learned the truth of Ron's machinations until after their marriage ceremony.

Oh, he had fooled her good. He had seemed so sincere, or perhaps—she was now able to admit to herself—she had been desperate for affection and acceptance. She had wanted to be normal…and there was nothing more normal than marriage. Right?

Ron's flattering lies, coupled with the desperate sexual hunger of her first *pava*, had made her capitulation to his studied seduction a sure bet. The intensely physical side effects of her sexual heat hadn't helped her rational thinking processes much and she acknowledged, ruefully, that she had been a ripe plum for Ron's picking.

Almost from the moment she said "I do" the relationship ran into problems, translating her dream of normalcy into nightmarish reality. Recalling the emotional desolation of those days, she swallowed sickly, leaning her head against the tiled wall of the shower and let the echoes of her ex-husband's angry accusations reverberate in her mind.

Grip me tighter, damn it! I'm swimming around in here. No way were you a virgin, Nnora. My own hand is tighter, you whoring slut! You're looser than a two-bit Harlem prostitute…

She idly swirled the cloth about her belly, lost in dark memories, wishing for the hundredth time she had learned the truth of her otherworldly heritage before embarking on her marriage fiasco. She'd been a virgin—still was, for that matter.

How could she have known the vast difference between her body's internal scale and that of a human woman's? Who would have guessed that Ron's cock—while impressive on a human scale—was incapable of matching her pussy's dimensions and could not meet her fevered needs, let alone extend far enough to breech her maidenhead?

After a few months of mounting frustrations and increasing bitterness on both their parts, the marriage had dissolved by mutual disagreement. Her foster family, in their uniquely wonderful ways, had formed a solid wall of support for her.

Explaining the break-up to her sister, Nnora had half-joked, "I guess I never stroked his ego enough, and he sure as hell never managed a stroke deep enough to *reach* my sexual cravings...let alone appease them."

Poppi Brewster, bless him, had absently noted that the divorce had taken longer than the entire marriage, then offered to hire some goons to rough Ron up.

However, her fondest memory was of Hattie Brewster herding her into the kitchen for one of her "momma-daughter" talks, sitting her down and gazing deeply into her eyes as if to assess the damage to her baby. Her foster mother, who had been vehemently against the marriage from the start, held her hand as she said, "Nnora, you just came through a mighty troubling time. Much as I wanted to steer you clear of this mess, it was your mess to deal with. Now, before you go off getting into some more mess, I have a story to tell you."

Nnora had settled down to listen, knowing the futility of trying to rush her mother. "All right, Mom, I am all ears."

"It was winter time and a newborn chick was freezing. He cried out for help. A cow, hearing the chick's cry, took pity on the little one and dropped a load of manure over the baby. Well, that made the little thing furious and while it sat in the steaming pile, fuming at the cow, a fox came along and plucked it out. Before the chick could say 'thank ye kindly', the fox quickly brushed the manure off the chick and ate it. And the moral of the story is: not everyone who drops a load of shit on your head means bad by you, and not everyone who plucks you up out of a pile of shit is doing you a favor."

Nnora remembered she'd felt a headache pounding behind her eyes. "Mom, I keep trying to associate this with my problem, but I just don't get it."

Mom Brewster had slapped her knees and pushed herself away from the table. "You thought you were pretty miserable not having any boyfriends or going on dates. Then along came that fox, Ronald and plucked you up. He dumped a whole load of dirt on you, as if making you feel an inch high added to his own height. Compared to what that devil was shoveling, that first pile of manure ain't looking so bad, is it, baby?"

"No, Ma'am!" Nnora had meekly replied. When Mom Brewster—world-renowned biochemist responsible for decoding the final key element of the human genome—spoke Ebonics, Nnora listened.

Before they left the kitchen, Mom had also addressed her fears of going home. "No matter where you go, you are always going to be our baby. Nothing's going to change that, Nnora. You just stop your fretting and go meet your other family. Your Daddy's been struggling to climb out of a pile of shit, too. You can either help each other out, or wallow in it. What's it going to be?"

Mom had been right, Nnora acknowledged, stepping under the spray to rinse off the peach scented suds. She had been afraid that embracing her biological family would mean losing her adoptive one. Fortified with her Mom's reassurances, she found it easier to anticipate the upcoming trip with a growing amount of pleasure.

Mom was right about so many things. Her life pre-Ronald hadn't been too bad. Since her failed marriage, she'd taken the time to appreciate what she had and find contentment in simply being herself. She had friends she had gained while in college and more importantly, she had a loving relationship with her foster family.

Perhaps most important, her failed marriage had driven home the fact that, annoying *pava* cycles aside, she simply wasn't the passionate type—she just hadn't cared that much that she couldn't get off with Ron.

Lost in thought, she yelped in surprise when the water suddenly turned from warm to icy cold. Ruefully cursing her wandering attention, she skipped back and away from the chilly downpour.

Reaching at arm's length to shut off the water, she hugged the back of the stall, determinately abandoning her painful train of thought. "I am damned sure not going to allow any past misfortunes to add to my worries concerning this coming trip."

Groping blindly for a towel, she snatched one off the warming rack. Wrapping her dripping hair in the warm terry cloth, she vigorously rubbed the moisture from her knee-length tresses, closing her contact-free eyes in blissful pleasure. She twisted a bath sheet about her chilled body, reveling in the instant warmth.

She stepped out of the shower and flipped on the overhead fan to dissipate the swirls of steamy mist floating on the ceiling. Bending under the sink, she took out the hairdryer for a quick blow-dry, careful to minimize the stimulation to her scalp.

Clenching her teeth, she fought the urge to fondle the beaded tips of her aching breasts, knowing just how fleeting the momentary relief would be. The flow of warm air wafting over her hair and scalp made her stomach muscles clench, squeezing a dollop of heated cream from her empty vagina. She squirmed, rubbing her thighs together, and the movement applied unintentional pressure to her aching clit. The pleasure slammed through her, weakening her knees and her determination.

She gave up trying to resist turning the blower nozzle of the hair dryer towards her spasming cunt. Dropping her towel, she played the sultry air across her swollen labia, letting it caress her throbbing vagina, and surrendered to the resulting volcanic rise of passion.

It felt so good.

She widened her stance, half-squatting against the cool tile of the wall as she played the warm breeze over her sensitive labia. Her clitoris swelled and stiffened, poking from beneath its protective hood. She held herself open with two fingers of her left hand while employing her middle finger to stab at the stiffened bundle of nerves, alternately circling it then pressing it hard against the floor of her pubic bone.

"Hhhmmmmm, sooo *goood*!" she whimpered, continuing to stimulate her ravenous cleft as the hot air blasted the folds of her pussy. She licked her lips, wetting the parched flesh as she ruthlessly directed the stream of heated air so it flowed over her aching clit and pussy. Placing the nozzle closer to her weeping entrance, her free hand forced her lips wide open, allowing the contrived breeze to blast its way into her hungry depths.

Her hips rocked forward as she sought to deepen the sultry contact, every move and every action only making her hotter and more needful of relief.

With a broken sob, wishing it were a lover's hand entering her, pleasuring her, she thrust two fingers into the liquid depths of her pussy, working them up and in. Moaning, she pumped her fingers in a frantic rhythm that soon had her hips bucking in a wild dance of arousal. Her inner muscles clenched as an upsurge of lustful explosions whipped through her, causing her fingers to spasm. The hair dryer slid from her slack grasp, thumping onto the carpeted floor while she brought both hands into play, one pinching and twisting first one then the other of her long, erect nipples, the other busying itself between the dripping folds of her rippling sex.

Stabbing pleasure darted from the hard tips of her breasts to explode in the clasping depths of her aching pussy. With a tortured gasping cry, she slumped against the wall, her breathing choppy and labored as she rode out the bucking thrill ride of a prolonged, explosive orgasm. Every inch of her body sizzled and sparked, quaking with multiple detonations of a pleasure so intense, it almost stole her reason.

Boneless with her momentary satiation, Nnora floated on a wave of euphoria.

* * * * *

Prince Glendevtorvas fumed as he led his small contingent of warriors past the saluting guards. He'd hoped to have time to court the *fem* fate had chosen as his *cherzda'va*. GanR'dari's news blasted those hopes. Newly explosive tempers and seditious events back home required his immediate presence. There would be no time to woo and win the good favor of the Princess he hoped to mate with.

With a regal nod of his head, Dev gestured the guards assigned to Glennora's safety off duty, replacing them with his own men. Narrow-eyed, he made sure the three colonists embarked on the vessel he'd designated to return them to their *Chyya*, Brevchanka. Satisfied the males were indeed gone, he ordered his men to deploy themselves about the living room and signaled to his second-in-command to follow him as he went in search of his future queen.

As they moved through her small apartment, Dev noticed the understated elegance with which Glennora had decorated her home. Each piece seemed to fit, to dovetail with every other element creating a seamless whole—a home not merely a house. His eyes took in everything, analyzing carefully every iota of information that pertained to his future mate. With each passing moment, he grew more anxious to meet her.

From the corner of his eye, Dev saw GanR'dari raise his right hand, signaling a halt. Catching the eye of his second-in-command, Dev quirked his eyebrow in question. When his friend gestured towards the closed door, Dev quietly crept forward, silently ordering GanR'dari to remain where he was.

The sound of running water assaulted his keen hearing as he approached the second door in the hallway. With stealth honed on the battlefield, he quietly turned the doorknob and eased the door open. The crack afforded him a glimpse into the room beyond the door, without betraying his presence on the other side. His breathing quickened. His heart slammed against his chest, beating a rapid tattoo at the incredible sight of the naked figure of the woman he would soon be bonded with.

Mouth going dry, he swallowed thickly, almost choking on a lump of lust. He grew instantly hard, his *cherzda* rising strong and vigorous, straining against the confining material of his jeans. Determined to see more, he moved closer to the crack in the doorway.

Glennora—with her long black hair curling under the plump, round globes of the most beautiful ass he'd ever seen—almost floored him. Holding his breath lest his panting give away his position, he watched as the *fem* ran a soapy cloth over her abundant curves. Her body, small and delicate, more finely formed than the *Rb'qarmshi* norm, twisted and turned under the spray of water, droplets glistening and highlighting her flesh. Her breasts were soft-looking creamy mounds, topped with inch-long jutting nipples. Her arms were gently rounded and her long legs and thighs nicely fleshed. Sweat sheeted his forehead as Dev envisioned her trim ankles wrapped about his waist as he sank into her luscious-smelling heat.

When she began to rub her cleansing cloth slowly across the concave valley of her belly, he released his held breath, mouth falling agape as his gaze was dragged in the wake of those trailing fingers. He didn't think he could stand it when she leaned against the cubicle wall and let her head fall back against the tile, the saddest expression he'd ever witnessed dampening the natural glow of her beauty. He wanted nothing more than to fling the door open and gather her in his arms, promising her that nothing would hurt her while in his care.

Glennora let out a yelp.

His nerves jumped. Was he discovered?

Peering through the crack, he saw her half-leap away from the cascading water to huddle at the back of the small space, muttering something under her breath about past mistakes and trips.

He figured out the stream had grown cold when he saw the raised flesh on her shivering body as she gingerly reached to shut off the spray. He drew back some, allowing the bulk of the door to shield him while she grabbed a towel and vigorously rubbed her long tresses with it before stepping out of the shower and retrieving a machine shaped like a pulsar gun. His fingers itched to thread through the drying mass while she employed the machine to hasten the drying of her hair. He longed to sink his hand in her hair and discover whether the strands were as soft and silky as they appeared.

He almost swallowed his tongue when she let the towel drop and began running the barrel of the dryer up and down her body, paying close attention to her nipples and her flowering *pava*.

Tears flooded his eyes as his nostrils flared; he drank in her heady, life-affirming scent. It had been more than twenty years since he had smelled the intoxicating aroma of a *fem's* flowering *pava*.

Eyes locked on her writhing form, he lowered his hands to his jeans-covered *cherzda* and palmed his demanding bulge. Leaning closer to the door, trying not to miss a moment, he felt his *terat* constricting, felt the tingling as they roared to life and softened. He barely managed to bite back a groan as he witnessed her solitary dance.

His own tears fell as he watched her slump down in utter despair after the last tremor of ecstasy faded away. He felt so connected to her, could almost read her thoughts.

He hurt for her.

Carefully, quietly, he eased away from the door. By *Deth*'s gate! She would never again have occasion to suffer through her *pava*, alone and lonely.

His plan to deliver her to her father changed in that moment.

* * * * *

Nnora rose at last from her crouched position, biting back a harsh moan as intimate muscles twanged and pulled. She bent over to retrieve the hair dryer, moving like a tired, old woman. She sighed worriedly as she turned the appliance off, wrapping the cord around the squat round barrel before storing it away. The pleasurable relief had not lasted nearly long enough.

Only twenty days into this second, yearlong *pava*, already she'd reached the level of constant arousal it had taken five months to arrive at during her first cycle. How was she to survive this constant agony of desire without losing her mind?

"Thank goodness," she murmured, reaching for the moisturizing lotion, "my biological father never stopped searching for me. If only there were more males like my father… Now, Dad is a major hunk!"

With a fond smile, she recalled her shocked disbelief when a gorgeous, seven-and-a-half-foot tall man had knocked on her foster parents' door, asking after the child they had taken in almost twenty years before.

On him, her height and brilliantly-colored eyes looked damn good. The king, her father, looked entirely too young to have sired her, but there was no denying their relationship once he had shown her the birthmark he bore upon his left flank—the same blood red, three-pronged flower that graced her rounded thigh. The mark, passed down through the royal family, was the mark of a ruler, or a potential ruler. *Rb'qarmshi* custom, her father had said, allowed only one who bore it to rule.

No matter how glad she had been to see him, her father had returned to Mars with his hopes of reuniting her with his new family unrealized. She'd refused to leave with him. After prolonged and escalating arguments, he had finally accepted her rejection, if not with good grace, then with diplomatic patience.

On his second visit, the *Chyya* sweetened the pot by introducing her to her three half-blood siblings and to their mother, the woman he had married once his grieving period for his lost queen was done.

At first, intimidated by the new queen-consort's height—she stood almost eight feet tall—Nnora had been reluctant to approach her, but the queen had proven to be a sweetie. Once past Nnora's initial wariness, Nnora and the queen had taken to each other, both thankful the other was willing to be friendly.

For Nnora's part, she was glad her stepmother was willing to share her knowledge of *Rb'qarmshi* biology. It was from Queen Rinalli that Nnora learned she had at least two more cycles—six Earth years—to endure before the eldest of the young *Rb'qarmshi* males would reach sexual maturity.

The queen had informed a despairing Nnora of the current dearth of eligible males. She blamed the shortage on the stupidity of males in general—and the long, violent rebellion that had caused Nnora's father to send her and her mother away to safety specifically. Raging over fifty years, the fraternal war had cost the colony greatly in the lives of its viable males. Their loss rendered the settlers ominously short of diverse genes. This lack had placed the future of the colony in grave jeopardy.

"Heaven help me," Nnora groaned. "Two more cycles! If each *pava* grows with this degree of intensity…"

She frowned as she heard the self-pity in her words. "Damn! I hate a whiner. Get a grip, Nnora," she fussed, addressing her image, her voice echoing loudly in the steamy bathroom. "What the hell do you have to cry about? You're luckier than most."

She giggled, thinking of what Lori would say should she come in and hear her talking to herself. She didn't care. She needed this pep talk, needed to reiterate her blessings.

"I've survived a shuttle-wreck, survived losing my real family and history and survived being different. I have weathered being alone in a world of strangers, have overcome the rejection of my childhood peers and on top of all that, I managed to find the best foster family in the world. I have a mother and a father who truly love me, as well as a cherished sister who helped nurture me through those rocky first years.

"Now I have an adventure to look forward to. In less than an hour, Father's ship will be arriving to transport me to his kingdom on the planet Mars. What are a few pesky *pava* cycles compared to that?"

I can hardly wait to see what outer space is really like! Does the Earth really look like a green and blue jewel, or is that just T.V. special effects? Wonder if I can talk the pilot into stopping off by the Moon for some pictures—I'd like to see the landing site where they planted the American flag.

She playfully hummed the music from the *Twilight Zone* series as she finished applying a silky lotion to her long limbs. She switched over to the theme music of her favorite sci-fi show, *Star Trek,* giving full voice to her excitement.

"Dum-de-duuum-de-dum-dum-de-duuum-de-*duhm...de-duuuhm*! Space... The final frontier," she intoned solemnly, snatching up the hairbrush to serve as her microphone. "These are the voyages of the Starship Enterprise! Its five-year mission...to explore strange, new worlds...to seek out new life and new civilizations...to boldly go where no—me, me!—has gone before!"

Thrilled to be embarking on her own voyage to the strange new world of her forgotten homeland, Nnora tried to imagine what was in store for her. At last, she would see the home her mother's great-mother had established after being forcibly exiled from her home world.

Honestly, she hated the fact that, try as she might, she could not bring herself to forgive her father. Her inability to let go of the resentment of her past challenged her personal view of her character. Having been on the receiving end of injustice and prejudice, she demanded fairness in all her personal dealings, holding herself to a high standard of behavior. She squirmed within at the knowledge that she was not living up to her own expectations.

Worst, she knew her father did not deserve her censure, knew she should not blame him for acting in the only way open to him at the time. Yet, though she hated seeing the hurt look on his face every time she pulled back or eluded his embrace, she found herself unable to let go her anger and move beyond the hurts of the past.

Mr. Spock would say it was illogical to blame her father for abandoning her, for leaving her to live as a human. Her father had been forced to abandon the search, and intellectually, she even understood his need to order the destruction of the wreckage to prevent any humans from gaining evidence of their existence. The resulting blast had destroyed the possibility of searching the site for further clues of her survival and possible whereabouts, thus hindering his subsequent attempts at finding her. She still found it hard to believe her father had never given up searching for her, had designated a group of people to do nothing but search for clues for her existence, day in and day out, reading newspapers, analyzing headlines, leaving no stone unturned in a relentless search to find a child…or a body.

Emotionally, she still held the *Chyya* accountable for sending her and her mother away. His protective measures had backfired and she had ended up abandoned, deserted and alone, forced to adjust, to hide her alienness. In a harsh world, surrounded only by those unlike her, she had finally learned to view her unique differences—her height, her *pava*-driven sexuality, her glowing tangerine eyes—as ugly aberrations and genetic mutations.

Deep down, she knew she would eventually return to her father's kingdom to take her rightful place as his heir. The Brewsters had instilled a deep sense of duty in both their daughters and she knew her duty as well as the next woman. Much as they might wish her to stay with them, her foster family would never voice that plea. They expected her to do her duty and take up her role as a leader to her people.

And she would...eventually. But this year, she fully intended returning to Earth in time for the fall school session. This trip, much as her father might wish he could order differently, was a fact-finding visit during which she hoped to learn more of her true culture and heritage.

Sighing, she clicked off the whirring exhaust fan, gave a final swipe to the shower stall and finished tidying up the bathroom. Tossing her washcloth and hair towel over the appropriate rail and applying the Velcro fastening of her bath sheet under her arms, she flung open the bathroom door—

And plowed into the massive chest of the most gorgeous male she had ever seen.

Chapter Two

His iridescent eyes declared him to be *Rb'qarmshi*. And Glennora was sure this glorious specimen before her—taller and more broadly formed than any *Rb'qarmshi* warrior she had ever seen—outclassed them all. He literally stole her breath away, left her gasping in instant awe and lust.

The male towered over her, his head just clearing the eight-foot ceiling. Her neck arched as her head tilted, her disbelieving eyes tracking up and up his imposing body, over long firm legs, lingering on the junction of powerful thighs that nestled a masculine bulge graphically molded by constricting jeans. Her eyes skimmed across the broad chest straining the material of a tight black tee shirt, then roved over a face covered by darkly tanned skin that stretched without wrinkle over a pair of blade-sharp cheekbones. His lips were wide and square, the bottom one fuller than the top, and his eyelashes and brows were thick and heavy, dark as a moonless night.

Stunned by the visual feast before her, she lifted her awed gaze again to the man's golden-bronze eyes, finding them as alien as her own when not disguised by the hated contacts...and hotly returning her frank perusal with a heated male stare that reminded her she was covered only by a skimpy towel.

She clutched the terry wrap against her chest with nervous fingers, accidentally scraping the rough material across her jutting nipples. In spite of her recent orgasm, need sparked along her nerve endings and she fought an involuntary shiver as prickling, tingling sensations rushed over her greedy flesh. In the strained stillness of the room, she became acutely aware of the man's pointed attention, felt his stare zeroing in on her stiffening crests.

She twitched her towel higher, her dry throat working to swallow the lump of lust threatening to choke her. Against her will, her gaze flicked down towards—then quickly away from—the stranger's jeans-covered groin where the thickening evidence of his maleness proved the sexual interest she was feeling to be mutual.

For an endless moment, she basked in a fantasy world where this huge male found her attractive, perhaps as attractive as she was finding him. Then her euphoria was shattered as she abruptly realized there was a *mature male* standing in her bedroom.

An uninvited man, a very *big* man, who had invaded her private space…and she had no way of knowing if he was friend or foe.

Backing away from the intruder, she assumed her haughty look—the one Lori called her "Royal Princess expression". Her voice not quite steady, she asked, "How dare you violate my privacy and enter my chambers without permission?"

Her question seemed to go right over the man's head. She wasn't even sure he had heard her. He was too busy growling something in his dark, husky voice, his eyelids slowly closing as his nostrils flared, chest rising on a deeply inhaled breath.

Good Lord! Was he sniffing at her?

He continued to speak and she found herself ensorcelled by the sheer loveliness of the sounds pouring from that beautiful mouth. Even his gruff, masculine tone could not detract from the splendor of the otherworldly cadence of—

A momentary panic dumped ice water upon her enchantment with the liquid, musical language pouring from the stranger. My father's edicts expressly forbid our language—Rb'qarmli—to be spoken anywhere but on the colony world, and his commands have the force of law, binding on all loyal Rb'qarmshi. Who is this stranger? Why does he flaunt his king's command?

Her mouth tightened as she shook off her unusual bemusement, her eyes angrily narrowing at his daring affront. "Who are you and how dare you insult and dishonor your *Chyya* by ignoring his laws?"

The man's mobile lips stretched into a slight smile while his eyes twinkled. His coloring was very like hers. Dark hair and softly glowing tangerine eyes proclaimed their distant blood connection. A flushed heat warmed her cheeks when she noted his gaze, riveted on her mouth. The heat moved lower, brushing her nipples and pussy with a tingling warmth when he licked his lips. His broad tongue smoothed over his full bottom lip then made the reverse journey on the curved highway of his top lip.

She experienced an almost uncontrollable urge to feel those intriguing lips crushing her own…a burning desire to taste more than his damp lips. There were, literally, miles of skin she could explore and sample, given more time than she had available now.

She gave her head a quick, thought-clearing shake and sternly reined in her lust. She strove to keep her outward stance towards him cold—frigid as Ron had often accused her of being, though she wagered this male could heat her quickly enough, if she gave him leave.

"Forgive, Princess, the unavoidable intrusion of your privacy." The male's stiffly formal phrasing sounded as if he struggled with an unfamiliar language. "Assured be, I mean to *Chyya* Glenbrevchanka, no disrespect. Your father, Lady, is not *my* sovereign. His edicts are not my rule." He frowned. "Do you speak no *Rb'qarmli* at all?"

She shook her head. "Nope, I only understand fragments from before the crash, a baby's vocabulary. I do remember the word for 'mama', though."

The stranger made a disapproving noise and his frown deepened, darkening his handsome face when he heard her nonchalant statement. "That is a...shame, yet fixable. You will learn quickly. We have medicines that will assist. Until then, I continue to say words in this planet's barbaric tongue. You would understand my words of greeting to you?"

She was sure her expressive face informed her uninvited visitor how unhappy his choice of words made her. She didn't much care for the way he disparaged her adoptive planet, not to mention his matter-of-fact assumption that she would be learning the language just to converse with him. *Not living likely!*

"Well, don't make me wait all day," she snapped irritably. "If you have something to say, spit it out."

Even before his brows drew together in a look of reprimand, she modified her words, appalled at her rudeness. She'd been taught better. Just a few years ago, Mom Brewster would have served her a dose of manners applied to her backside with a long wooden spoon.

"Forgive me. Yes, I would like to understand what you said to me." It wasn't the thought of her foster mother's swift discipline that had her scrambling to apologize. Even as she heard her placating words, she marveled that a disapproving look from this man had her changing her attitude, striving to please him.

Glendevtorvas narrowed his eyes as he assessed the reactions from his future consort. She was proving to be a feisty *fem*, but he liked that about her. It would not do for his queen to be a *fem* easily led or controlled. Hers would be a supreme voice of power on two worlds, second only to his, and it was imperative she become accustomed to wielding authority.

It was easy for him to read Glennora's guilt-fed irritation. He'd been informed of her negative reaction when her *Chyya* had first suggested she learn *Rb'qarmli*, how she had stubbornly refused, choosing instead, to continue nursing her resentment towards all things *Rb'qarmshi*. He also knew of her intense curiosity involving all things new and out-of-the-ordinary. Her father had informed him that Glennora instructed younglings and like her charges, had an insatiable hunger for information.

Now he wondered if she wished she had been more receptive to her father's wishes. Not speaking the language would make communicating with her future subjects a difficult feat. Luckily, her sister, Dohsan, whom he knew had visited with Glennora numerous times during the last two earth cycles, spoke English like a native and would be an able translator. She had volunteered to accompany Glennora to *Rb'qarm*, and he had permitted this since he wanted his bride to settle quickly into her new life.

"Mere words cannot express your impact upon me. You are beautiful beyond my wildest dreams of womanhood, fully mature and ripe for mating. Even from across the room, the hot smell of your *pava's* flowering, your recent pleasuring, is drawing me to you—"

"What?"

"The smell of your spilled juices is ripe upon the air. You danced alone in the cleaning cubicle for the last time. From this moment, I will be the one, now and always, to ease your need."

Chapter Three

As the lyrical cadence of his accented English washed over Glennora in sensuous waves, her instincts for survival awoke, and she squinted in sudden suspicion.

Who the hell was this guy? How could he know she had masturbated earlier? She wanted to sink into the floor from embarrassment, yet at the same time, knowing he knew of her actions and had expressed the desire to join her made her hotter and more aroused then she'd ever been in her life.

She should send him on his way; refuse to tolerate his intrusive, sexually threatening presence a moment longer. She should demand he leave, yet...she couldn't bring herself to do so. Just the low rumble of his voice engendered a sensual trembling response in the pit of her stomach.

Even while she cursed her instant attraction for this luscious male eye-candy, cursed her ever rampant curiosity, she could not deny how desperately she wanted to know everything about this stranger. She found herself driven to find out what his uninvited male presence in her bedroom meant, to explore his reasons for being here, to find out if he were eligible! And if he were?

His words did wonderful things for her ego; still she well remembered how Ron—the only man who had ever complimented her so effusively—had done so with a hidden agenda. What was *this* man's agenda? After all, she was a royal princess, in line to rule an entire planet, harsh and un-giving as it was. What were his intentions?

The insurrection that had caused the *Chyya* to send away his vulnerable infant daughter had ended in defeat of the opposition two years ago. Yet, she knew, there remained a small number of rebels at large that refused to accept her father's rule and had recently threatened to attack him at his weakest point—his family. The *Chyya,* fearing for the safety of his children, insisted upon guarding all his children at all times. She'd balked at his attempt to surround her with bodyguards, certain she would be safe while away from Mars since she had never been bothered or approached before. She'd lost that one battle, and had since resigned herself to her new shadows—

Her guards! How could she have forgotten her guards? Where were they and how had this man gotten past them?

God, don't let them be lying dead somewhere!

She slowly, deliberately took a step back from the man, meeting his eyes with a fearful, yet head-on gaze. "If you are not one of my father's subjects, then you are truly a stranger. Who are you, and what do you want with me?"

One confident stride narrowed the distance between them, bringing the intruder into her personal space. His air of unconscious command managed to set her teeth on edge even while it prodded the drowsing beast of her sexual need.

"Again, I must apologize, Princess. Your beauty froze my words, else I would have made known myself, right away."

"Fine. Who the heck *are* you and how did you get past my guards?"

The man executed a bow that was elegant and practiced. "I am Prince Glendevtorvas abri' *Chyya* Quasharel, ruler of both *Rb'qarm* and—since the ending of a two hundred years' war—also the planet *Rb'nTraq*. Your *Chyya* gave me a writ of passage. Your guards have been ordered home."

The elevated position of her visitor startled her. His name bore the Glen-syllable proclaiming his first-born status as heir like her own. This man ruled the home planet! The planet her father still spoke of with reverence mixed with greed. She had never heard of that second planet.

At least that answered one of her questions. She had nothing this man didn't already possess. Her status might equal his but she could never outrank him.

She struggled to keep her eyes on the intruder's face, resisting the urge to sneak another peek at the impressive bulge stretching the taut fabric of the man's jeans. A good long look tempted her more than gathering information, but, hell. Duty called.

"Welcome to Earth, Prince Glendevtorvas. I am sure my father is pleased you made this journey, but what are you doing *here*…in my bedroom?"

The prince spoke a rapid sentence in *Rb'qarmshi* before he caught himself and switched to English. "I have come for *you*, Nnora."

His stark words hit her like a speeding train. She was no superwoman to sustain such a blow. Her heart tripped, threatening to pound its way out of her chest.

"Ex—excuse me. What did you say?"

Glendevtorvas chuckled, the sensuous rumble sounding downright dangerous to an already frazzled Nnora.

"I have placed my claim upon you. Already have your father-*Chyya* and mine written our mating contracts—"

"*What* mating contracts?" The fine hairs on her shoulders rose up, the question growled between her grinding teeth.

The prince ignored her less than flattering reaction and continued. "I can allow but a few minutes for you to choose things to bring. Or not." He shrugged. "As my queen, have you the choice from the bounty of ten worlds—"

The prince's words sank in. She was shocked. She didn't know whether to scream or laugh. Surely this was a monumental joke. She refused to believe her father had meant to use her as marriage bait. *Please, God,* she silently begged, *don't let this trip I have looked forward to so much be just a political ploy on my father's part.*

"Prince Glendevtorvas, you are out of your egotistical mind if you believe I will just pack up and go anywhere with you. I don't know you from… I don't know you at all.

"I don't know how the females on *Rb'qarm* or *Rb'nTraq* are treated, and I'm not really sure about the status of those on Mars, but I do know one thing—I make my own decisions. I won't allow any man, and that includes my father, that kind of power over my life. I—"

"*You* should do as you are told!" Glendevtorvas frowned down at her, crossing his arms, an emotion that looked a lot like exasperation deepening the striking orange of his eyes.

She mocked him, frowning back, barely resisting the urge to stick her tongue out at him. Shockingly, he gave her an approving smile when she did not back down from his intimidating glare.

"Your spirit pleases me. While your surliness does not, I overlook this time. No doubt, your being in second *pava*—and unmated—has unsettled you."

"Oh, so now this is about *me*? I have PMS so you will humor me? Please." She mumbled under her breath, insulted. Why was it all the good-lookers ended up being jerks? She let her growing anger spill over into her tones. "Do me a favor, Prince—*don't* do me any favors."

"Yes, favor! Great favor have I done you. I am ruling Prince," he began, his words laced with growing agitation. "Total power and authority have I on two worlds. Women of ten worlds would fight and swoon with pride as my chosen *Cherzda'va*."

"Get over yourself." She snorted with laughter at his arrogant statements. "You are too conceited for words."

"And you are... I know not the Earth words," the prince shook his clenched fists at the ceiling, an impatient growl rumbling in his throat.

She wondered if the growl signaled impatience at his own less-than-proficient use of her language or his disapproval of her refusal to be instantly impressed. Whatever the reason, anger looked good on him. Despite her irritation at his highhandedness, she savored the thrill of watching his impressive chest expand with his deep, agitated breaths.

Speaking slowly, Glendevtorvas began again. "I know you were lost as infant. Took years, your father did...to find you. Now is he eager to fulfill his responsibility. To establish you in proper mating—*good* mating! Think you, that you are the only one..." He paused, clearly searching for a word more to his meaning. "...softly forced?"

"Compelled? Coerced...nudged in a direction you don't wish to go?" she offered, her years of teaching making her insertion and amplification automatic.

"Yes, that is the word. Coerced to duty. I, too, am under a father's rule. This duty, it pleases me...*now.* You are very beautiful—though very tiny and fragile. Yet was I prepared to accept you at my father's command, whatever your look. But, you! You give no thanks, show no joy! You are not...proper, are not—*Rojas!*"

She snickered when he cut his sentence short with what sounded like a curse and turned his back. She found it hard to hide her smile. As a ruling prince, he probably didn't have very many people opposing his will.

"Am I ugly in your sight?" The prince turned back to ask.

His face betrayed his agitation and she somehow knew he would be more upset if he knew she was reading him so easily. All at once, she was not so happy to cause him such discomfort. "Oh, you definitely are not ugly in my sight. I am sure you know just how attractive you are," she hastened to respond, her own embarrassment spiking when she noticed the direction of the prince's wandering gaze.

Although she lived alone in her one-room apartment, Lori, who still lived at home, was a frequent visitor. Out of respect for their parents' old-fashioned beliefs, Lori—though older than Nnora and sexually active for years now—kept her affairs from her parent's notice. Nnora's apartment happened to be a convenient trysting place and an even more convenient cover to use when she was elsewhere. All Lori's sexual toys and supplies sprawled across her side of the dresser. Sitting prominently at the fore was the emergency box of extra-large "horse" condoms.

Cheeks growing hot, she watched as the prince—whose muscular build, sweetly taut buttocks and firm thighs had her wayward pussy creaming in tortured anticipation—idly toyed with the items littering the dresser. She prayed he wouldn't notice or at least wouldn't comment on Lori's emergency stash. Of course, because she wished the opposite so desperately, the box was the next item he picked up.

Even with his back still to her, she could almost feel his eyebrows rising as he studied the suggestive pictures printed on the compact box. She huffed and expelled an exasperated sigh when he opened the box and pulled out one of the foil-wrapped packets. He turned to face her, the condom held on his outstretched palm, one raised eyebrow asking a question.

She refused to be embarrassed. This was *her* bedroom and *he* was the uninvited intruder here.

"They're called condoms. Human males use them to prevent pregnancies."

"Not yours, then." He chuckled, dropping the thing back onto the dresser.

She bristled, peeved by his statement. "What does that mean? I am so unattractive no man would want—" She broke off, appalled to hear herself blurting out her insecurities. Now it was her turn to swing about, hiding her mortification from his interested gaze. She gasped, forcing back a sob, feeling stripped bare and naked, vulnerable.

The sound of his laughter cut her fragile self-esteem to shreds. Nnora's fists clenched and a hot wash of shame heated her cheeks. She fought agitated affront, injured pride and the beginning of tears. "Get the hell out of my bedroom! I don't give a flying...*damn* what you think, anyway. For your information—"

"*Fem*, why are you angry?" Glendevtorvas' brows drew together. "Surely, your anger cannot be over my laughter? How could you not expect me to be amused by such a joke?"

He moved close behind her, using the bulk of his body to cradle her without actually touching her with his hands.

"You are beyond attractive, as you well know," he told her softly, as if he meant to soothe her irritated nerves, which she did not believe for one second.

"Stop making fun of me!" She snarled, pivoting on her heels to face him, her ire rising anew at his continued efforts to ridicule her.

Raising both hands in surrender, the prince backed a step. "My laughter was *with* you, not *at* you!" he quickly said, obviously attempting to stave off another verbal attack. "All males must desire you. All my men and I would worship you. Any human male...how could they not lust for you? But, these things—" he indicated the discarded condom "—what use have you of them? No human male can impregnate you."

Her brow furrowed at the matter-of-fact way in which he spoke the last sentence. "How could you possibly know that, for sure? Our scientists are still debating the issue. It has never been conclusively decided that inter-mixing among our two species is impossible."

"When the answer is obvious, still scientists debate," Glendevtorvas said, shaking his head. "It is matter of simple dimensions.

"You are a tiny thing compared to *Rb'qarmshi* and *Rb'nTraqshi fem.*" His eyes burned a path down her torso, lingering on the delta of her towel-covered thighs.

"Already you are in second *pava,* untouched, untaught!" He tsk'ed his tongue in seeming displeasure and continued, "I fear it difficult to mate you without much pain, yet I doubt you could even feel a human, no matter how well endowed they think themselves to be—"

The prince lifted his molten gaze to hers, and her nipples sprang to attention under the heated, ravenous look. No one had ever wanted her like he seemed to, as if she were the banquet at the end of a forty day fast. As if he would starve without her essence to nourish him.

She stifled a moan as the muscles of her pussy contracted, trying to milk a nonexistent cock. *Well,* she told herself drolly, eyeing the long thick ridge that seemed to be growing behind the tight jeans material, *it does, in fact, exist. It simply isn't where I need it to be.* She shook herself and had to put forth a determined effort to understand the Prince's continued conversation.

"—no human male could fill you, and never could one expand the walls of your sweet *pava*. Yet will I fill your—"

"Look," she interrupted rudely. "If you are going to talk English, do it correctly. As far as I am concerned, a *pava* is what I am *experiencing*. What I *have* is a vagina. You can even use pussy or cunt. I won't object." Inwardly, she thrilled at the sound of the naughty words. "Choose one of those words, okay?"

He nodded sharply. "Yet will I fill your pus-sy. Your va-gi-na. I will be steadfast in this duty."

She inwardly shook her head. What, did he think her moved by his reassurance of his competency as a lover? On the contrary, his expertise only highlighted her lack and escalated her fears of their future mating.

And he saw making love to her as his duty? She cringed at this new blow to her budding self-esteem. She had no experience, no knowledge. Was it her fault that no mature, eligible males existed among the colonists to help her explore her sexuality?

Her teeth absently worrying her bottom lip, she struggled to categorize the contradictory feelings assailing her. For him to call her a tiny thing and mean it made her feel dainty and feminine—something she had craved for a very long time. On the other hand, she floundered in uncertain waters. She had no idea how to handle this situation and so she rejected his allure, falling back on sarcasm to hide her insecurity.

"Was there supposed to be a marriage proposal in there, somewhere?" she asked snidely. "I hope not, since I'm afraid I'll have to refuse, Prince Glendevtorvas.

"Thanks just the same, but no thanks. Unlike you, I do not consider it *my* duty to accept you."

"What say you?" The prince's disbelieving words rang in her ears. "You dare dismiss me so?"

"Let me see..." Nnora tapped a deliberately insolent finger to the tip of her chin, pretending to consider her behavior. "Yep, I do. See, I may be in my second *pava* and unmated, but I'll never be so desperate that I have to be someone's *duty*," she said, her voice gone chill.

"So, as the saying goes—don't let the door hit you where the good Lord spit you."

With an imperious finger, she indicated the door to the hallway. "Bye-bye! What a pleasure it's been meeting you...*Not*. And you needn't worry your *little*—" she glanced disparagingly down at his crotch "—head about me, I'll just wait for the next crop of maturing boys."

She watched, heart-sick as the insult fell on fertile ground.

Growling, the Prince captured her gaze. His burnished gold eyes, grown hard, bored down into hers as he deliberately ripped off his black t-shirt. Another angry jerk loosened the fastening of his jeans. "I have offered you honorable marriage and plentiful fucking and you reject me out of hand—to wait on boys who may not even make it to manhood."

Glendevtorvas moved toward her, male arrogance personified and rolled up in one irate package. She backed up, not willing to tangle with the warrior, whose swirling emotions were an almost visible cloud about him. Tripping over the fringed throw rug in her haste to distance herself from the determined male stalking toward her with lust twisting his implacably masculine face, she shivered with a mixture of desire and wariness.

Strong hands snatched her into the air, preventing an ignominious fall, only to pin her against the bathroom door.

"But why wait, my lady?" Glendevtorvas gritted from between clenched teeth, forcing a heavy thigh between her legs and grinding his hips into her pubic mound. "I am a mature male ready to service you, since *servicing* seems to be all you are concerned with."

Chapter Four

That ripped shirt implied a sensual threat Nnora didn't think she could handle. Even while she flinched away from the thought of her inadequacy, she couldn't help staring hungrily at the taut expanse of his exposed chest, her eyes irresistibly drawn to his muscular physique. Something told her she was in deep trouble.

Oh, Hell's bells! This guy embodies the epitome of sheer masculine virility and I've just insulted his manhood.

She gulped, pushing against his shoulders to create some space between them.

Devtorvas yanked her against him, the steely fingers of one large hand sinking into the full curve of her ass. The jeans-covered solid bulge of his cock nudged the tender skin of her belly as he wrapped his arms about her, head lowering.

She parted her lips to apologize…to breathe…and his tongue surged in, claiming her mouth in a heated carnal foray that wiped away her ability to speak and sent jagged shards of electrifying excitement careening through her bloodstream.

"Ooooh, god…" she moaned, shuddering as his masterful tongue plunged into her mouth again and again, while one hand caressed her scalp, his fingers snagging in her tangled hair.

Oh, stars above, the man could kiss!

She melted into his embrace. Her breasts, flattened against the firm, warm flesh of his broad torso, tingled and burned. Beneath the terrycloth towel, her nipples jutted, lengthened into little diamond pikes that stabbed at his impervious flesh. Never had she felt such intense arousal from a simple kiss.

Simple? Lord, but there was nothing simple about his kisses!

His tongue forced its way into the moist space behind her teeth, filling her mouth with the hot and spicy taste of his essence and her pulse pounded. She moaned, all thought of resistance blasted from her mind.

Caught in his sensual storm, almost swooning from the unfamiliar emotions his touch ignited within her, she turned to flame in his sexual heat, returning his kisses with a fervor she didn't know she possessed. A river of need washed over her and flowed out of her. Her pussy throbbed, releasing a gush of liquid heat.

With an inner thrill of power, smelling her own tangy scent rising from between her slick folds, she watched Devtorvas fling his head back, nostrils flaring as he sniffed the air like a stallion catching the scent of his mare in heat. She felt his chest expand and press against her swollen breasts as he inhaled deeply, filling his lungs with the fragrance of her lust. His arms tightened about her, anchoring her to his rampant body.

"I smell the sweet bouquet of your pava flower! It tells me you want me, whatever words you might say. Do not fear this, fem. I want you as much as you want me. Maybe more."

Bold, he gripped the cheeks of her bottom and she squirmed as he wedged a knee between her legs. His thick thigh pushed the hem of her towel up as he dragged her body forward. His large palms kneaded her ass. He lifted her, rocking her on his steely thigh, rubbing her pussy and clit against the rough heat of his denim-clad cock.

"Feel how hard I am for you."

His mouth swooped down again, tormenting her with another mind-tangling kiss. They were so close, his alluring fragrance—essence of rampant masculinity, hot and exciting—inundated her senses. Desire roared through her as his unique scent seared her lungs, burning a fiery path deep inside her body. Her spine went limp. Her knees went weak. She dug her nails into the firm flesh of his corded forearms, holding on for dear life. Her wits reeling under his expert tutelage, she realized she didn't want to tear herself away. His cock, pressing into her belly, told her his arousal matched her own.

The feel of him against her body and under her hands, all mounded muscle and thrusting man, sparked her natural curiosity. She wanted to know everything about him…the textures of his skin, the depth of his emotions…the contrast of his hard, muscular planes against her soft, hairless silkiness.

She swept her hands up and down the warm flesh of his arms and chest, her earlier agitation forgotten. While their mouths and tongues tangled, her fingers spread and flexed, measuring, testing and tweaking beaded male nipples. She had never felt anything remotely resembling this firestorm of passion he evoked in her. She opened her senses to the experience, wanting to indulge in everything he did to her.

The stubborn streak embedded in her core would not allow the total escape she sought in his arms. Even now her inner voice screamed, telling her she should not allow the prince to think she had given in to his heavy-handed seduction. Regretfully, she struggled to pry her lips apart from his searing kisses. Placing a hand between their mouths, she quickly composed a salve for her pride.

"Don't think my reaction a tribute to your skill. You take advantage of the fact that I am in pava and not likely to resist even you. As horny as I am, any warm male body would illicit the same reactions."

While she spoke, he had been attempting to reclaim her mouth. Now, he paused, a fierce frown distorting his devilishly handsome face. A frown that gradually gave way to a knowing smile.

Shaking his head at her, he pulled back just enough to brush his chest against the towel covering the aching points of her distended nipples.

"I am not misinformed by your words, fem. I refuse to be upset by your insult. I know you but seek a way to deny your feelings for me," he growled, moving his lower body in a way that rekindled her flaming passion.

"The exchange of pheromones triggers Rb'qarmshi arousal. Without them, we could not take this first step in joining. The smell of your flowering has triggered my own scent, to which you are reacting.

"The joining has begun. The taste of me makes you hungrier. You want my tongue in your mouth."

She gasped, outraged at his words. "I have never heard a more arrogant statement!"

"I am not arrogant where you are concerned, fem. In fact, I am humbled. I have been ready for you since you danced in your cleaning room. My heart trembled as I smelled your spilled juices." He nudged closer to her, rubbing himself against her like a big, cuddly teddy bear.

She'd had a teddy bear. Hugging it had never caused her to react like she did now. Her breasts drew taut; her nipples stiffened and tented the towel, long and jutting. She shivered when he brushed the tips with his thumbs.

"You fool only yourself with this talk of responding to anyone. My vow...once I seat your nipples, complete our mating, you will no longer make such statements." His broad masculine hand rubbed intimately across the naked expanse of her hip. One long thick finger caressed the slightly raised mark of her royal birth.

When had he gotten his hands beneath her towel?

Shocked free of the dark allure of his sinfully arousing touch, she scrambled to regain control of her self-will. She railed at herself, aghast at his ability to bewitch her to the point where she lost all sense.

What's wrong with me? Where is my sense of decency? How does he make me forget the rules of behavior Mom Brewster painstakingly instilled? Why am I allowing a man I don't even know to make a docile meal of me? After all, I was never tempted or driven to give in to my sexual desires during my last pava—never like this!

But if he's telling the truth, I felt no desire for human males because they gave off no pheromones. What do I feel for him, then? Is it the beginning of love or do I desire him only because we've begun this joining-thing?

She shook her head. At the moment, none of that mattered.

Regardless of how I feel, how much I want this man, I refuse to be my father's puppet. Let him play his games of empire and dominance if he will. But until I can meet with father face-to-face and get some answers, this mating is so not going to happen.

Her mind made up, she sought a way to bank her passion, which didn't prove easy. While she had been thinking, his hands had been caressing her hips, running possessively up and down her flank. His lips had been nibbling her ear and pressing hot kisses into the crease of her neck. She had to find a way to deflect his attention and, at the same time, escape his clutches.

She decided upon attack.

"Hey, get your hand off my ass, buddy! I never gave you permission to handle me like that!" She made an abortive attempt at dislodging his wandering hands.

"Your kisses and full participation led me to think otherwise, fem." His husky voice rumbled next to her ear just before his tongue dipped and swirled into the sensitive opening. His hands resumed their devastating course.

Shivering and gulping, she bit back a scream of frustration. She wrestled with the surging lust that roared through her, battling herself more than him.

She so needed to end this swiftly…lest she give in.

Sighing dramatically, she went boneless against him, letting her considerable weight rest fully on him. She waited for his gallantry to kick in, for him to shift his hold to support her sagging body. He didn't disappoint her.

The moment he moved to secure her, she twisted out of his grasp and skipped away, tightening the fastening of her towel. She couldn't resist the victorious gesture of sticking her tongue out at him. The look in his eyes had her scurrying towards the door.

"I have a better use for that tongue, fem." Glendevtorvas flashed a marauder's grin as he lunged after her and caught the trailing towel edge. He gave it a hard wrench.

With a cry of dismay, she gripped her scant covering and refused to let it go. Holding on with grim determination, she pulled in the opposite direction. Her feet slid on the slick tiled floor and she fought for traction as she was dragged inexorably towards him.

His arm, a band of iron, tightened about her waist. He held her in place by fisting his left hand in her long hair.

"Do not make me hurt you."

"Let me go!" She twisted wildly, snarling.

"Stop fighting me! I don't intend to harm you." Tightening his grip on her, he nonchalantly brushed aside the vicious kick she aimed at his genitals. "I only want to know what changed your mind, so I can change it back."

She didn't deign to answer, too busy using her breath to fuel her struggle. Seeing she couldn't break his grasp, she knew she certainly couldn't win this battle of muscles. Yet she refused to quit trying.

They wrestled. She pushed at him. He shifted his grip and held on. She turned within his grasp, used her body to slam him into the furniture.

They struggled back and forth in the narrow space between dresser and bed. He controlled her easily, allowing only enough room for her to brush her body all along his. She vigorously kicked her legs and rocked her body, managing to knock over every lamp and table in the small bedroom. She had occasion to be thankful for the strong Velcro fastening of her towel, since she almost lost hold of it several times.

She couldn't believe how weak she felt in contrast to his easy strength. Always before, her denser molecular structure enabled her to best any opponent. She'd surprised Ron by tackling him and holding him down, the one time he'd attacked her after an especially bad session in bed. Against the prince, she could not hold her own. She shuddered, thinking what her fate would be if, instead of merely restraining her frantic struggles, he truly wished to hurt her.

A surprised cry flew out of her mouth as she felt herself falling backward. He had flung her backward across the dark wood-grained surface of the dresser. His hard body came down over her, pinning her down. Her toweling rode up in the skirmish, and his bulging crotch pressed intimately into the cradle of her splayed thighs. Her pussy throbbed with need.

Despite her body's insistent urges, she was still not prepared to give in. She would not live her life at her father's whim. She would never allow him to hand her over as goods in a trade deal. "Let me go! I'm through playing."

"I am not. Not yet."

He groaned then placed a stinging string of kisses down her jaw. His hand slid up from her knee, his fingers teasing the pouty lips nestled between her thighs before dipping inside her to test her honeyed interior. His fingers re-emerged, dripping with her juices. He licked them clean then delved back inside. His lips nuzzled at her shoulders as his fingers probed deeply.

Her hips arched up into his touch. A primal cry of need rang from her gasping mouth. He applied two more thick digits, stretching and playing her with his large fingers. The pleasure went off the scale, spinning her into a sudden climax. Her spine bowed, belly tightened, legs jack-knifed as she came, screaming. "Devtorvas!"

"I am here, cherzda'va and I like the sound of my name screamed from your sweet mouth. Take more, grasp more pleasure…then scream my name again."

His hand mashed against her mound, his fingers pistoned in and out of her, driving her swiftly to another, higher peak.

She tossed her head, desperately trying to throw off the escalating fireball. She feared the magnitude of her response. Her mind whirled under the powerful thrusting of his fingers, shocked to feel her body reaching for another flashpoint.

She convulsed, almost sobbing from the intense overload of sensations flooding her. Her nipples stabbed at the sky, the diamond-hard bits abraded by the terry cloth towel. Every muscle in her body clenched then released as she bucked under the power of the enormous orgasm. The muscles in her neck gave way, dropping her head against the dresser.

A cold wave of shame washed over her, icing her flesh. Humiliated that he had won her willing participation, she determined he should not realize just how much she had surrendered.

Eyes tightly closed, refusing to look at him, she groped sightlessly for something—anything—she could use as a weapon. Her scrabbling fingers closed over Lori's heavy silver hand mirror. Breathing an apology to her foster-sister, she brought it crashing down on his head.

His eyes closed, his grip went slack and she quickly darted out from under him. He dizzily reeled away, hands clutching his head, cursing in both English and his native tongue. He recovered almost instantly from the blow and, in a move too fast for her to counter, intercepted her escape.

"Fem, that hurt!"

Two grinding orgasms had weakened her legs and left them shaking. She managed only a few steps before he easily recaptured her. He quickly relieved her of the shattered mirror, growling a string of imprecations under his breath. He caught her hands from behind and looped them across her chest, using her own arms to shackle her. With each of her frantic breaths, his muscled forearms rubbed the up-tilted, painfully erect tips of her breasts.

"Ooohh!" The moan escaped her parted lips against her will.

He grinned, baring his teeth in a mocking smile. He deliberately brushed her sensitized crests again and again. His cock, solid and huge, pressed threateningly against the swell of her buttocks.

"You want to play rough?" His raspy whisper tickled her ear.

It wasn't laughter that shivered down her spine. She gasped, shaking her head no. He lifted her in his arms anyway.

Relentless, he walked over to the bed. Brushing aside her half-hearted attempts to deter his will, he forced her down onto the mattress, throwing a muscled leg over her thighs. He secured her with his greater weight. His engorged penis nudged her belly and thigh, its distended length heavy on her sensitive flesh.

Holding her gaze, he sent his hands roving over and under her terry-cloth cover, seeking the closure. His fingers snagged on the opening, and, undeterred by her defiant glare, ripped the towel away.

Chapter Five

"Chyya! Hoden bra'qu…? Malau ne macinee?"

A man sporting an immense weapon stood in the open doorway, his head bent to clear the bedroom's eight-foot ceiling. A frantic spate of words tripped from his well-shaped lips. The hilt of his wicked-looking sword familiarly clasped in one gigantic hand, the warrior appeared alert and ready for any contingency.

Over the loud thundering of her heart, Nnora hadn't heard the newcomer's entry nor did she understand the questions he asked the prince, since he spoke them in his native language. When he first came in, she'd been grateful for the interruption. Now, having recalled the predicament she was in, she found herself wondering whether this new intruder would prove to be friend or foe, one of her father's soldiers or one of the prince's warriors.

From his garb, he did not appear to be one of her father's men. Since her father's warriors tended to blend in with Earthlings as much as possible, they wore clothes that were the norm for the locale they guarded in. In other words, Levis and tee shirts, covered by trench coats to conceal their weapons.

This man's loose, belted tunic resembled those once worn by ancient Roman soldiers. The short skirt cut full to accommodate ease of fighting, ended well above his knees, exposed miles of hair-roughened legs and thighs.

Why was he here? And what had he asked the prince, something along the line of, "Is it my turn yet?"

She shuddered.

The man's unearthly neon-green gaze swept the dim corners of the room as if searching for an intruder. He turned, taking in every aspect of the disruption caused by her tussle with Devtorvas. She cringed—he'd probably heard everything that had occurred earlier, too.

Abruptly, the big man stiffened. Nostrils quivering, he swung his massive head about and turned sharply toward her, zeroing in. He shuddered, eyelids drifting to half-mast as he inhaled deeply.

Her face flamed as the man's cock jerked erect, rising hard and fast to tent the loose skirt of his tunic.

Oh, my god! She ogled the thick lengthy pole rearing against the thin material. If that's his cock, the thing is astronomical in proportion! No one has dicks that big...do they?

Frightened, she curled into a small ball of cowering flesh beneath the prince's bulk.

As her struggles against the prince had brought home to her, these homegrown *Rb'qarmshi* men were strong enough to force her against her will...to hurt her badly. The possibility stole her breath.

Does the prince intend sharing me with this behemoth and the other soldiers I hear milling about in my living room? I know he said he wanted me for himself, but after he finishes with me...what then?

"Stand down, GanR'dari. As you can see, there is no intruder here."

She sighed with relief when the prince shifted his body, gallantly shielding her nakedness from his man's interested gaze. She also gave him silent thanks for speaking in English, clearly intended to alleviate her anxiety. He had to be aware of her fear as she had tucked herself under him so tightly her body practically melted into his.

"You may leave. I have the situation...*the princess*...well in hand." His gently mocking glance dared her to contradict his statement as his thumb insolently brushed her beaded nipple.

Though she had to grit her teeth to do it, she remained silent. The pompous ass rewarded her with a softening of his predatory smile and another flick of his marauding thumb.

"Contact the surgeon for the injection I ordered." His autocratic voice sounded over her head. "If it is ready, have it brought to me. Here."

His massive cock boldly erect and swinging beneath his skirt with every step, the giant nodded his head curtly, and then eased from the room. The sound of raucous male laughter told her the other warriors had noticed their captain's lost control. She glanced over to find Devtorvas smiling in what looked like rueful sympathy. Was his sympathy for her or for his man?

"Excuse the intrusion of my warrior, Nnora, it was not intentional. Also, forgive GanR'dari's...condition. My followers and I have been without a *fem's* easing for far too long. We cannot prevent our bodies' natural response to the sweet smell of *pava*-flowering. You need never fear they would harm you, or that I would ever allow you to be harmed."

"It is you I fear, not them." Her uneven breathing sounded loud in the quiet room. "And do not think I wi—will allow you to cart me off or rape me without a fight!"

A tear slipped down her cheek. "Why won't you let me speak with my father?" Hiccoughing, she fought to contain the sobs rising against her will.

The prince caught the fallen tear on the tip of his tongue, delicately lapped at the others that followed. "Let there be no more talk of rape. When I take you—and I will—it will be with your full consent. With your eager participation. As for speaking with your father, I cannot…that is not possible right now. Perhaps later, when we are in route—"

"I want to speak with him now! How much later will it be?"

He sighed. "Nnora, when you make contact with your father, who contacts first?"

"He does."

"Yes, because any attempt at communication is not easy this close to Earth transmissions. Always there is a danger the communication will be captured.

"Intercepted?"

"There is danger of interception—thank you for supplying the correct word—if I try to bring communications with your father's colony now. It would be the worst course of action I could take. My ship and my people might come in danger and that I will not do. Not even for you."

Before she could ask another question, a knock sounded on the bedroom door and the same hulking warrior stuck his head round the portal. He was very careful not to look in her direction as a flow of liquid syllables cascaded from his mouth. He opened his hand, and she caught a fleeting glimpse of an ampoule glistening on his outstretched palm.

With a relieved sounding comment, Devtorvas eased away from her, rose and went to the door.

As soon as he turned his back on her, she hurriedly snatched up her towel, retreating back to the bed where she sat down, clutching it over her heaving breasts with both hands.

He took the ampoule from his captain and closed the door behind him, then proceeded to engage the lock with a deliberateness that started her pulse pounding and her cunt juicing. He turned. When he saw what she had done his lips twitched up in an amused smile.

She straightened her back and firmed her jaw. Her heart pounded with a mix of anticipation and dread as she watched him approach, his bold eyes drilling into hers, silently challenging her to admit the mutual desire sparking between them.

His face was arrantly beautiful, his body a graceful rhapsody in motion. Though massively built, he moved lightly, silently on nimble feet. The defined ridges of his muscular chest, unmarred by hair, rippled and contracted under his smooth dark skin with his every movement. For the first time, she noticed a slight indentation about three or four inches below each flat, wide masculine nipple. The circular, smooth depressions looked like scar tissue, a little darker than the skin around them. What could have caused the circular scarring?

His voice interrupted her musing. "Nnora, tis no disgrace to be bested by a more able foe. The fighting ends now. Or…" he grinned, "…must I have my men in here to assist your surrender?"

Even as he spoke the threat, she knew he did not mean it. The locked door testified against him. She was convinced she need not worry on that account.

"You will remove your covering and submit to me, now."

She knew he would brook no further resistance.

The growing heat in her loins compelled her to admit she wanted, no *needed* what the prince offered. Her curiosity grown enormous, she desperately wanted to explore this erotic landscape with the prince—the most intriguing man she had ever met. Still, she had questions regarding her father's plans and his involvement in this situation.

Silently, provocatively, hoping her tremors of fearful lust were not visible to him, she let the towel pool about her waist. Her skin pinkened under his focused gaze. Her nipples crested in blatant arousal and she fought back the urge to shelter her breasts behind her hands. She wanted him to see her, to desire her. She wanted him to find her breasts alluring and irresistible. She had one more question, however.

"Surely you do not intend to mate me with your men listening in the next room?"

He came up to her, smoothed his hands over her bare arms. He ran his fingers across the top of her chest, skimming the yearning flesh of her swollen breasts. "Were our situation different, I would consider waiting until after the Acceptance Ceremony on *Rb'qarm* for full mating, however—"

"Will you wait if I promise to accept this marriage?" She would bargain, willingly offer anything that would buy her some much-needed time to think. To plan.

"No, Nnora, I will not." He shook his head. "You bargain falsely. You mean to placate me now, while you plot your later escape. I admire your tenacity, *fem*, as it will serve you well in your new role as my mate and consort." He sighed.

"I know you are as attracted to me as I am to you. The flowering does not lie. I truly regret having to snatch you away against your will. If only I could spend more time courting you, if only I were not so desperately needed back home—" He shook his head again.

"I do not care to see you unhappy, my *fem*. I vow I will make everything up to you. I will shower you with the gift of my affections and will grant you whatsoever else you desire, up to the half of my kingdom." He smoothed back her hair, gaze lingering on her face.

What was he looking for? What did he want from her? She tipped her head back to lock gazes with his fascinating eyes and felt him capture her left arm in a firm grip. He pressed something into her forearm.

The ampoule he had received from his henchman—she had forgotten in her fear and scheming. It dissolved quickly and painlessly into her skin. She recoiled away from him in terror, staring at her arm.

God, was she poisoned? Had he drugged her to ease his kidnapping plans?

"What did you do to me? What did you give me?"

Dare I trust your answer?

"Be calm, *Nippa*. It is merely a nanotech learning device." He sought to soothe her by allowing her to place distance between them. "It is a miniature translator which will not only allow us to communicate more effectively with each other by attaching a node to your cerebral cortex—it will gradually give you a complete database of the emotional context of the words and phrases, as well as the grammatical usage. You will soon be speaking and understanding our language as if you were born to it, which, in fact, you were.

She rubbed at her arm, frowning. She narrowed her eyes, glared at him. "I don't like that you did that without asking me. I have a right to make my own decisions, Glendevtorvas."

I will give you all the choices I can—all but the choice to deny me, now."

"That is no choice, at all," she snapped.

"I realize this situation is not fair to you, Nnora. Again, I regret I do not have the time or the self-control to withhold myself from you, to court you as I wish to. It has been many years since my *terat* have softened for a *fem*. I had thought myself resigned, used to the lack, and then I peeked into your cleansing room. I saw you touch yourself, smelled the flowering of your sweet pussy. I tell you..." He gathered her close as he stared into her eyes. "You will never know how close you came to being taken against the reflecting wall. I have yet to regain that lost control, and for that I give you my apologies. I make no apologies for anything else."

He bent to press a soft kiss against her lips.

Nnora turned her head away.

His fingers snagged her chin, turned her face up to his.

"Resign yourself, *Nippa*. As sure as the stars burn, we shall share sex...and *soon*. I dare not allow you to remain unmated the length of the journey home. My men are as cruelly deprived as myself, and you present a heady temptation. I will not chance having to kill a friend over you. I want you too desperately to delay for long, but I will give you the choice of when and where we seal our bond…here and now? Or tomorrow, on board the ship?"

"I choose tomorrow," she said quickly, thankful for any reprieve, marveling at how open he was being with her.

"You do truly mean me for yourself? You do not plan to share me with your men?"

"*Share a life-mate?*" He drew back, his face contorted in a horrified scowl. "By the stars, *fem*, where came you by this blasphemy? What perversions have been spawned on this *Rojas*-forsaken planet?"

His shock seemed so unfeigned and deep, it convinced her of his sincerity. She slumped in relief. "It is not the practice among my father's people, as far as I know, though it has been known to happen here on Earth. I was unsure of your intentions."

"My intentions, this day, are to influence your *pava* and flowering towards me. I will *seat* your nipples, and if you are cooperative with that, I will grant you the day's delay of our full joining." He shrugged. "More than that I cannot do."

"*Seating*…not just sitting down. I seem to know that it is something sexual, something important to do with a couple becoming mates." Her gaze went without thought to the circular indentions in the prince's chest. "What does *seating* have to do with your scars?"

His thick brows drew together. "I was told you were raised among Humans, but I cannot believe you were allowed to grow to maturity uneducated about your own sexuality and biological legacy."

She didn't especially care for that note of pity she heard in his voice. "I wasn't found until after my first *pava*. But since you seem to enjoy using *seating* to threaten me, I'll let *you* do the explaining, Prince."

"That you can label it a threat tells me how woefully ignorant you are. I have issued you no threats. I have only made the very real promise to make you my *cherzda'va*.

"As for the *seating*, I'll gladly explain if you'll stop trying to convince yourself you are in danger. Come. Sit here, beside me." He patted the mattress.

"I'd rather stand, thank you!"

He gave her a level stare from beneath down-drawn brows, silently waiting.

Sighing audibly, trailing her towel, she flounced over to the bed and flopped down. "All right, I'm here. So talk!"

He didn't say a word. Instead, taking her hand and placing it brazenly in his lap, Devtorvas forcibly folded her hand around his hot, mammoth, and still expanding sex, anchoring her fingers under his own. Directing her hand in a slow glide, he drew their linked fingers over the rough denim, slowly tracing the changing contours of his stiff, pulsating cock. "This," he instructed calmly, "is my *cherzda*." He pressed her palm into the soft mass of his balls, "And these are my *sirat*. *You* shall be my *cherzda'va*—the only woman my *cherzda* rises for."

"The biology lesson would have been fine as a verbal tour, you know." She yanked her hand free. "You could have instructed me without the tactile assistance." She was embarrassed and at the same time unbearably aroused by his bold words and bolder gestures. Her fingers and the palm of her hand tingled with the remembered heft of the Prince's arousal, the weightiness of his balls. She had never felt anything so huge in her life. Ron-the-"Rocket's" firecracker member was an ice cream stick in comparison…no, *a toothpick*. She smothered a guilty laugh by covering her blushing cheeks and mouth with both hands.

"I could have, yes," Devtorvas agreed. "But you need to learn how to handle me, grow accustomed to me."

How unbelievably arrogant of him. As if his huge cock was enough to convince her to give in to him totally. She fully anticipated enjoying their foreplay, and had no intention of forgetting her plans to call a halt before the actual lovemaking, no matter how her insides were screaming for a chance to be filled with something other than her "Jumbo."

Her thoughts disintegrated, blasted into nothingness by the feel of his hand upon hers. Her heart tripped in renewed excitement when she heard him say, "There is much to teach you during our journey home. I believe we will begin here."

Chapter Six

Leaning forward, Devtorvas touched his forefingers to Nnora's nipples, pressing and releasing the buds, circling smoothly. When they responded by tightening and lifting, he cupped a breast in each hand, creating a masculine frame for her feminine flesh. "Look at how beautiful you are," he invited, his voice rich and deep, his hands tightening around her breasts, fingers pinching hard on her beaded crests.

She shuddered, a sudden rush of hot fluid filling her cunt and oozing out to glisten on the hairless lips of her pussy.

The feel of his long, elegant, very masculine fingers, the warmth of his callused palms enclosing her aching flesh made her wild, invoking another pungent flowering. She groaned in concert with him as her sharp scent flooded the air. Squeezing her thighs together, she shifted restlessly in a futile attempt to ease the growing emptiness between her legs.

"You have long, pouty nipples." He carefully squeezed her sensitive tips. "Stiff little delights, just the way I like them. I want them in my mouth. I want to suck them up like hard treats."

At the heavy, hungry look of sensual greed in his all-seeing eyes, she wished she wore a pair of panties to hide her growing dampness.

"You are in for a surprise if you have truly never been *seated.*" His lips turned up in a slight smile that bore a hint of sexual teasing.

"So when are you going to get around to introducing me to this surprise?" She did some teasing of her own, and walked her fingertips up the broad, naked chest before her. She dipped her nails into the shallow depressions below his masculine nipples and thrilled with the enjoyment of her feminine power when he shuddered under her hands. So much masculine power under her control.

He drew back from her, trying to ease her fingers away from his chest. The tightness of his grip almost crushed her fingers. Curling her hands about his and rubbing them against his taut skin, she avidly tracked his response to her playful touches.

His lips drew back in a hiss of barely controlled lust and he growled from between clenched teeth, his words harsh with need. "You play with fire, *fem*. I am very near the brink of my control. Let me, I beg you, lead this dance—"

"If I don't, what will you do?" she asked archly, reluctant to give up the heady feeling of controlling their play.

He paused, gazing down at her beneath hooded lids, his expression thoughtful. "I keep forgetting you were not raised on the colony, so you have very little idea of what you are putting me through." His mouth widened into a rakish smile. "I rejoice that I will be the first to give you a good nipple-suckling."

She swallowed hard, had to try twice before managing to force the words from her constricted throat. "I have had my nipples sucked, before. I *have* been married, you know. I—"

"To a *Human!*" His disparaging tones made plain his low opinion of the breed. "I consider you untouched—a canvas waiting for the artist's hand, a wild, open field that I shall enjoy frolicking in. Moreover, I shall make sure you enjoy our romp, also," he bragged. "You have never been attended to the way I shall care for you, my own."

Sliding his large hands under her breasts, he hefted their heavy weight. His broad palms made her Dolly Parton wannabes appear, if not dainty, then certainly smaller and lighter than she was wont to think of them. In his hands, she felt small, feminine, and…desired.

"You sure don't need a town crier to blow your horn." She battled to subdue the fluttering butterflies in her belly. Stars above, how she loved the feel of his big hands on her flesh.

"I intend to prove my every word upon your luscious flesh," he purred, bending his head and carefully lapping at a diamond-hard point. His rough tongue sent splinters of jagged sensation arrowing straight to her cunt. "And I shall show you what you have been missing."

"You think your mouth so talented, then?"

He laughed aloud before pulling the nipple right into his mouth, pressing the tip between the roof of his palate and tongue and suckling hard.

Her back bowed under the stream of fire burning her from the inside out. Mewling, she buried the fingers of one hand in his thick hair and tugged his head closer to her full breast. By the time he released her reddened nipple with an audible pop, she was panting.

"Actually, yes, my mouth is that talented. But I won't be using my mouth when I suck you raw," he informed her. "I am going to insert these luscious berries into my *terat!*"

Bending his head, he took the other nipple in and treated it to the same fixed attention, sucking it deeply into the humid cavern of his mouth and pulling strongly. His fingers twisted and tugged her free breast, rubbing her areole with the palm of his hand.

The strong tugging called both her nipples and her pussy to strict attention. The muscles in her belly tightened then fluttered as her cunt throbbed, begging for his touch. Her clit was swollen and aching, as were her pussy lips, the entire area awash in her spilling juices. She wanted him to stroke her *there*...but she was too shy to take the initiative and move his hand to where she needed it the most.

Between the intense stimulation and her own heavy breathing, she could hardly articulate her next question. "You say *terat* and I hear suction holes or breast cups. Why am I hearing this at the same time I hear you say something else? I wish you would speak English."

He lifted his head and laughed at her. "Little Princess, I haven't been talking English since I gave you the injection of nanofyles. You are hearing the translation of our language through your new implant."

His casual attitude exasperated her. "So I can expect no let-up of this confusion, huh?"

Another laugh rumbled from his throat before he bent back down to lick and nip at her erect nipples, interspersing each word with a heated swipe of his tongue. "To answer your question, *Rb'qarmshi* men have *terat* to milk their mate's *tlinis*."

Ceasing his tongue play, Dev gave a last lingering swipe to each pebbled crest before slowly releasing her damp flesh. "By *Deth,* I hate to stop, but I think you're ready now."

His fingers still plumped and tugged on her breasts as if he could not get enough of the feel of her beneath his hands. Finally, he ceased his heated caresses, drawing back, sliding his hand down her arms until he reached her hands. He curled his fingers around her hands, lifted them to his mouth and planted a kiss in each palm.

"Watch and feel." He took her hands and brought them to the indented circles below his flat male nipples, then touched her pointer fingers to his chest. Her fingers sank into a shallow dip about three quarters of an inch deep, where strong inner muscles caught and held them. She jerked in shock, instinctively moving to pull away. He countered, his hands holding hers firmly to his body.

Her eyes opened wide and she gasped. "What—? How—?"

"When the *Rb'qarmshi* male is aroused, these soften and a mouth is created. This is how we *seat* our woman's *tlinis,* drawing her essence, her gift, into our bodies. The *seating* is the second point of joining, intensely pleasurable for the *fem.* The gods' gift to both parties."

The rhythmic pull on the tips of her fingers set her mind racing. What would that strong pull feel like with her nipples buried areole-deep in his chest? Clamped around her swollen clit? She bit back a moan at the wild thought.

His hands returned to her breasts and she moaned aloud. His fingers meandered over her swollen, hot curves in maddening patterns that etched erotic magic, worked upon her flesh until she cried out at the spiraling need he awoke. Her breathing quickened, shortened, making her words a jumble of sounds. "Wh—what is the...*ahh*...the first point of...joining?"

"This." Releasing her captive fingers, Glendevtorvas brought her lips to his. His kiss was neither mild nor tentative, but bold and audacious. Adventurous, inviting her participation in the open-mouthed feast, he bit at her, nibbled her lips, surprising her into a gasp. He took quick advantage of her startled reaction to thrust his tongue deep into the recesses of her mouth, brazenly laying claim to the territory behind her teeth.

She opened to him, giving him her tongue, which he sucked into his mouth, chewing lightly on it, gathering her moisture and sharing his with her, drawing forth an echoing wetness that pooled between her legs.

Hands fisted in his hair, she drew on his tongue in return, drinking in his essence and losing herself in his heady taste. Her breasts felt tight and swollen against his heavily muscled chest. Shifting her legs back and forth, she rocked against the bulge of his cock, trying to stimulate her clit.

Shaken, transported, she opened her eyes and was stunned to find herself flat on her back, her legs spread vulnerably open. Unnerved, she sought his gaze.

He fixed his brilliant orange gaze on her as he wedged himself more firmly into her crotch, snuggling his massive cock between the splayed lips of her seeping cunt. He pushed himself up, straightening his arms, and reared up over her—Zeus to her Leda.

She blushed to see the front of his jeans damp with the dew of her weeping pussy. She barely had time to recover from that provocative sight before he was pushing against the juncture of her thighs, rubbing his jeans-clad erection across her clit.

A keening cry clawed its way out of her throat as pleasure poured over her. She cried out again, dragged her hands down the broad slick back of the man working the rough cloth of his jeans into the opening of her vagina. Almost frantic with lust, she rose against him, urged him to press into her again and again.

Their mingled scents wafted heavy on the air, a loamy, perfumed aroma reminiscent of a steamy tropical forest. Like some primal animal, she slid against him and he responded, moaning and growling his gratification.

She speared her fingers into the thick growth of his black hair, reveling in the silky slide of the curling strands against her hands and wrists as she caressed his scalp.

He choked back a groan. His cock surged against her lower belly, jerking and growing impossibly larger under the erotic stimulus. His *terat* softened and dilated.

With another dark groan, he gathered her breasts in both hands, aligning her nipples with his *terat*, then slowly, slowly eased down over her.

Fascinated, she watched her nipples disappearing into his chest, watched as her areolas were also engulfed.

He looked down, caught her gaze. A dark glitter of lust shone in his eyes. A strained smile stretched his handsome lips. As his mouth swooped down, parting her lips for another lush, wet kiss, he began a gentle undulation. Using his chest muscles in a way surely designed to drive her mad with desire, he rose and fell against her. He crushed her under his weight, his *terat* opening to force more of her flesh into the cavity of his powerful chest. Alternately, he lifted his chest away from her, his *terat* clamping tight to the swollen nipples, elongating her mounds. He proceeded to milk her with a strong, rhythmic suctioning.

"Ooooooooohhhhhhhhhh! Oh, my god!"

This was where her nipples belonged! These glorious feelings were what her breasts were designed for. No wonder her ex-husband's mouth and tongue had never satisfied her, never called forth her passion.

Every single nerve in her nipples was on fire. Something, some enzyme or substance inside the prince's *terat* seeped into the buried crests and stung like a thousand tiny mosquito bites, swirling together both stinging pain and escalating delight. The pleasure was as sharp as the pain, the two intertwining in such a way that she could not separate them. The alien sensations spilling through her drove her half-wild. She screamed, thrashing beneath him, her captured nipples throbbing, burning, and igniting in the grip of his rapture-inducing *terat*.

Caught up with her in this storm of sensation, he ground his cock hard against her juicing mound, cursing aloud the barrier of his clothing. His muscles trembled. Sweat poured from his skin as he drove his hips at her.

"Come for me, *Nippa*!" He growled at her, lifted her hips, dragging her pussy across his jeans-clad cock. He pressed himself to her, chest to breast, and pushed her swelling mounds up with his hands, feeding more and more of her flesh into the hungry, dilating mouths of his *terat*.

"Gift me with your life-changing fluid!"

Shivering and quaking, she fell deeper under his spell of pure eroticism. She mewled and panted as his heavy body blanketed hers, pounded against her, bore her down into the soft mattress. He wrapped her in heated darkness until her only thought, her only reality, was the hot, liquid pleasure bubbling up within her, building to an explosion, the magnitude of which she had never before experienced.

Her head reeled. The tips of her breasts stretched. Her areolas puckered. She whimpered, drowning in sensation, awash with lust and teetering on the edge of a massive orgasm. It felt as if a cauldron seethed within her, filled with bright, effervescent juices threatening to bubble over. Every muscle in her belly clamped down.

In blind reflex, her hands locked about his shoulders. She clasped his waist with her legs, held on for dear life. Her thigh muscles clenched against his heaving flanks. "Devtorvas! Help me…I feel…I…oh—*oooooohhhhhhh!*"

It started in her toes. Lapped around her ankles and rushed up the backs of her legs. Skimmed across the plateau of her flat stomach to sparkle through her system. Her senses ignited. Achieving lift-off, she screamed and convulsed. Her spine bowed, thrusting her breasts into his *terat*—a flood of liquid lightning burst free, gushing out of her spasming nipples.

Freezing above her heaving body, he let out a mighty shout as her ejaculation flowed into him.

She screamed again, writhing in a maelstrom of sexual delight.

She went limp with momentary satiation. Above her, chest heaving as his *terat* muscles milked every drop of what she could only think of as cum from her spilling crests, he chanted his praise of her.

"Yes! Yes, my own, come for me! Give me all your cum! Let me milk you dry!" He locked their mouths together in a torrid kiss as the exchange, the pleasure, went on and on…and *on.*

Chapter Seven

Wordless moans escaped Nnora's lips. Her body performed a series of slow, sensual undulations, riding out the dwindling surges of the ecstatic completion pulsing through her. Never before had she orgasmed so completely, never had the relief from her *pava*-driven arousal lasted so long. But even now, she sighed with reawakened longing as Devtorvas leisurely shifted his body.

He lifted his chest away from her, sliding gentle fingers between them to help ease her reddened nipples from his still-contracting *terat*. She couldn't help the despairing mewl that escaped as her flesh slid free of the hot confining grip of his chest cavities.

"Are you sore, *Nippa*?" he asked, clearly mistaking her inarticulate moans for ones of distress. "Poor dearling, let me soothe you." The prince lowered his head and brought his facile tongue into play, tenderly licking at her still inflamed tips.

His tongue was anything but soothing as he unhurriedly lapped at her breasts, already overly hot and sensitive from the special treatment Devtorvas insisted on lavishing upon them.

Moaning, she bunched her fists in his hair and pressed his head to her flushed skin. Incredibly aroused, she squirmed beneath him, begging without words for more of his attentions.

As if he could read her mind, he gave her what she wanted. He took first one straining bud, then the other fully into his mouth, drawing on her erect flesh with firm pressure, finally drawing forth a cascade of words.

"Yes! Yeeees! Oh, God! Please, please…please don't stop!"

Cupping his cheeks in her palms, she trailed her hands across his jaw. The hollowing of his cheeks as he pulled at her tight, engorged tips, sucking them into the heated cavern of his mouth, had her hissing with excitement. Through the connection of his skin and her palms she *felt* the tugging, biting movements of his lips and teeth as he fed at her marble-hard nipples.

Incredibly, a pounding, relentless climax ripped through her. Liquid fire gushed from her spasming cunt. She marveled at how easily he seemed to bring her to the edge of grinding orgasm with just his mouth at her breasts, when she had never managed a single one from Ron's cock.

A second, stronger delightful thrum of pleasure rippled throughout her body and she cried out, shivering. All thought ceased as her muscles fluttered and her nerve endings snapped and tingled. A wave of bliss swept through her. She felt all light and tingly, as though the finest champagne sparkled in her cunt.

Her pussy contracted on nothingness and she pumped her hips up toward Devtorvas, instinctively seeking a deeper mating, seeking to fill her yawning emptiness. She bit her tongue, barely resisting the urge to beg Devtorvas to *please* fuck her…

Damn it all. Much as he had the ability to rock her world, she didn't know this man. Beside all that, she never fucked on the first date.

Oh, but he certainly knew how to use his mouth to weaken a woman's resolve.

Every inch of her skin registered the wet sweeps of his tongue, the boiling heat and pressure of his suckling mouth, the hard firmness of his teeth as he bit down upon the ultra-sensitive tips of her breasts. Those sharp nips, bordering on the knife-edge of pain, shot clear down to her pussy, igniting a firestorm of lust. Though she struggled, ever conscious of the sharp-eared guards in the next room, she could not constrain her cries. Raw shouts of pleasure rang through the air.

Long minutes went by before he lifted his head from her heaving breasts to meet her heavy-lidded eyes. His gaze possessive, he grinned, his wide smile infectious enough to coax forth one of her own. "So, *Nippa*-mine, there was nothing to be affrighted of, eh? We have shared now—lips, breasts and *terat*—and the sharing was sweet. *Your* sweetness has taken away the pain of my long years of waiting." His voice sounded strangely gruff.

She dragged her sex-dazed eyes open. The liquid sheen of tears blurring the beautiful burnt gold of his irises shocked her almost as much as her powerful surge of protectiveness toward him, witnessing his strong response to their lovemaking. If this man bottled his potent masculinity, he could patent it and make a fortune. Yet he watched her from behind eyes drenched in tears, gazing upon her as if she were his only salvation, his green oasis in a dry desert. The thought that he trusted her enough to allow her to see inside him like this moved her deeply.

"You are crying," she whispered. The area about her heart grew tight as she fought welling emotion. Incredibly awed, she searched his expressions, trying to read all the emotions flashing across his face. She lifted a tentative hand towards his cheek, touched a tear with the tip of her finger. "Why?"

"I cry with joy, *Nippa*...with thanks to the Creator of All for fashioning you for me. With joy in knowing I have finally found the one woman who completes me." He seemed unashamed of his tears.

She marveled at his openness, at his willingness to share the depths of his emotions with her.

The prince had a way of constantly surprising her. His reactions threw her, not fitting the normal "male" responses. Most of the men she knew were so busy being macho they often forgot—hell, never learned—how to be sensitive.

"For long, empty years," he continued, his quiet words recapturing her attention, "I struggled to be a worthy leader for my people, yet in all that time, my heart remained locked away, frozen by grief and despair. While I mouthed platitudes and hawked hope to my people like a deluded priest, exhorting them to look to the future and work toward a better tomorrow, I never really believed my own words. I didn't believe that you—your existence—was possible. I never dared trust that the realization of my own deeply held hopes and dreams could happen. Yet, here you are—here we are, together.

"You will never know how the feel of you, the sight of you beneath me, fills my heart and satisfies my soul's greatest longings. To see your beautiful breasts—plumped and pink from the working of my *terat*—heaving with the pleasure I have given you, to feel you limp and satisfied...I am content. Together, we will build upon the good beginning of our bonding, explore the limits of your body's capability to withstand the pleasure I will heap upon you.

"But for now, I need to rest."

The prince's half-smile looked both winsome and weary, making her want to offer him her breasts as his pillow. But such an offer would reveal to Devtorvas the successful outcome of his deliberate seduction. Still she admitted, if only to herself, that the prince had thoroughly seduced her by his gentleness, his openness and finally, by the mind-blowing, muscle-clenching multiple-orgasms in his arsenal.

Orgasms that lasted, by damn. She stretched boneless beneath the heavy body of the man who had reduced her body to a puddle of orgasmic completion.

"Yeah, I'm tired, too." A sudden yawn stretched her jaw. Her lack of manners embarrassed her, but those three—or was it four?—orgasms had worn her out, leaving her too limp to lift a hand to politely cover her mouth. Well, at least the prince could see she had all her own teeth.

"I have not slept since before arriving at your father's realm and the enjoyment of your irresistibly abundant charms, while a delectable treat, has taxed my reserves. The only weapon I can lift right now is the one pressing against your sweet pussy…and that because it requires no effort on my part. My *cherzda* rises for its mistress as the sun rises for the new day."

She blushed, both at his blunt words and at the feel of his arousal pressing against her clit through the scratchy material of his jeans.

"I may be momentarily weakened by our love-play, but you may be at ease, *fem,* and worry not that your rest will be broken." His hand absently soothed the pebbled skin of her abdomen. "Nothing and no one can slip pass the force field GanR'dari has set up in the outer room. My men will guard us vigilantly. We need fear no intrusion as we refresh ourselves with sleep. We will need our stamina when we take the last step together."

He repositioned them, snuggling close to her, allowing his head to rest upon one full breast. With a sigh, he nestled his cheek against her, rooting for a nipple. Finding the stiffening crest, he slurped it and the surrounding flesh into his mouth and settled down to suckle.

"What last step?"

Suspended in the lingering euphoria joining with him had brought her, physically drained by her orgasms and that peculiar breast thing, she admitted to being confused. She had never before ejaculated from her breasts, yet pearly liquid had flowed from her nipples in an ecstatic stream and like a starving cat, Devtorvas had greedily licked up the residue not absorbed by his…chest cavities, his *terat*.

She really needed to have a talk with her stepmother. Barring that, she'd just have to overcome her monumental embarrassment, her reluctance to appear ignorant in his eyes, and ask Devtorvas for an explanation. She was a teacher, for God's sake—her hardwiring demanded she have answers to every question. And boy, did she ever have questions.

She cocked her head, trying to get a glimpse of his face and snorted, finding he had drifted off to sleep. Obviously, her questions would have to wait. While he slept, his body a dead weight atop her, his possessive grasp had slackened, but his mouth remained latched onto one of her nipples. She squirmed under the forceful pulling—this was no babe at her breast—feeling the tug at her nipple clear to the center of her cunt. Her womb contracted and the pungent smell of arousal wafted on the air. Not again!

At her slightest movement or heavy breath, Devtorvas' lips tightened on her crest, his cheeks hollowed with the strength of his suckling. He would draw on her nipple rapidly, only to ease back into slackness as he eventually slipped deeper into his snooze.

Biting her lip as need spiked anew, craving his mouth's attention at her other breast, she carefully, slowly, eased her nipple out of Devtorvas' slack lips, and replaced it with the neglected one.

The muscles of her belly clamped down and her cream spilled out to slick her upper thighs as his mouth performed its instinctual work, drawing hard enough to hurt before softening into a series of gentle pulls.

Through all this, he slumbered on. She tentatively draped her arms about his muscular frame, filled with conflicting emotions. This man had invaded her home, threatened her with abduction and taken gross—*all right, so there was nothing gross about it*—sexual advantage of her.

She should be terribly angry, shouldn't she?

Instead, lying here beneath him, she luxuriated in the first lasting orgasms of her *pava* cycle. For once, the *pava* cravings had been satisfied. For the first time in a long time, she experienced freedom from the perpetual ache of unrelieved arousal.

She shifted her hips a little, settling into a more comfortable position. Lying under the sleeping Prince, she had plenty of time to delve into her emotions and motivations. Without her *pava* cycle influencing her, she realized she felt an intense attraction for this man. She could no longer blame it on physiological needs…it wasn't just her body involved. Her current state of arousal had nothing to do with being in *pava* and everything to do with the man draped over her.

She craned her neck to garner another glimpse of him. He had proved a selfless lover. The muscles in her cunt clenched as she relived the pleasure he had given her. For that, alone, she felt like falling on her knees before him and—*hhmmm…Now, there was a thought.*

She chuckled.

She had never tasted unflavored cock as Ron, who had a "thing" about oral sex, had sipped at a glass of wine the two times he had eaten her pussy and insisted she drink wine the rare times he allowed her to suck his cock. She'd never known if the wine was to purify her mouth for him or to make his dick palatable to her. She no longer cared, but the fact remained…she had never tasted unfermented cock. And she wanted to.

Suddenly she wanted to know everything about his…what had he called it…his *cherzda*? Yes, that was the word he'd used.

Her eyes drifted closed as she imagined unzipping his pants and slowly pulling them down to reveal the long, heavy cock she had handled only through his jeans. What color was it? Did their people practice circumcision? Could it really be as thick around as it had felt to her wandering fingers? She hadn't felt the head of it—was it tapered or flared? What would he taste like? His body gave off a heady forest-like smell that made her want to set her tongue to his flesh and lick…*everywhere.*

Down, girl! She admonished her libido. Let's not get sidetracked, here. Who cares if he looks like Adonis and

Apollo all rolled up together? Who cares if he's hung like a stallion with a dong a mile long? Who cares if he has thingies in his chest that dole out orgasms by the dozens?

I do! Her libido screamed, jumping up and down and waving her arms madly. This is the first relief we've ever had from the pava pains. The man is a sex god and I, for one, am hooked, addicted and strung-out on the pleasure he gives.

He may do and be all that, she argued back, but let's face it, girl, the man has a barbaric tendency to ignore my right to make my own decisions. On top of that—and here's the biggie—he's from another planet. It's one thing to consider moving to Mars—at least I could still make frequent visits to my Earth family. But this guy lives out of the neighborhood. Way out! I can so not do the galactic moving thing!

Where in the hell are Rb'nTraq and Rb'qarm, anyway? What kind of distance are we talking? If it isn't so far away that a semiannual visit home could be a possibility—

Her eyes popped open. She had to stop stressing! Right now, she had enough to worry about without adding future events she had no control over. Better to live in the present.

Speaking of the present, she had a sleeping god snuggled next to her, up close and personal, slurping down on her nipples. Instead of taking advantage of this situation, she was having a two-sided argument with herself. How lame was that? There just happened to be some prime real estate close by. No better time than now to take the opportunity to let her fingers explore uncharted territory.

Not wanting to wake him, she gently caressed his back, ran her hands over the enticing bands of muscle lying beneath an immense expanse of smooth dark skin. Devtorvas stirred beneath her hands and she froze, fingers coming to rest lightly against his skin. She held her breath, waiting to see if he would awaken.

Her pussy clenched and she drew in a shaky breath when he roused enough to suckle at her straining nipple before nestling his head back between her breasts.

Once sure he would not awaken and catch her pawing his body, she let her hands and her imagination rove on to new territory. Her fingers crept down his back, edging under the waistband of his jeans until she was brushing his ass cheeks, ruffling the short hairs that lightly furred the crevice delineating his tight, hard globes.

She licked her lips at the luscious feel she was copping. She so loved a well-turned male ass. Despite having been married, this was her first chance to fondle one. Ron had always pushed her hands away, telling her he was no rump ranger. She'd always wondered if it had been a case of the person protesting too much.

She gave a mental shake of her head, dismissing all thought of Ron. That loser was in her dead past and she sure the hell didn't want to dwell on *him* when there was Prime Intergalactic Rump Roast beneath her questing fingers. She patted it experimentally.

Damn, but his ass was tight and round. Taut enough to beat a tattoo on.

Oh, hell, I think I'm sunk! Nnora sighed, resigned to lusting after this man. Exhaustion dragged at her, and she yawned, but refused to let go the hands-full of male flesh she was clutching. This ass was hers! She'd gone on finger-safari to find it and she was sho nuff keeping it.

911? Help! I'm trapped beneath an Adonis-Apollo look-alike god, possessed of a tight firm ass, who is intent upon suckling me to death.

I've fallen and I don't want to get up.

* * * * *

Glendevtorvas came awake, cock fully aroused and throbbing. Warm, feminine fingers possessively tucked into the crease of his ass made his eyes cross with lust. Mind whirling, heart thrumming with the urge to sink into the sweet confection beneath him, he propped himself on his elbows and, with barely restrained passion, gazed down on Nnora's sleeping face in wonderment.

He hadn't known her long, but he knew she would be mortified to be caught holding on to him in such a revealing way. The princess' slumbering actions were the very opposite of those she confessed to while awake. The way her fingers curled into his flesh, gripping him in a determined hold, told him she wanted him. Driven by the need to establish her ownership, she had laid claim to him in much the same way he'd placed his mark on her.

His lips curved in an exultant smile. Shifting his weight to his left arm, with his right forefinger, he gently circled the red, swollen areolas of both her breasts. His private mark of ownership. He planned to keep her nipples buried in his *terat* often enough for them to maintain that rosy hue and sensitivity. Every time she breathed, every time an article of clothing encountered her well-used flesh, she would know his possession of her.

He felt no qualms about his agenda for her. He fully intended to addict her to the pleasure he would willingly shower over and in her. He was going to enjoy taming her and training her to his needs, while making sure to meet hers. From the way she had howled and bucked under him, he was fairly certain his Nnora had never received the sexual pampering and care adequate for her well-being.

He placed a caring kiss on her relaxed lips, his heart clenching at the thought of the escalating pain and sensual deprivation she must have endured during her current and last *pava* cycle. Well, she was under his care, now. He would see to it that she never suffered another uncomfortable *pava*. He was able, willing and ready to fuck his woman all day, every day, giving her all the orgasms she required. Above all, he would give her his child. Once she became pregnant, the pain of her present *pava* cycles would cease.

He shifted to get more comfortable and Nnora's arms tightened around him, curtailing his movement and drawing him back to her. He chuckled, flattered by her obvious, though unconscious, attachment to him. He applauded her actions by inserting a bold hand between them, dragging it down to her juicy folds. His finger slid through her slick cream, sinking past his knuckle into her hot, tight cunt. He withdrew his hand and ran his tongue over his finger, licking every drop of her tangy taste from his flesh.

Deth, she tasted delicious. He wanted more.

Easing down her body, using his shoulders to hold her legs open, he soothed her sleepy protests with gentling sweeps of his hands until she stilled beneath him once more.

He covered her breasts with his palms, plumping and worshipping the soft flesh. He rotated his hands, massaging her stiff nipples until they grew incredibly harder, stabbing up into his curved hands. Taking the aroused tips between thumbs and forefingers, he squeezed down, pinching the sensitive flesh, rolling and tugging at them until they stood sharply erect in all their crimson glory.

A low groan brought his head up and he met her unfocused gaze head on. Even as her eyes cleared and her muscles bunched, preparing to move, he flung an arm over her breasts, holding her down, holding her still. She trembled under him. Not wanting to frighten her, he reared back, reining in his need to take her, stake his own claim.

"I only want to taste you," he grated, his voice gruff with longing. "Please, don't deny me."

His heart almost ceased when he felt her body relax, accepting his dominance. But she did more than relax. She made of her surrender a regal gesture. Lying quietly, eyes wide open, gaze entangled with his, she bent her knees and splayed her legs, offering him free access to her *pava*.

His cock twitched and throbbed. In his chest, his *terat* contracted and softened, anticipating her insertion. He wet his lips, starving for the feel of her plump nipples embedded deep in his *terat*, filling the masculine cups evolved for her sole enjoyment. He wanted her breasts, badly, but he'd had a taste of her succulent—what had she called it? Oh, yes—*pussy*, a small sampling that didn't begin to satisfy. He needed more, needed to gorge on her honey, to sate his hunger with her sultry, tangy cream.

He breathed deeply, drawing in the heady aroma of her spilling juices. The lust-inspiring scent made him ravenous. He moved an inch nearer, urging her legs further apart so he could get as close to her as possible. He licked his lips in greedy anticipation as he moved into position, eyes locked on the beautiful sight of her pretty crimson cunt.

"You have no idea how beautiful you are." He traced her folds with a reverent finger. He had traveled the galaxies, visited hundreds of worlds, but her tender, dainty *fertile* pussy was the most beautiful sight he had ever seen. Bending his head in reverence, he parted her nether lips with his thumbs, exposing her pink, glistening entrance. He dipped his tongue inside in a kiss of homage, vowing his thankful, eternal loyalty. His *cherzda* jerked, letting him know it wanted inside to kiss her, too.

"I want to fuck you so badly," he crooned, pulling back from her just enough to settle in to a comfortable position. "Since I have to wait for that, I'll make a long meal out of your luscious pussy, instead."

Placing his thumbs on each side or her labia, he caressed her silky skin, carefully pulling back the fleshy folds to reveal her pussy. He drank in the sight of her. She was all ripe, succulent flesh in shades from pink to dark strawberry, highlighted by her glistening juices. Her inner petals pulsed with the fragile echo of her distant heartbeat, the rhythmic movement irresistibly drawing his gaze.

He leaned in close to swipe her shallow channel from bottom to top, gathering the silky liquid spilling from her small opening. His tongue lapped at her, flicking against her clitoris at the top of his arch and her taste sizzled on his tongue, zesty with her natural spices. He tried to hold back, to be tender—to give her a gentle loving, but his hunger peaked, grabbed him hard. His hands came up and gripped her upper thighs. Spreading her wide, he ate at her cunt.

"Mmmmmmmm! So good! Yes, oh, please…eat me!"

Her sexy mewls and whimpers spurred him on. He exalted in the sharp tug of her fingers in his hair.

"Oh, God, Devtorvas! Don't stop…never stop!"

He lapped at her, rooting in her folds for the heavy honeyed syrup oozing from her weeping *pava,* smearing her juices over his face, luxuriating in her sweet fragrance.

It wasn't enough.

He returned his mouth to her entrance, taking her clit between his teeth. With teasing tugs, he jerked the little bundle of nerves. Only when her clitoris was stiff and red, fully distended from under its covering hood did he stop. Slurping her up into his mouth, he suckled hard on the engorged button, alternately drawing and nibbling on it.

He slowed when she began to quake beneath him, her knees locking tight to trap his head between her shaking thighs. He clamped his hands down on her thighs, holding her still while he rammed his tongue up her narrow channel and rimmed it around her vaginal walls, only to retreat back to her clitoris to worry it with his teeth and tongue.

Her taste burned its way into his mind, etched itself upon his heart and he drank, taking suckle. Still he thirsted. He knew his thirst for her would never be slaked—

"I can't…stand it…ohhhhhhh…yessss…eat me… mhhmmmm, like that…hard! Harder! Ohhhh…I…I think I'm coming!"

Her pussy clamped down on his tongue, and he knew she was on the brink. He hummed into her, vibrating her stiff little clitoris with one last stimulus.

Her screams echoed off the walls of the bedroom as her pussy pulsed around his pistoning tongue, gushing out her creamy fluid. Moaning himself, he locked his mouth on her pussy to catch very drop of her cum. He didn't stop until she collapsed back against the mattress in a boneless heap.

Lifting himself from between her legs, he flung himself down on his side, arm bent, his head resting on his palm. He gazed down at Nnora. Her eyes closed, legs and arms sprawled, she fought to catch her breath. He grinned, licking his lips, taking her inertia as a compliment to the massive orgasm he knew he'd given her. His *Nippa* appeared the very picture of a well-loved woman.

While he watched her, his smile slowly faded as he became aware of his demanding *cherzda.* Swollen and throbbing, it pressed insistently against the constricting material of his jeans.

Chapter Eight

Slipping from within her loose embrace, Devtorvas reared up on his haunches, his hands yanking at his clothes, fingers fumbling over the working of his zipper. With a smothered imprecation, he manhandled the catch, and then worked his tight jeans down over his swollen rod. Carefully maneuvering around his jutting staff, he tugged until the jeans cleared his hair-dusted buttocks. He panted heavily when his weighty sex finally sprang free.

Floating on the edge of total relaxation, her gaze followed the path of those descending jeans. She came alert quickly and jerked upright, awed, when his *cherzda*—a monster far too large to label a mere penis—was revealed. She swallowed sickly, watching the massive cock spring up. And up…and up!

Was there no end to the thing? Was there a Human male born with even a quarter of the equipment the prince possessed? More to the point, was there a woman alive who could take that organ and survive? She'd been insane to fantasize about having that mammoth beast in her mouth—she'd have to unhinge her jaw in order to accommodate a cock that size without choking.

Panic threatened. "What are you doing?" She scrabbled breathlessly toward the headboard of her bed. "You said we were going to wait! I-I thought…?"

"And as *hard* as it is proving to do, I shall keep my word." Devtorvas grinned wryly at his stiff cock. His hands, though large, barely contained the enormous erection. "I refuse to go around with my *cherzda* bent double inside these tight pants. I need relief, and since you are not of a mind to accommodate me—" He paused, slanting a questioning glance her way.

She shook her head back and forth, frantic. "I have never been suicidal."

"—I'll deal with the situation, myself. But I give you fair notice," he warned, grimacing, "I intend to be inside you at every opportunity, once we have mated. I have had enough of my own hands to last two lifetimes."

"Once is all you'll get with me." She was only half-joking. "I'll be dead, split in two by that megaton heat-seeking missile you're thinking about stuffing me with."

"You will be surprised at how easily we fit, *Nippa*." His teeth flashed in a quick grin. "You are a small thing, yes, but I believe your *pava* will stretch to accommodate me. How often must I reassure you we are mates, preordained for each other?"

As he spoke, he cupped his pendulous balls, rolling them between the palms of his hands. His fingers lightly squeezed his testicles, and he licked his lips. "My pleasure increases when I envision your soft hands on my hungry flesh." He groaned, gaze dropping to her crotch. With another, deeper moan, he gripped his cock in his other hand, working both at the same time.

His shaft jerked and stiffened under his ministrations, spurting to a greater length and girth. Despite her very real fear, she wanted him still.

It wasn't his fault his cock was so big. Maybe they could ring it halfway down so he couldn't bottom out and accidentally hurt her. For some unearthly reason, she firmly believed he would never intentionally harm her.

"What do human males call their sex?"

Gaze riveted to the motion of his hands, while he caressed and tugged on his imposing staff with firm jerks of his hands, she hardly noticed his question. She had never seen a man masturbate before. What an education.

"Men."

Wow. Up and down. Up and down.

"Nnora..."

Dayam! I would love a chance to get my hands and my cunt around a mega-cock like that. Hell, it won't half fit in any hole of mine, but I can certainly salivate at the thought. What I wouldn't give for the opportunity of having to, just once, deal with the problem of a cock that is too large, rather than having to cope with one that is too small—

"Nnora!"

The sharpness of his tone brought her mind screeching back to the moment. "Whaat?" She didn't take kindly to having her fantasy interrupted.

"Humans call their *cherzda* 'men'?" He sounded confused.

Blinking, she ran over the last sentences in her mind. A bark of laughter escaped her. "No, I... I must have been thinking of something else."

"Answer my question." His hands became a blur on his rampant flesh; his breathing roughened.

"Oh." What to call it hardly seemed important at the moment. "Ummm, they have all sorts of names for it. Dick. Penis. Member. Rocket. Joystick. Shaft. Cock. Dong..." She faltered. He was torturing his straining flesh, moaning harshly. His poor cock took on a deep crimson hue under his forceful handling.

Men obviously don't appreciate cock like women do. If I had all that luscious meat in hand, I would never handle it so roughly.

"Strange. We have only the one word. *Cherzda.*"

"Which makes sense, since you only have one cock." She held back a smile at his expression. He was so cute when he was confused.

A short burst of laughter escaped him when he got her jest. "True, *fem.*" He stroked his thrusting length from its wide base to the tapered tip. "But, which of the Earth terms do you like best?" With firm hand-over-hand motions, he worked his cock. The swollen head of his *cherzda* engorged with blood and deepened in color, resembling a ripe plum.

He gripped the blunt, ridged crest between thumb and fore-finger, squeezing ruthlessly. Flinging his head back, he let out a garbled, moaning plea.

The almost agonized expression of stark sexual hunger on his lean face touched a deep, unexplored portion of her soul. Fascinated by his ability to control his urge to come, she sensed the raw display of masculine power calling to her femininity. Her own arousal spiked in response.

She loved the way the corded muscles in his neck stood out in stark relief under his warm, dark skin. Loved the sight of his defined and buffed deltoids powering his pistoning fist. Her pussy gushed in response, releasing her fragrant musk.

Watching a man resort to hand-fucking himself in order to honor his word proved an unbelievable turn on. Just how badly did he want to fuck her? It couldn't possibly be as badly as she wanted him. She locked gazes with him and their eyes communicated what their mouths would not.

"Nnora! *Which one*?"

She'd lost the thread of the conversation in her rising excitement. Again. "Which…uh…what?"

"Which of the terms do you like best, *fem*?"

"Oh. I like cock." She swallowed thickly as he fondled and squeezed his, strong fingers as agile on his own flesh as they had earlier been on hers.

"I'm glad to hear it!" His husky laughter sounded strained over his continued pumping of his steely erection.

Her body quivered in primal response to his sexual motions. A primitive pulse throbbed to life in her wet sex. She gulped air into her starved lungs, hoping he didn't realize just how much he affected her.

Her nipples caught fire, tingling and burning when he began a rhythmic thrusting. She burst into flame watching him slide his arching hard-on through the tight, narrow ring of his fingers. The long, thick length tunneled through his hands, forcing his fingers apart. Her lips parted on her labored breaths as she visualized how that thick cock would feel forging through the tight portal of her cunt, stuffing and over-filling her almost virginal channel.

It would hurt, she knew. Just the thought of being fucked by his massive cock—having her pussy reamed by that huge schlong, pounded by the inhuman strength she knew he possessed—almost scared the arousal right out of her. At the same time, the thought titillated her like nothing ever had.

She didn't notice him climbing up between her legs, not until his large hands gripped her legs, forcing them wide apart. But she certainly noticed his monster cockhead thudding against the high mound of her pubis as he tugged her close, grinding his hips into her crotch.

"What are you *doing*?" Her strained whisper was barely audible. Fear battled with almost uncontrollable desire. Oh, god, was he going to fuck her after all? Break his word and try to fit that enormous cock in her unprepared pussy?

"I...need..." he panted, "need...to...see...your...beauty, *Nippa.*"

Embarrassment heated her cheeks while he pried her thighs wider apart, opening her to his burning gaze. He stared at her pussy. The heat of his passionate, hungry gaze on her slick cunt scorched through her nerve endings like molten lava. She felt pinned, like a captured butterfly with outstretched wings. Her body thrilled to the fact he wanted her so badly.

Taking himself in hand, he rubbed the dripping, bulbous head of his cock through her pussy lips, mixing his pre-cum with her slippery juices. When the heavy, wide glans thudded against her clitoris, her womb contracted, muscles fluttered and she shuddered. Her breasts swelled, nipples came stiffly, instantly erect. Hot cream spilled out of her pussy and ran down the crease of her buttocks to pool beneath her on the bed.

"I want in, Nnora." His deep voice rumbled beside her ear before his tongue rimmed the canal and his teeth nipped at her lobe.

His huge glans wedged itself between the lips of her pussy, pressing against her vulnerable opening. A wash of excitement lubricated the walls of her cunt. He pushed the wide head slowly into her. It forced open the first ring of her entrance, stretching her painfully wide.

Fear flared up in the wake of the growing discomfort. Her cunt muscles tightened down on the intruder, trying to expel it. "No! Stop!" Her voice shook with fright.

He stopped immediately, cursing as he eased out of her. "Then touch me, *Nippa, please...*" His eyes burned hotly. His voice, dark with need, almost managed to cut through her fears. "Help me reach completion. I beg you, take me in your hands."

"You're on the edge." She gulped. "I don't want to be...forced if you should lose control."

"Please, *Nippa*," he pleaded when she didn't move. "Help me, before I lose this fight...and give in to the urge to fuck your delicious pussy into oblivion."

She shrank backwards as far as her captive position would allow. "I don't think touching you is such a good idea then," Nnora whispered, hesitant, and, at the same time, sorely tempted, to sample that masculine need and heat focused so narrowly upon her.

He pulled back from her, then, and released his cock. His gaze intent, expression solemn, he cupped her face with his palms, absently running his thumbs along her jaw. "My *cherzda'va*, I promise I won't. My life's vow I give. I will never harm you. Did I not stop at your command?"

She nodded, too uncertain to speak.

"I always will."

When she searched his earnest gaze, the honest caring in his eyes persuaded her more than his words. She worried her bottom lip as she weighed the pros and cons. She did trust Devtorvas not to hurt her—he had never done so yet...and she *wanted* to get her hands on his cock, to test its girth and heft for herself. She just didn't want it inside her. With the safety net of his promise, it was an easy enough decision.

"All right, Devtorvas, tell me what you want me to do."

"The first thing I want you to do," his voice came light and gentle with good humor, "is to call me Dev. We are naked together. I think that means we can dispense with formality."

She nodded her head jerkily. "I can do that."

"Good." He smiled, helping her to her knees. Taking her hands, he wrapped her fingers about his rampant cock, his breath hissing through his clenched teeth. "The next thing I want you to do is get familiar with my *cherzda*. I am yours, forever. Learn me…learn *this*."

Keeping his hands over hers, he slid her fingers up and down his cock, showing her the motions he liked.

"Yes, like that!" he encouraged as she took up the rhythm on her own. "I need to come. I'm so hard, I hurt, *Nippa*. Please…ease me…help me."

When she looked up from her preoccupation with his cock, he had twisted his mouth in a parody of a smile. His glittering eyes, strained expression and labored breathing revealed the extent of his lust. She marveled at his control, praying it would hold.

Gauging his every reaction, she went back to teasing his engorged flesh, running her hands over his out-thrust length, inquisitively cataloging his attributes. "Oh! You are very different from human males—I mean, besides the obvious difference of size."

She hefted the long, thick shaft in her hands, the heat pouring off it almost searing her palms. The majestic organ rose from an impossibly wide, thick base in a bed of dense black hair to flair even wider at the summit, and though there was no foreskin, it was easy to see no circumcising knife had ever been laid to the exposed head.

"Why are we females naturally hairless when you males have so much genital hair?" She twisted her fingers through the thick mat surrounding his sex, while glancing up to look at him.

"I don't know," he gritted out, pressing his palms to her shoulders and rubbing in a circular motion. "Perhaps the gods willed it. By *Deth's* pillars! Don't stop."

"Don't rush me." She was determined to take her time searching out all his differences.

His cock was magnificent. Prominent, ropy veins stood out along the entire length. Except for the dimpled eye resting in the tip of his cock and the dozens of tiny apertures encircling the entire shaft just below the bulbous head, the skin of his cock stretched taut and silken over the steel rod of his muscle. Not a wrinkle disrupted the velvetiness of the skin just below the ridged crest.

Hot. Hard. Smooth.

Alien.

She tried and failed to palm the enormous ball sac containing his *sirat*. It was too large to fit her relatively small hand. The sac, swaying heavily between his legs—buttery-soft and covered with a silky pelt of hair resembling mink fur—drew up and tightened when she palpated it with gentle squeezes, signaling his impending ejaculation.

He sank his fingers in her hair. "I love the way you touch me, so delicately—*Yesss!* Squeeze my *sirat*...like that...*Uuhhhmmm*."

Her own excitement growing at his groaning sighs, she returned to fondling his *cherzda*. Though still frightened at the thought being fucked with it on some fast-approaching date, she couldn't get enough of it now.

"Harder, *Nippa,*" he urged breathlessly. "You may be rougher. Let me feel you."

She obeyed, gripping him with both hands. Forming a ring, she stroked up and down, harder and faster, pumping his cock until her hands stung from the friction.

"Oh! Yes…ye—ee—sss, *Nippa!*"

His breath catching on a sibilant hiss, Devtorvas broke away, his cock swinging outthrust before him as he paced the length of the bed, grasping the head of his cock between the iron pincers of his fingers.

"Why did you stop me?" She swung her legs over the side of the bed, coming up to a seated position. Her nakedness forgotten, she felt totally at ease with the man standing at the foot of the bed, stiff cock jutting away from his body, throbbing head clamped between steely fingers.

"Do you trust me?" There was a look in his eyes she could not interpret. Trepidation? Did he care enough to be frightened that her answer might not be what he wished?

"Yes," she answered, meaning it. Somehow, sometime during this strange, surreal afternoon, the prince had gained her trust. She didn't quite understand how he had managed it, yet it was so. "Yes, for some strange reason, I do."

He swallowed hard, a smile lighting his features. "You humble me and honor me both at once," he whispered, eyes devouring her. "I will strive never to betray your trust, *Nippa.*"

"I believe you," Nnora said softly, her mouth widening in an answering smile.

"What do you know of the sexual attributes of *Rb'qarmshi* males?"

"Not very much." Where was he going with this line of questioning?

He nodded. "This is what I suspected. May I give you a short lesson? I assure you it is necessary. I do not want you to say, later, that I took advantage of your ignorance."

She frowned, her curiosity flaring to life.

"Like the *fem's* gift—the fluid which flowed from your *tlinis* at completion—there is an enzyme in the male's sperm which heightens the pleasure threshold of their mate. When introduced into the *fem* by ejaculation, our seed enhances orgasmic frequency and duration. When applied to the dermis, it enhances the sensual receptors of the nerves embedded in the skin, causing a greater tactile sensitivity leading to heightened pleasure."

She resisted the urge to tap her foot. "Gee, Prince," she teased, "let's see if I can rephrase all those big sounding words in twenty words or less. Your cum is an aphrodisiac…right?"

"Not quite. An aphrodisiac makes you *want* sex while our sperm makes the sex *better*."

She felt her eyebrows arch, echoing her rising speculation. She thought back to the orgasm she had achieved while being *seated* and her belly went hollow as her womb spasmed. Arousal hit her so hard it frightened her, tightening her nipples to pinpoint hardness and swelling her clit. "Damn, Dev, if that's true, what happens if you swallow it?"

An arrested expression swept his face and he fidgeted under her inquisitive gaze. "I don't...personally...know."

Nnora's heart tripped, her breathing hitched. At the same time, she wanted to howl with laughter. Oh, the tables had turned with a vengeance!

"You mean, you have never had your cock sucked?" She deliberately mimicked his earlier phrasing about the state of her un-*seated* nipples.

Dev had moved to stand before her while he spoke, so she had to look up to catch his reaction. His height and her seated position placed his cock mouth-high. She could wait no longer. She gave in to the temptation of finding out what cock—*Dev's* cock, unflavored with the cloaking bouquet of wine—tasted like.

Leaning forward, she swabbed the broad glans with a bold lick of her tongue. Dev's cock leaped in response, causing it to jerk away from her mouth. It thudded against her nose on its downward arc.

"Ouch!"

"Uzak!"

Simultaneously, she grabbed the swaying cock, stilling its wild gyrations and he shouted, clasping her head between his hands. Her nanofyle implant fed her a string of words, some she didn't understand, but "shit" seemed to be the consensus.

"I'll take it that means you liked what I did. Maybe there is something in *Rb'qarmshi fem* saliva that enhances the pleasure receptors of their males' cocks," she suggested with a grin just before repeating her actions. This time, she slid one hand down to his *sirat*, cradling what she could of his ball sac. Her fingers feathered through its silky, mink-like covering. She lapped at the base of his cock, and his stones did a happy dance in her palms. She laughed low in her throat, her merriment sending vibrations along the jutting shaft as she glanced up from beneath her lowered lashes to assess her effect upon Dev.

He stood braced above her, sweat beaded on his brow, lips drawn back from clenched teeth as his eyes glittered with naked lust. His hands kneaded the back of her skull, bunching in her long black curls, opening and shutting as if he couldn't make up his mind whether to pull her forward or push her away.

"*Nippa*," he groaned, "You burn me up with your sweet mouth. I never knew such was possible. Let me give you pleasure now…let me spill my seed over your sweet pussy and your plump, beautiful breasts. I wish to see my seed adorning your body, marking you as mine."

She drew in a shaky breath. Her breasts quaked and her pussy tightened, pulsing at his erotic pleas. If he fucked half as well as he talked, she'd be in sexual heaven.

His hands left her head and soothed over her shoulders before he pinched a distended nipple in each thumb and forefinger. Catching her gaze and holding it as firmly as his fingers held her captured nubs, he asked, "Still trust me?"

"Yes," she managed on the third try, her voice raspy with the effort of speaking at all. Her breasts tingled where he gripped them. Her blood-filled clit throbbed, eager for equal attention.

"Then lie back on the bed and spread your legs for me."

For just a moment, she hesitated and then she lowered her body on the bed, arms raised, and hands open-palmed beside her head. With a seductive, deliberate movement, she brought her feet up to the mattress and planted them wide, opening herself to him, wordlessly submitting to whatever he planned.

He grabbed a couple pillows and gestured towards her hips. "Up!"

When she lifted her hips, he stuffed the cushions beneath her, elevating her to an angle where she was sure all her intimate parts were exposed to him. She wasn't sure how she felt about having her ass on blatant display, but she didn't have time to worry about it before he spoke again.

"Spread your pretty pussy for me, my Nnora."

Creaming at his words, she obediently reached down and pulled back her swollen labia, revealing her stiff clitoris and her drenched cunt. She had never felt hotter and wetter than she did now, lying spread-eagled before him.

"You are so beautiful it hurts me to look at you—" he praised, delving for her entrance with a thick finger, sliding through her slick sea of wetness "—to be deprived of the sight of you would hurt me more." He moved closer and bent his knees, bringing his cock into contact with her pussy, carefully rubbing himself between her juicy nether lips.

With exquisite control, he pressed the blunt head of his seeping cock against the dripping mouth of her sex, hard enough to cause the ring of muscle to quiver, yet not hard enough to enter. Pulling back, he positioned his cock at the tight ring of her puckered little asshole and repeated his actions. A nasty thrill shot up Nnora's spine, exploded throughout her nervous system.

She had never before considered anal sex and couldn't believe the pleasure knifing through her as his hard maleness pressed against the tightly closed sphincter of her ass.

God, but the feeling of his cock at her back door had her nipples stabbing at the sky. Her thighs clenched in terror and titillation.

Eyes locked on hers, easily reading her reactions, he positioned his cock right over her anus, pressing just hard enough to open it.

She grunted, impaled on a stake of flesh that felt a mile wide, her ass stretched beyond belief. Yet, she knew he had not entered her, would not enter her. In fact, she felt no pain, only an intense sense of pressured openness.

He lowered himself over her, catching his weight on his extended arms. The length of his cock enabled him to remain lodged against her sphincter while he pressed against her clit. He rotated his hips, mashing the little bundle of nerves between them and she cried out, arching her pelvis into his grinding strokes.

Reaching up, she clasped her hands about his biceps, holding on to the only stable point in her universe. Her nipples begged for his mouth or *terat*, her clit burned and swelled under the abrasive strokes.

"I want to suck your cock."

He lifted himself off her and she felt bereft, her anus and clit aching for the lost stimulus. She slid to her knees as he sat on the side of the bed.

Eyeing the oversized lollipop, she wrapped her hands about as much of it as she could and went right to work devouring the banquet set before her, licking her way all around the broad circumference of his shaft. She savored the differing textures, leaving the head for last. He tasted of...*her*, fresh from her peach-scented shower and of a flavor all his own—a wild, green, living taste that flowered on her tongue, activating her saliva glands.

She giggled at his shocked reaction to the finger she circled around the tight entrance to his ass. Enjoying herself immensely, she slurped her way along the solid cock to the meaty glans. The head glowed a deep magenta, the shaft an angry red. Her lips tingled as she nibbled on the soft-on-hard flesh.

"Uhhmm! Feels good—yes!" He hissed his enjoyment of her actions.

The accompanying sounds of his harsh groans and masculine sighs of lust inspired her to greater feats of erotic imagination. She strove to push him over his limit, driven by a need to participate in his explosive pleasure.

She dipped her head and took in what she could, pumping his cock and fondling his balls as her tongue flicked the underside of the ringed head. She noticed a clear liquid seeping from the puckered slit in the blunt head. The fluid also issued from the tiny apertures lying along the broad circumference of his rod.

The viscous, slippery substance looked and smelled nothing like Human ejaculate. Hot and slick, it caused her hands to glide and slip as she ran them over his jutting manhood and down between his legs.

"What *is* this stuff?" she asked, her fingers playing slip 'n slide over his responsive cock.

"It is...my *zhi*. It presages my seed. It will...ease my way...help me enter you without too much pain. "By *Deth, Nippa!*"

He sucked in a loud breath. His eyes squeezed shut as his body danced beneath her busy mouth and fingers. The muscles in his lower belly visibly bunched and contracted in jerky spasms that caused his rock hard erection to thud against her cupped hands. His hips bucked frantically as he choked off a harsh, primal cry of ecstasy.

"Enough of this!" He dragged her up, capturing her mouth in a desperate kiss.

Lush. Wetly primal, the kiss incited her to partake. She twined her eager tongue with his, bent on shattering his last defenses, on giving as good as she got. Reaching down between them, she grabbed and squeezed his balls, adding the final touch to his defeat.

He let out a lusty groan, then arched his bucking hips into her palms, a jet of cum spuming from his pulsating *cherzda*. He came a long time, flooding her hands and breasts, her thighs and her mons until he collapsed down beside her in spent ecstasy.

The smell of his glistening seed was strongly evocative, reminding her of scent from her childhood. She could not bring to mind the exact aroma; the scent eluded her. Nnora could not resist swirling the tip of her pointer finger through the shimmering layer of cum decorating her right breast. Determined to know his taste, she brought the finger to the tip of her tongue—

Anise stars danced behind her eyelids.

Licorice novas exploded through her body.

Her body bowed under a brutal orgasm. She jack-knifed up towards his crotch. His cock, still erect and firm, thudded hard against her clit. She howled like a bitch in heat, screaming as her hands, clenching and unclenching, pounded the mattress at her sides.

Oh, god, what is happening to me?

Her head thrashed from side to side, eyes wide open yet blinded by the maelstrom raging throughout her bucking body. She felt on fire, hotter than firecrackers on a July Fourth evening.

"Help…me…help…*oh, god!*"

Incoherent pleas poured from her lips as her body burned and sizzled, dark need and grinding completion battled within her, searing her flesh. She didn't feel him moving her, rearranging her body.

She knew nothing until Dev eased her thrashing thighs further apart, murmuring assurances and stroking calm into her taut flanks. Sinking his head between her thighs, he clamped his open mouth over her weeping cunt.

Every flat-tongued swipe seemed designed to drive her higher; every swirling lick caused the flames to burn brighter.

"Dev, I'm burning up…you're…burning me up."

She wept as he relentlessly devoured her cunt, loudly gulping and slurping the flowing streams of her slick cream. Lapping, biting at her, he worked her pussy until once more she climaxed, climbing again, screaming again.

Like a ravenous beast, he feasted in her cunt, seeming never to have enough. He tongue-fucked her, his driving tongue a fiery lash spearing into her churning depths.

"Oh, yes, oh, yes…eat me! Ream me," she shouted, climbing from plateau to plateau of pleasure, sobbing out her satisfaction through orgasm after orgasm.

He fed on her quivering flesh until he had reduced her to a moaning heap, no longer capable of producing so much as a whimper out of her raw, abused throat. Took her to height after height, until she lay beneath him limp and satiated, unable to sustain another drop of pleasure.

He lifted his head and met her dazed eyes, a measuring look in his own.

"You can take more." Relentlessly, he pinched and twisted her abraded nipples, reddening them more. Their spurt of erect growth only met with firmer handling. "I love to see you come, *Nippa*. Dance for me, again..."

Giving her a wicked grin, he lowered his head once more to take her clit between his teeth.

Chapter Nine

He motioned for her to precede him through the open door. "How long will you be angry with me, *fem*?"

"Until you can give me an acceptable explanation for making me pee with an audience, you high-handed, overbearing *male*."

Nnora was still fuming over the fact that Dev had refused her request for privacy. After their amazing love-play and shared shower, she had been feeling in harmony with him until he had issued his high-handed edict that she was not to leave his sight until they reached his ship.

Disregarding her frantic pleas for a few moments alone, he had pointed out their earlier intimacy, reminding her he had already seen everything she had.

She gritted her teeth at the memory of his typical male response, becoming angry all over again. Men! Why couldn't they seem to realize that some things were just more intimate than sex? In her humble opinion, using the bathroom definitely fell in that category.

The irritating lout had rejected all her well-reasoned, logical points. He had lounged against the mirrored wall, arms crossed over his wide chest, his large presence stealing the very air, filling the extra space in her small bathroom. Under his gimlet eye, she had made several abortive attempts to empty her bladder. Frustrated, teeth floating, she had begged him to turn around, to allow her, at least, the illusion of privacy. He'd agreed to her request and she'd been so thankful, she had failed to notice his trickery.

She'd watched anxiously as he turned his back. With a long, relieved sigh, her tense muscles relaxed enough for her to take care of business. Her ire forgotten, she happily contemplated their recent sexual indulgences, excited about where their relationship might be going…until, in the midst of her happy thoughts, she glanced up and met his watchful gaze in the mirrored wall. The tricky dog had been watching her all along. With an angry cry of embarrassment, she'd thrown the roll of toilet tissue at his head.

After that humiliating interlude, she knew she should have no problems facing down his soldiers, though she definitely did *not* look forward to running the gauntlet of alien warriors milling about her living room. In actual fact, she still dreaded becoming the focus for the knowing eyes of his personal guard, every one of them privy to what had been occurring in her bedroom. Even if nothing could be worse than Dev watching her pee.

Damn him, anyhow. After that explosive series of climaxes engendered by her tasting his sperm, he had brought her to completion several times more during the course of the afternoon, twice with his mouth and hands and once with his *terat*. Until she'd become too hoarse and too exhausted to make a peep, her screams of ecstasy had probably penetrated all the way out to the street, let alone into the next room.

How could she have known she was a "screamer"? Her lips turned up in an unwilling smile.

Oh, she'd gasped and moaned her way through many Jumbo-induced climaxes, but hand fucks required a certain level of control. She'd never before had the opportunity to find out how giving up control to another during orgasm would affect her—before Dev's whirlwind entrance into her life, she'd never had an orgasm with anyone else.

Now, standing in the doorway of her crowded living room, head bowed, cheeks burning hotly, she prepared to pass through the congregated men. At her side, Dev whispered encouragement, taking her upper arm in a broad palm.

She started out, eyes lowered, yet she fancied she could feel the intent gaze of each soldier burning through her layers of clothing. Were they envisioning the shape of her nipples, the roundness of her buttocks?

From what her quick, furtive glances garnered, every single member of the prince's personal cadre of guards exceeded the standard—*hers* anyway!—of masculine beauty. Each epitomized the height of manly strength and form.

The thought of being the focus of these men's sexual fantasies caused a wicked spurt of hot excitement to blossom in her breasts and in her cunt. Her nipples perked up and preened for their audience, pushing boldly against their thin covering of silk. Horrified, she snatched her arm out of Dev's grip and rushed past his men, intent on getting on the other side without them smelling the heated flow of her arousal.

In her wake, she vaguely heard several of the warriors making comments in the melodious sounding *Rb'qarmli* tongue, but the loud pounding of her heart, the ringing in her ears, prevented her from comprehending what they said.

Catching up with her just before she reached the door, Dev recaptured her arm, whispering reassuringly, "No need to feel discomfited, *Nippa*. They only remark on your regal bearing and uncommon beauty, knowing I would allow nothing more personal—"

"You claim to know what I'm feeling, Dev?" she asked scornfully, using the informal diminutive of his name as he had requested. Considering the intimate activities they had shared, it would be hypocritical to balk at familiarity now. "You think you can read my thoughts?"

"What need have I to read your thoughts, *Nippa,* when I have only to read your expressive face—" he opened the front door , letting in the sights and sounds of the busy San Francisco street she lived on "—or smell your *pava's* sweet release of juices."

She wanted to slap that smug smile off his too-handsome face.

So much for her aroused state escaping the men's detection...

She made no excuses for her body's responses. She would have had to be dead not to react to all the testosterone floating free in her living room. Any normal woman—and Dev had proven her just that, this afternoon—would have responded in the same manner.

"Keep your nose out of my business, Your Highness," she snapped. Immediately, she wished the sentence back, sure he would take offense at her unthinking words. "Devtorvas, I—"

"Sh'tai, craal i nohtan'ka!"

The living room emptied as the warriors instantly headed for the bedroom in obedience to their prince's irate command.

Her mouth worked soundlessly, unable to articulate an apology as Dev advanced on her with eyes narrowed and lips drawn tight in anger. Before he could speak, she rushed into words. "Please don't send them in there, Dev! I didn't strip the sheets—"

He took hold of her, his pectorals flexing as he lifted her up against the wall, the strength of his arms easily holding her in place. He growled, "Fuck the sheets! You dare *flower* in the presence of my men and declare it not my business? Know this, Glennora, my *cherzda'va*...when you are ready to *dance*, I will be your *only* partner."

"I didn't mean it like—"

Dev's mouth crashed down on hers, cutting off the rest of her sentence. His tongue stabbed at hers, swiping the walls of her mouth, skimming the edges of her teeth. He thrust his tongue in her repeatedly, mimicking how he had thrust it into her cunt earlier, demanding her response.

She helplessly gave him what she knew he wanted, entangling her tongue with his. She suckled on his marauding flesh, losing herself in his spicy, erotic taste.

Why did he, how could he, cause her to forget everything in his arms...even her justified anger?

He leaned into her, his considerable bulk holding her still while he snaked one bold hand up under the hem of her dress, snarling a word her implanted translator couldn't or wouldn't handle. Holding her gaze, he shredded her panties as if they were paper. His hand returned to plunder her wet folds.

He flicked her clit with a heavy swipe of his thumb while he sank two digits into her contracting pussy. She tensed, fighting the response, but pleasure washed through her, darkening her sight. Against her will, her clenched muscles loosened. Her clit throbbed beneath his rough handling. Her cream flowed heavy and thick around his fingers, easing their path. He shoved them in and out of her until her hips were thrusting back at him, wordlessly begging for more.

She was addicted, a junkie for his sexual expertise. He knew just what she wanted, what would turn her on, burn her up. For a moment, she hated him, hated that he had such control over her. The next moment her arms were encircling his shoulders, her legs rising to clasp his waist as she rode his thrusting hand, her thoughts disjointed and chaotic.

She forgot the open door and the men huddled in the bedroom, forgot everything but the lust zinging through her. Dev worked her clit with merciless pressure, driving her higher and higher as his fingers shuttled in and out of her weeping sex.

She needed him, needed this. With each grinding, shattering climax, her pussy felt emptier and hungrier. He was conditioning her. Soon, she knew, he would have her begging for his cock, not caring how its size would stretch her, hurt her. She shuddered, muscles trembling as fire swept through her, building and burning as the first convulsions of a massive orgasm took her.

He yanked his fingers from her cunt. Dread washed over her, icing her womb and freezing her flesh. A river of cream gushed out no longer contained by his fingers. Her thighs were coated in rapidly cooling liquid, adding to her discomfort.

"Noooooo!" She moaned and wailed, bereft, lost, her culmination fading as if it had never been. She wanted those fingers back, wanted them buried in her throbbing cunt, needed them. "Please, Dev," she begged. "Please don't stop...not now, when I need you so much. Please finish me."

"'Finish me' isn't what I wanted to hear," he growled. "I'll give you a hint. The word starts with the same letter."

He rubbed his soaked fingers across her lips, bathing her in her juices. She gasped in affronted shock, and he pressed his fingers past her lips and teeth to wipe them on her tongue, giving her a taste of her own essence. He lowered his head beside hers, his tongue outlining the rim of her earlobe before he thrust deeply into the sensitive chamber, fucking her ear as he had her mouth, her pussy.

"Suck on my fingers," he demanded in a harsh whisper. "Taste yourself on my flesh. Have you ever tasted such sweetness?"

She could only moan as her lips closed over his fingers. Her tongue swirled around and between the two thick digits crowding her mouth, exploring her own unique flavor. All the while, a steady stream of tears fell from her closed eyes, wetting her face and the front of his shirt.

Abruptly, he stilled. A heavy, masculine groan brought her eyes open in question. His eyes met hers and he shook his head. "I should leave you aching for completion," he told her. "But as angry as you have made me, I still cannot bear to see you sorrowful or hurting." He sighed deeply. "Do not cry, *Nippa*. I will make it feel better."

He eased his hand away from her mouth, replacing his fingers with his tongue. While he explored her lips and the area behind her teeth, he worked his hand under her skirt and located her dripping pussy. Plunging his fingers inside her, he pumped them in and out of her with a forceful, rapid cadence that soon had her climbing toward orgasm again.

She flung her head back, reveling in the sensations of heated pleasure swamping her body, drawing up her nipples and tightening the muscles of her abdomen.

"Yes!" She clamped her fingers in the hard flesh of his shoulders, holding on for dear life as he rocked her lower body with the movements of his hand. "Please, Dev! I'm sorry. Don't stop. Harder…more!"

"Oh, *Nippa*." Dev dipped his head to lave her swollen lips, increasing the lustful rhythm of his fingers. He leaned back to watch her face as she thrashed in the beginnings of her climax. "I love to see you come for me. You melt all my anger when you call my name so sweetly."

His thumb rasped over her distended clit. She screamed out his name, overcome with ecstasy.

Wave after wave of pleasure rushed over her, drenching her inside and out, with the liquid joy she had found with no other.

* * * * *

Slamming the living room door, Dev stalked over to where Nnora sat perched on the edge of her couch. They waited for word the shuttle had arrived. Hands on hips, he glowered down at her.

"Silence will get you the same treatment I dished out earlier—only this time, there will be no relief," he warned her.

She continued to ignore him, knowing his empty threat to be an attempt at goading her into speech. After his so-called lesson, she'd made no more remarks about him minding his own business. In fact, she'd made no further remarks at all...though her curiosity was eating her up on one particular subject.

"Why are *you* dressed in normal earth attire—jeans and such—when your men are all dressed so differently."

"That is easily explained." He smiled tentatively, looking thankful she was talking to him again. "Originally, I was the only one disembarking to meet with you. When word reached us of a possible attack launched by your father's enemies, I thought it wise to have several of my men accompany me. There was no time to set the replicator to produce costumes for the others."

"This is news to me." She fought a rising tide of panic "I haven't heard anything about a pending attack. I should have been notified. My guards usually keep me well informed. So what happened? Did...anyone get injured during the attack? Is my father all right?"

"Be calm, *fem*." He turned away from her to gaze out the window. After a long pause he glanced at her over his shoulder. "All is well. The malefactors are merely a group of unorganized rowdies. They will be easily captured. I doubt they are part of any real rebel force."

For some reason, his answer sounded stilted, studied. She narrowed her eyes at him. "You were silent a long time. What are you not telling me?" Suspicion ran rampant through her.

"You read too much into the situation, *Nippa*." He chuckled, reaching for her arm on the pretense that he was helping her up.

She knew better. The truth was the man couldn't keep his hands off her. He'd had them on her one way or another all the long afternoon. What bothered her most about that situation was the increasing pleasure she found in his addiction to her. Forbearing to mention that aloud, she pushed his hand away, "No, thank you. I prefer to sit. But you can tell me something... *Nippa,* what does it mean? You called me that before. For some reason, it's not translating."

Dev opened his mouth to answer, paused, and then closed his lips on his response. It disconcerted her that she couldn't figure out the emotion behind the intense look he gave her.

"No, it wouldn't be in the database. I believe I will save that answer for later, *Nippa.* But do ask me again...during our mating."

Her mind raced ahead to that looming event. She didn't know how she would handle the situation when it arose. She wanted him more each passing moment, craved his touch and his smile, yearned for his approval.

He just might turn out to be the perfect man for her. Intelligent, kind, a wonderful lover, *and* he had a body a god would envy. Only two things hindered her complete acceptance: not knowing her father's level of involvement in this situation and her pending loss of the Brewsters.

She refused, on principle, to be party to her father's empire-building plans, and she really didn't want to live anywhere that made visitation with her foster family impossible. As far as she knew, *Rb'qarm* could be a billion light years away. She didn't say any of this to the prince. She contented herself with a social lie. "I don't want to know that badly."

"Oh, yes you do!" Dev smiled wickedly, his tiger-topaz eyes luminous with mocking humor. "In fact—"

A high-pitched beeping interrupted his words. He bent his mouth to a device on his arm, toggled a switch and spoke into it, acknowledging the message he'd received.

"Come, *Nippa*. The shuttle has arrived."

This time, she accepted his help, allowing him to draw her up off the couch. Tightening his hand on hers, he led her to the open front door, where a sudden wayward updraft caught the hem of her lightweight skirt, swirling it about her legs in a flirtatious dance.

"Another gust of wind like that will have my *cherzda* rising again," he whispered, leaning into her to keep their conversation private. "That glimpse of your beautiful thighs reminded me of what lies between them."

White-hot need stabbed through her midriff. She couldn't speak to reply.

"This is the second time I have rendered you speechless," Dev teased, then stepped away from her to converse with GanR'dari.

Yeah. Not counting the numerous times I screamed myself hoarse beneath your tongue and terat.

Dev's second-in-command, busy coordinating the men guarding the approaches to the apartment, paused to attend his commander.

"Is…*everything*…in readiness, GanR'dari?"

The guard sang into a small hand-unit, asking all units to report in, and Nnora had only to concentrate a little to catch the cadence and then the meaning of the words. Since Dev had shot her with that biological teacher, her understanding of *Rb'qarmli* was growing by leaps and bounds.

Aha, a third point she had against His Highhandedness. How dare he take it upon himself to decide how and when she would learn his language? The nerve!

Her attention snapping back to the present, she listened as the captain sang a few phrases more, and then closed the device with a flick of his wrist. Was it an alien cell phone, shades of her favorite show? She really didn't want to be beamed up, but it looked like there was no hope for it. She was going on a star trek of her own.

"Everything is in order, and all command-posts reports ready, *Chyya*. We leave as soon as you and your…" his eyes flicked to her and away before he corrected his words, "…the princess are aboard."

Dev released her hand and placed his arm about her shoulders. "Ah Dari, you see I am unable to control the giddy happiness that keeps bubbling up in me. Your inclination was correct, my friend. You may inform the rest of the men that henceforth, they are to address Princess Glennora as *Chyya'va*, for she shall rule beside me. We will arrange the oath ceremony once we are underway."

GanR'dari bowed stiffly in Nnora's direction, right hand over his chest and left hand on his weapon hilt. "My greatest pleasure would be to die in your service, *Chyya'va*."

She blinked. She gaped at the crazed warrior. "Are you off your gourd? What the hell kind of statement—"

"She is honored, GanR'dari" Dev adroitly interrupted.

"I am? No, I am not!" She dragged her feet as he bodily moved her away from his grinning warrior. Testosterone poisoning! All these men were suffering from an overdose of male hormones. Clearly, they needed the calming influence of a sensible woman. She guessed that would have to be her.

Herding her ahead of him, Dev steered her towards the vehicle hovering at the curb.

"Will you stop manhandling me? I had more to say to that warrior of yours—"

As she yanked her arm away from him, she caught a glimpse of the vehicle parked in front of her apartment. She drifted towards the curb to get a closer look at its underside. The darned thing floated above the ground. It had no wheels. Now that she thought of it, there weren't any engine sounds either.

"Hey, how does it *do* that—hover like that?" she mumbled more to herself than Dev. She walked into the street to see the opposite side.

He thought he would swallow his tongue. Fear ran like ice through his veins as he tugged on her arm, removing her from the path of an oncoming car. Engrossed in her perusal of the sleek vehicle, she hadn't even seen it heading for her.

Heaving a sigh, he tucked her tightly to his side, hopefully out of the path of danger and signaled his readiness to depart.

"Let us get underway, *Nippa*." He hurried her aboard the shuttle. "You may examine the *Lorme* to your heart's content—another time. Right now, we need to get to the Mothership. I have problems awaiting, situations I need to deal with immediately."

* * * * *

The spaceship was huge. Nnora watched the immense shape grow to fill the view-screen of the fast little shuttle speeding her towards the rendezvous with her future. It was larger than a 747 jet, but smaller than the Enterprise. Something this big had to be hard to hide—how had the *Rb'qarmshi* eluded the satellites and tracking systems the various governments kept stationed around Earth?

The shuttle pilot, a youthful warrior who looked just this side of gaining his maturity, supplied the answer before she could work up the nerve to ask.

"Isn't she a beauty, *Chyya'va*?" The boy was plainly in love with the ship. He needed no encouragement to share his enthusiasm. "I still get excited when I look on her. Our shield technology hides our heat signatures, enabling us to approach the less advanced worlds without being picked up by their primitive tracking systems."

She frowned. She didn't like the note of superiority she heard in the young pilot's voice. "I thought Earth had a very advanced tracking system."

"Don't they use sonar or radar or a simplistic heat signature technology? In school they called it ultraviolet rays or something." The boy scratched his head. "I don't recall the elementary subjects well, I'm afraid."

She swallowed the impulse to defend the jewel-like world spinning lazily beneath her. Instead, she probed him further. "Okay, tell me about your superior system. How do you deflect our scans?"

"Once we achieve stationary orbit, we project a camouflaging hologram that bends light-polarized ions around the hull. Most primitive planets still use sonar or radar technology, but bounce light or sound waves off us and we show up as a sinkhole, a solar flare-up anomaly, or stellar debris. Heat seeking won't work either—the ions radiate at sub-zero temperatures, cloaking the ship's heat in a blanket of cold. Ingenious, isn't it?"

"Very," she agreed, and meant it. How would humans react if they ever learned the truth really was out there, looking at them?

"And that's not all. We can—"

The pilot suddenly jumped to his feet, snapping to attention, his eyes trained on a spot over her shoulders. "Sir!"

She turned, curious to see who had startled the boy so much his skin had blanched. She groaned when she saw GanR'dari standing over the youth, his stern gaze grilling the younger man. "We were having such fun, too," she muttered loudly enough for the youngster to hear, smothering her grin when she heard him choking at her words.

"Did the *Chyya'va* ask you for information, pilot?"

The young Rb'qarmshi stiffened further. "No, sir!"

"Ah. Then she asked to be entertained?" She didn't like the sneer she heard in GanR'dari's voice.

Somehow, without losing his stiff military posture, the poor lad wilted where he stood. "No, sir!"

GanR'dari's eyes narrowed. "How dare you bespeak the *Chyya'va* without the permission of our *Chyya*?"

"Excuse me," she butted in. "*Whose* permission?"

"You young fool." The second-in-command ignored her, acting as if she weren't even there. He stared at the young warrior in angry disbelief. "Do you have a death wish?"

She threw up her hands. "Okay! I've had it! I'm fed up with all this macho bull crap. Stop bullying the boy, sergeant, or whatever the hell your rank is. He did nothing wrong. If you must know, I was about to ask him for information. He probably saw the question marks plastered all over my face."

"GanR'dari is not bullying him, Nnora." Dev had left his post at the command center in enough time to catch her tirade. "And none of my warriors are *boys*. They are strong, intelligent, dangerous men who have earned their place among the ranks. A ruling prince may call fifty men to follow him, to give their allegiance to him—and in time—to his immediate family. Each and every one of them deserves the respect due my personal vanguards."

Dev turned his sights on the pilot, addressing his man in a cold voice. "They also deserve a reprimand when they venture beyond the boundaries of their position. GanR'dari will pilot this craft. You will confine yourself to quarters for the duration of the trip."

The young warrior saluted smartly, face flushed with shame. "I obey at once! Thank you, *Chyya*. I-I b-beg the forgiveness of my *Chyya*. I meant no disrespect to you or yours."

"You have it—this once. You are dismissed."

The young pilot slipped away, quickly distancing himself from the scene of his disgrace. Before he made it to the corridor, the prince called out to him.

"Stay far away from my Earth-bred Princess, Conlan, lest your enjoyment of her company brings about your early demise at my hands. I will not be so forgiving should there be another encounter, for I tell you truly, I find I am of a possessive nature."

Conlan nodded his head and scurried out of his leader's sight.

"All he did was speak to me." The show of rampant male hormones frustrated her. "Where was the harm in that?"

"He broke discipline." GanR'dari turned sharply to face her. "What a scandal he could have caused. That young pup is lucky our Prince does not hold grudges. That a subordinate would dare to accost a half-mated *fem*—"

"You are in *pava*, Nnora," Dev broke in to explain. "I have *seated* you, but we are not yet fully mated. Any man, the merest commoner, could kill that forward novice and be well within his rights. It is lawful for a *Rb'qarmshi* to kill any other male who approaches his intended during this interval.

"You need to know that I will not hesitate to destroy anyone who challenges my claim on you. That warrior owes his life to you. He would be lying dead on this deck if you hadn't taken the edge off my hunger back in your apartment. But he can also blame you for the dangerous position in which he finds himself now."

"I should have known this would somehow turn out to be my fault." She snapped, colored hotly at his indiscreet, public reminder of what had passed between them earlier. She was not used to speaking so freely of such intimate matters. In fact, she had never been *involved* in such intimate activities. What she and Ron had done hadn't even been foreplay for her—or for him, if she were to judge by her memories of his numerous complaints.

"Come sit beside me, *Nippa*." Dev took her by one arm and half-dragged her behind him, ignoring her sputtered protests. "I have enough on my mind without the added troubles your *pava* sparks among my entourage," he said in a louder voice.

"Send me back, then. I did not ask to be here."

He halted in his tracks at mention of her leaving. Jaw muscles knotting as his teeth snapped together, he turned abruptly and snatched her into his arms, ignoring their audience of over thirty men. "I will never let you go, nor send you away," he snarled. "I thought this afternoon taught you how I felt. You are mine. If any question remains in your mind, I will prove it definitively, here and now!"

Ensnared in the cage of his arms, she beat her fists against his chest, her words pouring out in an angry torrent. "You try it, Buster! You just try it! You're nothing but a bully, a two-bit dictator, a...a...a despot!"

"Who is this Buster?"

Nnora gritted her teeth in frustration. *How in hell did you insult someone when he didn't understand plain English?* "You are, you dweeb!" Nonplussed, she brought his hand up to her mouth and bit down on it. *Hard.*

He released her with a startled cry, brows beetling as he glared at her. Total silence reined on the bridge, every warrior there waiting to see their Prince's reaction.

"Furthermore," she ranted while he examined the damage to his skin. "I'll have you know I will never meekly surrender just because you threaten me in front of your men. It will take all of them—and more—to hold me down."

He burst into laughter, shocking her. He hauled her back to his side and nearly smothered her in an enveloping hug, utterly ignoring her renewed struggles to escape his possessive embrace. "Your fighting spirit makes me proud." Grinning like a loon, he loudly addressed their audience of crew and officers. "I have captured a mighty fighter."

His warriors stared at her with mixed expressions of horror and slack-jawed respect.

Then Dev turned away from the crowd. "I ask forgiveness. Let there be peace between us until we reach the ship." His voice was soft. "It was wrong of me to bait you when I can see the tiredness in your eyes. I do not enjoy being at odds with you, *Nippa*."

"I'll agree to your momentary peace." She stalked over to the observation screen to look out at the stars. "But once we reach your ship, all bets are off!"

Reflected in the material of the ship's window, she saw Dev incline his head, white teeth flashing in an anticipatory grin. "As you wish, my own, but know this. Once we reach the ship, your 'bet' is not all that will be off, *Nippa*. We will resume this war of passion in privacy."

Chapter Ten

Unfortunately for Dev's high-handed plans, their private war had to be postponed.

In the heat of passion, he'd forgotten the problems that caused their hasty departure from Earth. As soon as they came onboard, he was met with news of a fresh development involving the old dilemma of their civil war—a development his frantic counselors claimed only he could solve.

"By *Deth* and the hurdles of *Pythin!* Will this stupidity never cease?" He cursed under his breath, conveying his ire in low-pitched tones, his words meant only for Nnora, who stood somewhat stiffly tucked into his side.

"I am loath to be parted from you, yet I cannot shirk the demands of my rule. I promise to return as soon as possible. GanR'dari will escort you to your cabin. Until then—"

Dev pressed a hard, openmouthed kiss on her, as though determined to *thoroughly* convince her of his reluctance to delay their skirmishes. His kiss rocked her traitorous libido into high gear.

His big hands clasped her head. He speared his stiffened tongue into her mouth over and over and rubbed his hard-on into the quivering bowl of her belly.

She brought her own hands up to frame his face and captured his tongue. They dueled, tongues intertwining—his long, thick tool that had brought her such heady pleasure in the past thrusting at and around her sensitive, more delicate one. She groaned when he enfolded her, sweeping her straining nipples against the hard muscles and skin of his chest. Lightheaded from the onslaught, her legs barely supported her lust-weakened knees. She fought for air and to stay on her feet.

When he at last released her from their heated joining, she sagged against the bulkhead. The high-voltage kiss short-circuited all rational thought. Dazed, she watched as Dev—cheered on by his warriors—quickly took his leave, rushing off to deal with the unexplained emergency.

Gradually, the sensual fugue dissipated and her senses returned. She found herself standing in a corridor empty but for GanR'dari. He stood before her, patiently waiting to escort her to her quarters.

"The sleeper awakens. Welcome back to our galaxy." A thunderous rumbling in his massive chest accompanied his words.

Could that grating noise be laughter? Did the jerk have the nerve to laugh at her? "Don't even go there, Lurch." She bared her teeth. "Hey! Didn't you talk to me without my—how did you put it?—express permission? So what gives you the right over poor Conlan, huh?" Frowning fiercely up at the behemoth, she pushed away from the wall and advanced upon the hapless warrior. It gratified her to see the monster backpedaling before her, his face wiped clean of the amused smirk he had been sporting.

"Yeah," she drawled, "seems like there are some advantages to being this '*Chyya'va*' person you call me, after all. So, unless you want me complaining about your inappropriate behavior to your *Chyya,* I suggest you keep your tongue between your teeth, get me to my cabin and then get the hell outta my face." Stars, but that had felt good. She was flying high on the combined adrenalin of Dev's kiss and her anger.

She didn't fly very long.

She followed the hulking, now quietly sulking GanR'dari down seemingly endless corridors, shame growing within her with each step.

Some leader you'd make taking your frustrations out on innocent bystanders. You had no right to snap at the man just because he witnessed how badly Dev's kiss rattled you. So what if the man observed your discomfiture? It is no excuse to come off as the Bitch of the Spaceways and bite his head off.

Her kiss-induced, shell-shocked behavior had probably been downright hilarious to the seasoned warrior. He'd likely never seen a drooling, horny, middle-aged, sex-starved *fem* stuck to a bulkhead, making goo-goo eyes at his ruler.

Damn. I'm going to have to apologize.

She exhaled a long, self-pitying sigh. Politeness, respect and personal honor were the three things Poppi Brewster had always taken the strap down for. Having had the principles ingrained in her by numerous spankings, she had no trouble seeing her error. There was no getting around it. She had to say "sorry".

While she was ruminating over how to phrase her apology—it had to be sincere, yet not abject—they came to a halt before a closed metal door.

In continued silent obedience, GanR'dari indicated a lit panel. "If I may break my ordered silence to instruct you, *Chyya'va*?"

At her nod, he continued. "This door has been programmed to grant you entrance in two ways. First, you may speak into the voice sensor while placing your hand, palm down upon the recessed area, here. Alternatively, you may undergo a retinal scan. That sensor is over here." He pointed to another panel at the side of the door.

He paused, raising his eyebrows in a wordless questioning.

"I see. Go on..."

"You may be assured of your total privacy since the *Chyya*, whose voice code overrides all others, is the only other person who can activate your door. It will open for no one else.

Guilt ate at her as she listened to his stiff phrases. She'd obviously ruined any chance at friendship with this guy and she really hated that. Other than wanting to die for her, GanR'dari seemed to be a sensible character.

Might as well get this over with... Gathering her resolve, she quickly began her apology, wanting the distasteful chore over with. "Look, I screwed up, okay? I was wrong to jump your crap like I did, and I am...uh...*abjectly* sorry. There was no excuse for my behavior and—" She broke off her convoluted apology, stunned to see the large man had gone down on his knees before her.

When he attempted to touch his forehead to her feet, she jumped back in alarm. "What are you doing?"

Now what? She warily watched the man kneeling before her. Good grief, all she needed was some upset, suicidal male deciding his best apology would be his death.

"I am awed by your greatness," he proclaimed. "Truly, our *Chyya* is blessed in his selection of a mate."

"Sheesh!" Placing her hands under the hulk's shoulders, she tried to heave him off the floor. He didn't budge. "What brought this on, my apology?"

"The fact that you didn't have to make one." GanR'dari rose easily from his bowed position. "Not to me, anyway."

She felt a momentary touch of jealousy at how he maneuvered all that bulk. For a big person—and a man, at that—he sure had her beat in the grace department.

"I angered you with my nonsense. Even though the prince and I have been friends all our lives, you had but to speak the word to have me executed and the prince would have upheld your command."

"That's sick!" The thought of having so much power repulsed her. She swallowed thickly, fighting the sinking feeling in the pit of her stomach. Bile rose up to burn at the back of her throat at the thought of what could have occurred if she had jokingly cried, "Off with his head!" in front of witnesses.

Surely, Dev would never enforce such a command. She couldn't believe it of him, though the look on GanR'dari's face told her the warrior had no doubts.

"Is that why you were so silent? You thought I would have you killed?"

"I was contemplating my stupidity." The warrior chuckled wryly. "You are the *Chyya'va*. The only voice higher then your own is that of my *Chyya's*.

"I have grown accustomed to the loose discipline our Prince allows his cadre and I overstepped my bounds. Making mock of you, no matter it was only a gentle teasing, could have cost me my life. Worse yet, it could have cost my Prince the loss of a seasoned battle commander.

"In these times of turmoil, Glendevtorvas relies upon the expertise of every loyal man, and I let him down. It is a humbling thing to find I am no better at discipline than our young Conlan."

"Any idiot could see how close you and Dev are to each other, GanR'dari. There is no way I would ever order your death as it would hurt him too much—"

"Do you hear yourself?" GanR'dari smiled, almost sly. "I think you are beginning to love our Prince. You are already concerned with his emotional well-being."

Striving to maintain a straight face, she gave the smiling warrior an evil look, then quickly dissolved into laughter. "I've changed my mind. I think I'm gonna have to kill you for the crime of providing unsolicited information."

Looking about the empty corridor, she pretended to see a contingent of soldiers. "Come, men. Take him. Off with his head!"

The hardened soldier choked on barely suppressed laughter. She snickered.

"That's better!" She straightened to her fullest height and raised her head to meet the brilliant glowing green eyes of the man she wanted to befriend. "I got off on the wrong foot with you. If you are willing, I would like to start over…to be friends."

Executing another of those disgustingly graceful bows, GanR'dari said, "I would be honored, *Chyya'va.*"

Holding out her hand, she smiled. "Hello. My name is Glennora Brewster 'abret Glenbrevchanka. And you are…?"

Taking her hand, he bestowed a kiss upon it. "GanR'dari 'abri GlenglanR'on at your service, *Chyya'va.*"

Nnora turned her hand so it gripped GanR'dari's and vigorously shook it, grinning from ear to ear. "Glad to meet you. Okay, here's the deal—I will only have you killed off in private if you will only tease me in private."

* * * * *

One pleasant conversation later, in which Nnora learned little but enjoyed herself greatly, the door to her quarters swooshed open. "Wow, talk about shades of Star Trek! Beam me up, Scotty! No, wait, I've already been beamed up."

She laughed as GanR'dari shook his head at her antics. "You are obviously not a Trekkie, my friend." Chortling, she pressed her hand to the panel so she could see the door retract once more. "Cool! But why doesn't it open when I approach? How come I have to put my palm on the panel every time?"

"The door is locked, *Chyya'va*. It would be best to leave it so, for now. Until your mating—"

"Off with his head!" She playfully shook her finger at 'Dari. "No mentioning my future mating or my future mate. The man drives me crazy. When I'm not salivating over him, I am angry with him."

He canted his head to the side, watching her with a twinkle in his eyes. "I do not believe there is a man among the Cadre who would accost you. Beside the matter of their proven loyalty, every one of them knows I, or the *Chyya*, would kill them for the offense.

"However, there are others aboard this ship—men we have not had the time to test, to train. When it comes to your honor, I am not willing to take a chance on those unknowns. If you want your door unlocked, you will have to ask the *Chyya* to show you. I have no desire to be killed in public for failing in my duty to protect you."

She stuck her tongue out at him, feeling totally relaxed and at ease with the gentle giant, able to enjoy their mutual teasing. "'Dari, you are a coward."

Her new friend produced an exaggerated sigh. "*Chyya'va,* more and more I am finding that to be true."

"I didn't mean it literally, friend. I know you are no coward. I guess my joke fell sorta flat, huh?"

"Not at all, milady." He bowed. "I need to go check the duty roster. Press this button here, to contact me if you need anything. Lock the door behind me, *Chyya'va.*"

Fascinated as she was by her quarters and the high-tech items it held, she waved absently as he took his leave. Like a child let loose in a toyshop, she pushed every gadget, opened every compartment and pulled every knob.

During her search she found the insta-bed and then lost it again, discovered the toilet in—to her way of thinking—a very strange place. She accidentally started the shower while she was standing in the cubicle, trying to puzzle out what the heck it was. It turned out all right, since when the system finished cycling through, both she and her clothes had been thoroughly washed, rinsed, and dried.

She stepped out of the stall with a thoughtful backwards glance. Those gusts of sultry air had been a mighty interesting and enlightening experience, one she couldn't wait to try again, preferably with a partner...*sans* clothes.

Chapter Eleven

The blaring of a shrill-toned siren shattered the clinical silence of the ship, interrupting Nnora's single-minded explorations. Frantic steps sounded outside her quarters, anxious voices shouted through her door speakers and a pale, hard-breathing Dev burst through her portal before she could find the intercom and inform everyone she was totally fine.

"*Nippa*! Are you all right? Where is the danger?"

He flung his frantic questions at her as his head twisted left and right, scanning the cabin with narrowed, deadly eyes.

"I'm fine. Honestly. I guess this is just a false alarm. I didn't mean to set anything off. I was just messing around—"

His head swung back to her, gaze grilling her. His shoulders relaxed but his frown grew. "False alarm? You were messing around?"

She fidgeted, shifting from foot to foot. Her heart dropped down to her knees under his condemning glare.

"Have you any idea the chaos you have set off? How many men have been mobilized on your behalf, because you were *messing around*?"

Her mouth tightened, jaw firming. Her glance flicked over to the men crowded in the open doorway of her cabin, avidly listening while their Captain chewed her out. She did not like being reprimanded in front of all those weapons-bristling strangers. Still, all these people were here because they were concerned for her. She couldn't find too much fault with the Prince for overreacting, all things considered.

"I apologize, Your Highness. Perhaps I used the wrong word... While I familiarized myself with my quarters, I inadvertently set off some sort of alarm. It was not done maliciously, I assure you."

He took a deep breath, looked hard at her. He must have seen her mutinous expression and guessed its cause, for he went to the door and quietly spoke with his warriors before sending them all away.

He turned around and studied her, saying nothing.

In turn, she searched his face, wondering how angry he was, wondering how he handled his anger...wondering if she needed to fear his temper.

His silent treatment unnerved her. She stood before him, hands clasping each other in a nonverbal display of her inner anxiousness, butterflies beating a whirlwind in her tummy.

He finally moved toward her, still silent. She quickly began speaking, "Please! I didn't know...I...didn't mean to..." Her shoulders slumped. "I apologize abjectly."

His hands bit into her shoulders as he yanked her up against his tense body. "You frightened a hundred *Faels* off my life! Show me how abject you are." He groaned heavily before burying his tongue in her mouth. He consumed her, took her with strong hands that swept down her back, pressing her close.

When they broke apart to restore their oxygen supply she gasped, "Oh! I am very abject, indeed! I'd better apologize again..."

This time, her apology took the form of intense one-to-one interpersonal interaction at the highest level of lip diplomacy. She licked at his lips, worried his full bottom lip with her teeth. She could taste the frenzy of his desire for her, his concern transmuted into boiling lust. Her hands clutched at his waist, slid down and back to grasp his tight buttocks.

A heavy groan tore its way out of his throat. "*Nippa*, you will be the death of me!" He moaned again, went back to showering kisses over every inch of her face.

She tightened her fingers on the firm flesh of his ass cheeks, snuggling closer in a rare moment of mutual understanding. "I'm okay," she assured him gently. This close, she could feel the racing thud of his heart. His arms—those strong pillars—shook even while holding her in an unbreakable grip.

"When I heard the alarm, I was in the middle of a vidcom. I have never felt such fear! I broke my own rule of not translating within the ship and made them drop me right outside your door."

She felt so bad about causing his scare that she let him to devour her mouth once more. She even helped him, opening her lips to take him in, to suck on the bold, spicy tongue that surged and retreated. She enticed him, encouraging him to thrust deeply into her mouth, nurturing his need to affirm her safety.

When he finally lifted his head, allowing her to snatch a few breaths, she explained. "I was just familiarizing myself with the items and gadgets in here, trying to see how everything worked—"

"*Nippa*." He shook her a little. "Didn't you see the notice under that toggle? You couldn't have missed it—"

"*Hello!* Is anybody home?" She tapped her knuckles gently against his forehead. "That injection you slipped me lets my brain understand spoken *Rb'qarmli* which is all well and good. However, I still can't *read* a lick! So...yes, I saw the toggle and writing. I thought the toggle might be a hat rack or something. The writing I thought a little boring for room decoration. A nice landscape would have been more to my taste."

Dev laughed, laying his forehead against hers. "Now I am the one who must say I am sorry, my Nnora. I did not think of that. We communicate so well I forgot you did not, in truth, know our language. I will arrange for a tutor."

His face sobered. He sighed, sounding weary. "I shouldn't be here. I am stealing this time from my meeting. If all goes well, I will be able to spend longer with you tomorrow."

"I understand you have more important things occupying you."

"Nothing is more important to me than you. That's why I am here. But there are urgent matters coming to a head that I must deal with now. Why don't you take this reprieve to accustom yourself to your new authority?" He pulled back, a smile widening his mobile lips and creasing his cheeks. "By the way, GanR'dari informed me of what transpired between the two of you. Thank you for making the effort to befriend him. He is like a brother to me."

She stepped out of his arms and pouted, planting her fists on her hips. "Why, that rotten traitor! He promised not to tell tales—"

"Draw in your claws, *Chyya'va*. He is, first and foremost, my man, bound by oaths...though you have certainly made a conquest there."

"I didn't want a conquest, I wanted a friend." Feeling betrayed, she swallowed hard, battling tears. "I thought I could trust him, but the minute you two get together, he spills all my beans."

"You have a friend, a good one. And you *can* trust him in all things—even to keep secrets from me, now that I have given you his service. Unless we go to war and I need to call him to my side, he will be head of your personal bodyguard. There is no better person I could trust with your safety. Use him well. He will be a good source of information for you. Now before I head back to that conference—"

He released her to stride over to the door. Then, he swiped his hand down a panel at the side of it, speaking a rhythmic sentence into the voice grid and the light on the panel turned from amber to black. A heavy metallic thunk reverberated through the room.

Why was he locking the door?

He unzipped his uniform top and peeled it off his arms as he turned back to face her, leaving his chest and torso exposed. "It has been several hours since your last orgasm, *Nippa*. I would not have you suffering from *pava* pains."

Nnora licked suddenly dry lips as confusion turned to consternation. "I wish you would stop that!" she wailed, feeling like a neon light, her arousal flashing for all to see.

"Stop what, *Nippa*?"

"Stop *smelling* me! It's so humiliating. Do you have any idea what it is like for me, knowing all the men on this ship can smell my lust?"

Lips quirking in a half smile, he reached out a hand to her. "I cannot help smelling and reacting to your needs. In fact, I relish the fact that I am able to respond to your sweet siren song. I am your mate and there should be no embarrassment between us, *Nippa*. Moreover, you need not endure the pangs of unrelieved arousal while I am here to care for your needs. Such is not necessary."

She ignored his outstretched hand.

"Uh, I'm okay." She instinctively denied her rising need. She didn't want his pity. "It isn't anything like it was before."

Her hands curled into fists at her side, nails biting into the flesh of her palms. Closing her eyes, she concentrated on beating down the pulse of lust throbbing in her pussy. Off-kilter, needing him, she couldn't move. Couldn't think—

"And I will not allow it to become what it once was, my *Nippa*. Bare your breasts to me." His voice sounded as matter-of-fact as if he were informing her that the sky was blue.

Her hands flew up, splayed across the expanse of her round curves. Her nipples stabbed into the palms of her hands. "Excuse me?"

"In fact, remove all your clothing and lie on the bed, legs spread. I am hungry for your fresh cream and we might as well fulfill both our needs at once."

Swallowing thickly, she watched him as he sauntered toward her, his masculine form a study in primal grace and power. She felt herself responding to his allure. The first swirling wash of liquid yearning flashed in the bowl of her belly. Her inner muscles contracted, releasing a heated flow of juices. Her labia throbbed. Her clit filled with blood.

"Uuhhmmm." She gulped, eyes drawn to the bulge between his muscled thighs. Lust swamped her. She didn't even know what drivel she stammered out almost incoherently. "I…there's no…you don't have to…put yourself out. I mean—"

"I am not sure what you mean, but I know what you *need*. There is no time for me to…put myself out, *Nippa*. And if you continue to waste what little we have, it is you who will be doing without. I have no intention of *seating* you until I have had my fill of your sweet-tasting pussy."

His eyes glinted as he reached her side, leaning down to place his lips very near hers. "Now get those clothes off and prepare yourself."

Heat poured off her in waves as she saw the implacable desire stamped on his face. Breasts tight and hurting, womb contracting with renewed *pava* pains, she let her gaze rove the man standing ready to pleasure her. God, but he was the hunkiest piece of eye candy she had ever seen. He made her panties wet just looking at him.

Tall and muscular, he had shoulders wide enough to bear her burdens. His ripped chest was bare and his *terat* drew her eyes. Her knees weakened in remembered ecstasy. Her blood raced and sizzled through her veins. Her heart-rate quickened at the thought of sinking her nipples into those sexy suction cups again. To top it all, Dev packed the most delicious-tasting, addictive cock.

She would eventually have to leave him, but nothing hindered her from accepting all he had to give her while she awaited the opportunity to escape. When all was said and done, she didn't really want to escape Dev. She simply objected to him robbing her of the right to make her own choices.

If only he weren't so overbearing. Still, she could handle his macho crap for while longer. No woman in her right mind lightly gave up multi-orgasmic sex, especially when it was so freely, even enthusiastically, given. She'd had more orgasms in this one day than she'd had in a lifetime. What more did she want from him?

Sex? Definitely! She knew once he began, Dev wouldn't stop pleasuring her until he had pushed her to her sensual limits, demanding she take all the pleasure he could dish out. He had a way of turning up the heat until just the thought had her cunt awash with her impassioned dew. She'd already soaked her panties and had to keep her thighs clenched to stop her juices from flowing down her legs.

Romance and attentiveness, perhaps? He offered her a feast of sensations, never ceasing to tell her of her importance to him. At the merest thought of danger, he rushed to her side, leaving an important meeting, making heads of state wait on her convenience…and she stood here, waffling over whether or not she should allow him to give her multiple orgasms. What flavor of fool did that make her?

Slowly, then more quickly, she drew one arm and then the other out of its sleeve, lifted the lightweight dress over her head, exposing her bra and panty clad-body.

His eyes caught flame, and in response, her wayward clitoris stretched and rose up from under its protective hood, pounding like a damned metronome, beating out the cadence of her lustful desires. Her nipples echoed the traitorous action, swelling and stiffening until they were painfully erect, eagerly outthrust and hungry for the *terat* suckling she feared she had already grown addicted to.

Before the dress had time to float to the ground, Dev pounced, hands clamping tightly on her forearms, head bending to worry a beading nipple through the semi-sheer material of her Bali bra. A bold hand slipped inside her panties to explore the crease of her pussy and slid in her natural lubrication. His finger brushed against her there, and suddenly penetrated. Her clit became the site of an electrifying storm, generating jagged bolts of delight that burned through her inflaming her nipples and cunt.

She gasped with the overwhelming sensations and his mouth slammed down on hers. Their tongues dueled while thick male fingers joined the first one, spreading and stretching her, delving between her parted labia and deep into her pussy.

His thumb skimmed upward to flick against her clit. The explosive pleasure sent her hips pitching forward, forcing her mound into the palm of his hand.

Her hands closed convulsively over his forearms, nails digging into his skin as her fingers and toes curled. Under her sensitized flesh, her nerve endings burned. Deep in the pit of her belly an ache throbbed to life, an ache that only he could appease. She turned her head to the side, breaking off their torrid kiss. "Please, Dev, please...I need you!"

His lips trailed down her neck, mouth open over her tender flesh, pulling on the cord beating out her pulse, teeth nipping, tongue soothing. She raised one leg, wrapping it about his thigh, trying to settle his hard erection into the cradle of her heated pussy. "I need you...want you..."

Suddenly, his mouth was gone. His hands twined through her hair, holding her seeking lips away from his

"That wasn't entirely true this morning. What part of me do you want, Nnora?"

Her eyes flashed down to the hefty bulge at his crotch and she drew in a deep breath. "I…uh…I want…*that*!"

He watched Nnora's expressive face as she struggled to answer him.

"Are you telling me you want my cock?"

Taking her hand, he plastered her fingers over his straining cock, drawing her palm up and down his outthrust length. He cut short her dithering.

"I know you want my tongue, my fingers and my mouth, yet earlier, you rejected my cock. Feel me. *Me!* My cock is part of me, *Nippa*. Feel how my cock grows harder at the thought of being buried in your tight *pava*…your pussy." His hips swayed forward, pushing his cock into her palm. "So tell me again, *Nippa*, what part of me do you want?"

He buried his face in her neck. She had the feeling he hid his face from her to shield his vulnerability.

She smiled, looking up at him. Even when his hand fell away, she continued milking his cock with firm, long strokes.

"I really do want all of you, Dev." She kept her own head bent as she shared her thoughts with him. "I finally figured it out in the shower." She smiled, smoothed her hand up and down the growing bulk of his sex.

"We're not human, you and I. We are *Rb'qarmshi* and we will fit." She snuggled her cheek into the hand he lifted to frame her face.

"I might not be the medical genius my mother and sister are..." she laughed a little, "but even I know a human's pussy could not have withstood the prolonged, ferocious tonguing, sucking, biting and licking you subjected mine to. I should be too sore to breathe. I should be walking bow-legged. Instead, my pussy reveled in your attentions. My nipples get hard at just the thought of being inside your *terat*. My clit is so stiff my thighs rub against it when I walk. I've never come so hard or so much in my life, yet I am ready for more.

"So to answer your question once again..." She dipped down and kissed his cock through his flight suit. "I want every part of you...your hands, your tongue...your *terat*...but most especially, I want your cock—inside me!"

His hands captured her head against his loins. His cock surged against her lips.

"Oh, *Nippa*, you shall have me! I will never let you deprive yourself of any pleasure I can give you. Soon, I will fill your hot pussy with this cock while I sink my fingers into that rosy little bud buried between your sweet cheeks. I will impale you, cunt and ass, inundate you with erotic sensation until you lose your mind and your fears. I intend to pleasure you until you scream."

Nnora shivered as her eyes drifted closed. He felt the tension rise in her body as his words flowed over her. Her nipples wound tighter and harder, pressing against his legs. Sharp desire speared him, lancing down to his *sirat* as he felt and smelled her heady response to the lusty images he crafted for her.

Her head fell back against his shoulder as she gave herself over to the spiraling sensations, so far gone in lust he knew she never felt him lifting her, carrying her over to the bed and removing her panties and bra.

"You know what I want?" He thrust a thick digit into her creamy center and pumped slow and deep, resisting the urge to shed his clothes and join her, join with her. *Damn it! I wish I had more time.* "I want to fuck your mouth, feed you my cock till my *sirat* bounce against your chin. Then I want to sink into your pussy, stretching it wide with my thick, hot meat."

He used his provocative words to burn through the last of her inhibitions. He guessed his erotic words, along with a second thick finger stretching her tight sheath, would send her over the edge. He thanked the stars this morning's foreplay had revealed her weakness for dirty talk. The knowledge was proving a priceless weapon in his arsenal. He needed all the weapons at his command to woo and win this fascinating lady.

"I want to impale you on my shaft. I want you to watch me pumping in and out of your slit and I want to hear you howl as you come with my cock embedded deeply in your pussy." He blew on her nipples, plying her breasts and cunt with sensation layered upon sensation, his words like touches on her quivering flesh.

He made sure she felt his ruthless need, his relentless hunger as his mouth drew on her, latching on to one nipple and sucking it up between his teeth. One hard draw, one biting nibble and he left the aching bud, using his stiffened tongue to prod the tip into another level of stiffness. Repeating his actions with her other nipple, he lavished attention on her pert tips. His mouth roved over the smooth skin of her midriff, dipping into the shallow pool of her navel before meandering down the sloping plane of her belly. He hummed against her pubes, sending vibrations through the skin to resonate in her womb.

She bucked beneath him, panting as she speared her fingers through his hair, holding his head against her.

Sliding a hand between her thighs, his fingers parted her slick folds, skimmed the shallow cleft of her sex. Lifting her hips, he bypassed her pussy to lick the groove of her ass, running first his hands, then his tongue over the plump round globes of her luscious derriere.

"Oh. My goodness. What are you doing?" She tried to jerk away. "No one's ever…I've never…"

His heart seemed to swell within his chest. A flood of tender feelings swamped him. Lifting his mouth from her, he let her see his smile. He liked the fact that he would be the first to teach her about anal play. "There is no spot of your body that is not delicious to me, my *Nippa*. Let me show you…"

Lowering his head back to her, he laved her from clit to collapsed rosette, using his teeth on her nether lips. He explored her tightly furled opening, caressing her insistently until she squirmed under the lash of pleasure that sparked incendiary flames along the nerves rimming her small, virginal entrance.

Her cunt muscles fluttered out of control, cream oozed out of her, escaping her body in heated, pulsing gushes.

He gathered her slick fluid, smearing the natural lubricant around and just inside her rectum.

He knew his hands were big and his fingers long and broad, knew they would stretch her uncomfortably at first. He swirled his fingers in her slippery fluids again, applying another anointing to her tiny hole.

She stilled, stiffening up as he began to push his finger into her tiny aperture. He stopped, finger pressed against her anus, denied entrance by the tightness of her clenched sphincter.

"I want in here, *Nippa*. Give me what I want?" he murmured, smoothing more of her wetness into the clenched entrance and resuming his steady pressure. "Relax. It will hurt if you tighten up."

"I'm afraid it will hurt too much. But if you are sure I will find it pleasurable..."

"I hope to make it feel good to you after a while. If it doesn't, if you dislike it, I will cease. My word..."

She nodded, relinquishing control to him. "Then I want to try it...with you."

It was his turn to shudder.

"Thank you for your trust, my own. Open your thighs for me. It will help you relax your sphincter." He pulled her to the edge of the bed so her legs dangled over the side and wedged a pillow under her hips. Going to his knees, he splayed both hands against the inside of her thighs and spread her, lapping her sweet pussy lips with broad strokes of his flattened tongue. Slowly, he inched his finger in a quarter inch and halted, inched in a fragment more then held, halting his inward movement to give her some relief from what he knew had to be intense pressure. Her tiny hole stretched about his finger so tightly he feared his circulation would be cut off. Visions of what it would feel like to bury his cock in her constricting passage brought a savage upsurge of lust.

Gradually, he felt her muscle relax, signaling her growing adjustment. "Is your ass burning with the tightness of my finger buried inside you? Is the pain mixed with pleasure?"

"It's...hurting me," she gasped, panting.

"Too much?" He paused, waiting for her answer.

"Your finger is so big… It feels as large as a club."

"Do you want me to stop?"

She didn't answer right away. "Do you want to stop?"

"By *Deth's* balls, no!" He gritted his teeth, reluctantly eased back. "I will, though, if you so choose."

She shook her head. "Make it feel good, Dev!"

"So, you want a little something to take your mind off that pain, huh?"

Lifting his head, he locked gazes with her. He flashed her just a glimpse of his smile before he lowered his head between her thighs, captured her clitoris between his teeth and bit down. He suckled her clit hard, wanting her pleasure.

"Yessss!" She thrashed frantically. Grabbing fists full of his hair, she tugged his mouth hard against her clit. "Suck me. Harder, Dev…eat me, harder… Ream me with your finger! Fuck me with your tongue!"

When he looked up from the delta of her thighs to catch her gaze, there were tears rolling down her face. He felt a surge of satisfaction at the agonized ecstasy he saw on her face.

She came, screaming.

Her hips bucked and she exploded into his mouth, pulsing and throbbing as her juices flowed in a copious stream. Her pussy slammed up against his mouth and he released her clit to plunge his tongue into her hot slit. Splaying one hand on her flat belly, anchoring her body to the bed, he kept his other hand busy at her anus, circling and probing, stretching her.

Her cream ran over his tongue into his mouth, the addicting taste flooding him with almost painful shards of pleasure as beneath his hand, he felt her womb ripple. Her spasming muscles sucked his tongue deeper into her pussy. She relaxed her sphincter as her climax faded and he surged inward, his finger sliding home in her tight little anus with no further impediment.

In his flight-suit, his cock, bent almost in two, felt as hard as battle steel. Groaning at the hot, clasping grip of her little hole, he nearly came at the thought of one day ramming his hard cock in there.

His mouth and lips tugging on her clit, he pumped his finger in and out of the tightly furled opening. Her juices ran down from her cunt, bathing his hand—made her dark passage slippery. Its virgin tightness made the pressure heavenly.

All the while he reamed her tiny asshole, he supped voraciously on her, biting and rolling her hard little soldier between his teeth, burying his tongue deeply in her clasping cunt.

Finally, breathing heavily, he pulled back and reared over her. His tongue swiped out to lick her tangy cream from his lips. With two fingers into both holes, now, he worked them deep inside her steamy slits. His hands flew in counterpoint, powering his digits into her pussy as the other withdrew from her back entrance, then vice versa. His forceful, rhythmic movements set her hips rocking under his command.

"Oh, god! Oh, Dev, it feels so good…too good!"

"Come again. Come for me, now. Let me see your pleasure." Without ceasing his ruthless finger-fucking, he smiled wickedly up at her, urging her on. "I love it when you talk dirty, *Nippa*. Love to see you convulse with the pleasure and ease I give you. Once we are mated, I shall see to your satisfaction every day—as often as you have need of me—"

"Don't talk. *Suck!*" she moaned, mashing his face back onto her clit.

He laughed out loud, happy to comply. Flicking her nub with rapid flutters of his tongue, he changed the rhythm and direction of his thrusts so that both fingers shuttled inward at the same time.

She bowed up into his embrace, shoulders and heels the only part of her touching the mattress as she surrendered to a third climax. Her juices poured from her in torrents, on the cresting wave of another orgasm.

Falling deeper under her thrall, he drank her down.

Releasing her death grip on his hair, Nnora fell back against the pillows. "Bring your…*terat*…up here and…suck my nipples. *Now!*" Her tone pleaded while her words demanded. She punctuated each needy word with a sharp tug on his locks.

"You seem impatient for me to join you, little one." He teased her as he carefully withdrew his fingers from her pliant body and prepared to receive her nipples.

"Quickly!" She lifted her body to him, plucking and playing with the desire-swollen tips. "If you hurry…" she bargained, letting her eyes play over his rampantly aroused body, "I'll suck your cock…drink your delicious come—"

"You'll go wild," he cautioned, "like the last time…" Coming over her, he fitted her stiffly jutting nipples into the dilating mouths of his softened *terat*, hissing at the immediate pleasure-inducing fullness. He loved being stuffed with her pouty nipples, loved the tightness and friction as they worked their chests against each other.

"I swear, *Nippa,* I can feel you all the way to my navel!"

"Yesssss," Nnora moaned, rocking her mons against his cock as her hard little points sank into his chest organs.

* * * * *

Shut up by herself, Nnora quickly became bored. She needed the stimulation of person-to-person contact and didn't enjoy being by herself. She was a people-person, which was why she'd chosen to be an elementary school teacher, for God's sake! She hated being isolated. Alone, she had little to do but dwell on Dev and their loveplay.

In the end, he had not allowed her the taste of his come, though he had forced so many orgasms upon her, he'd left the flesh between her thighs sore and tender, her inner thigh muscles protesting every move. The soreness wasn't as bad as it could have been, due to Dev's thoughtfulness in making sure she had a session in the hygienic chamber. Actually, she'd had two sessions, since the first cleansing had triggered their last bout of sexual gymnastics.

He'd stripped off his clothes to join her in the shower, tenderly holding her as the rejuvenating unit cleansed her inside and out.

She blushed anew, recalling the way she'd yelped when he'd inserted the dual-headed sinuous auto-bidet first into her vagina for a thorough cleaning and then up her rectum for more of the same. She'd reacted shamelessly, ravenous desire rising in her sharp and fierce, surprising her with its power.

She'd begged him to fuck her. Frustration stark on his face, he had roped one muscular forearm about her waist and used the flexible bidet hose in a most innovative way, thrusting the pulsating hose in and out of her clasping sphincter and pussy as he alternately pinched and tugged on her hard, thick nipples.

He'd made them even harder, readying them for insertion into his *terat* and when her crests had stood proudly erect, distended to their full length, he had turned her and *seated* her, keeping the cleansing hose inserted in her rectum. The stream of warm water mixed with gentle cleansing agents had flowed gently between her buttocks as the powerful muscles in his chest had surged against her tender breasts. One hand spread wide on her back, pressed her flush against his hungry mouths.

His *terat* had greedily engulfed her straining nipples and surrounding areolas in a rippling, suctioning vise-grip and he had surprised her with his pleas.

I love the feel of your hard nipples stabbing in me! Please take me, Nippa…fuck my terat…come in me!

She couldn't believe how hot his pleas had made her. Her orgasms had hit her with the impact of a speeding train. Three in quick succession, the first derailed her thought processes and weakened her inhibitions. Her second had her taking control, leaping up on the ledge of the tub to slam her breasts against him, taking his *terat* with a mindless ferocity that had them both shaking. The bliss of the third orgasm threw her into oblivion.

When she'd come to, she'd found herself cleaned, dried and splayed spread-eagle on the bed, Devtorvas' mouth and teeth greedily eating at her cunt while two thick fingers stretched the entrance to her rectum.

"I didn't mean for the shower to be anything but relaxing," he'd admitted ruefully after two more muscle-grinding climaxes. "But the sight of you coming is so beautiful; it twists my heart—and my cock—in knots. I had to have you again."

Thank goodness for her Rb'qarmshi stamina. Because he'd had her, all right…gloriously, repeatedly, magnificently, seemingly intent upon making up for all the orgasms she'd missed during her first pava…

Drifting back to the present, she closed her eyes on a longing sigh. The weary muscles in her thighs fluttered in a futile attempt at tightening as his parting words replayed in her mind.

I want so badly to be inside you, Nippa, but I won't fuck you with my cock until you willingly sign the marriage papers. When I finally have you, I'll bury my cock so deeply in your pussy, we will both feel your heart beating.

"Oh, Dev, I want that, too," she whispered despairingly to the empty room. "Right now, I need some cock so badly, I could scream. And I don't want just anyone's…I want yours. I think…no, I know I'm falling in love with you."

Alone in her cabin, she could admit she had fallen hard and fast for the alien Prince. But how could she forgive him for taking her choices away? How could they build a life together if they were unequal partners? What information was he withholding from her? And what was her father's role in this situation?

She paced the narrow confines of her room, wanting activity, needing something to take her mind off the dilemma of loving a man she was afraid to trust totally.

Despite the repeated, exhaustive orgasms, she'd never felt so wide-awake and antsy. Her blood sparked through her system, and she couldn't sit still. She'd promised not to do any more exploring in her quarters, to leave the gadgets alone until a tutor could instruct her on their proper usage. She waited as patiently as she could for the promised tutor.

When another hour had passed and no one had come around to check on her, she decided to explore the ship.

I made no promises about curtailing my explorations regarding the spaceship, only my quarters, she defended her plans, even though knowing Dev believed he had caged her by her given word, trusting her to abide by her promise. She felt a momentary shaft of guilt over her tactics, knowing her reasoning was self-serving and downright rebellious. She shook off the uncomfortable feelings.

She told herself semantic trickery was acceptable when dealing with the enemy After all, no matter how sex with him curls my toes, until we resolve our situation, he remains my enemy.

Sticking her head around the edge of her door, ready to pull it back at a moment's notice, she glanced left and right, furtively scanning the deserted steel aisles. To be safe, she waited a few minutes more before she easing out of her cabin and tiptoeing away. Picking a direction at random, she started walking.

Not wanting to get lost while traipsing about the featureless walkways, and having always thought Hansel and Gretel the stupidest characters trapped between the covers of a fairytale—who marked a trail with food, for God's sake?—she uncapped the tube of Cherries Jubilee lipstick she'd grabbed from her luggage. Armed with her inedible trailblazer, Nnora felt ready to explore.

As she walked, she lightly scored the bulkheads with a brilliant red line, blazoning her path back to her cabin. She brought along her tube of make-up remover and some tissues for cleanup on the return trip. After all, she wouldn't want to leave lipstick smeared on Dev's pristine walls. Knowing men, Dev would be as enamored of this spaceship as human men were of their trucks.

The ship was even bigger than she'd realized. She stood staring down an empty corridor in indecisive silence. She had worn her once new lipstick down to a nub and she had yet to wend her way through even half the ship.

She sighed. She wasn't ready to return to her lonely quarters. Nevertheless, she was contemplating turning back when she heard a voice that sounded familiar, raised in uncontrolled anger. The shrill altercation came from up ahead and she quickened her steps, anxious to see if her suspicions were correct.

Chapter Twelve

Nnora rounded the corner and skidded to an abrupt halt, only to come face-to-face with the owner of that familiar voice. Her younger sib, Dohsan, appeared to be in the middle of a rowdy brawl. Two patently unhappy guards were attempting—with little success—to restrain Dohsan while she mauled them, inflicting bites, kicks, scratches and all manner of mayhem upon their hapless bodies.

Dressed in a skimpy hot orange short-set that showed off entirely too much of her amply curved body, Dohsan screamed at the top of her lungs, her usually lovely features distorted by the force of her anger. Her iridescent red hair flew wildly about her agitated face as she spat out some of the most disgustingly vile curses Nnora had ever had the privilege of hearing.

Nnora stood a few moments, just watching and listening in awe. Dohsan, with her typically bold impudence, spewed insults indiscriminately, casting scathing aspersions on the soldiers' lineage, their bodily functions and their abnormal sexual inclinations. As far as she could tell, her sibling was having a wonderful time.

Her little sister had a real talent for stirring up trouble wherever she went and this location was obviously proving to be no exception. Yet much as she was enjoying the show, the time had come to intervene. From their brooding looks, the guards had grown fed up with Dohsan's antics. Their responses to her attacks were growing more physical; their fingerprints were beginning to mar her pale skin.

Chances were, her sister deserved her present treatment. Even so, she couldn't stand by while big men manhandled her sib.

"Guys, I think that's enough rough-housing. You should release my sister."

When they hesitated, she prayed Dev hadn't been exaggerating when he'd said her word was law to his warriors. "Stop. Right now."

She breathed a sigh of relief when the two men released Dohsan at once.

"*Chyya'va!*" They obviously recognized her. Both faces wearing twin looks of shocked dismay, the men bowed from the waist, rushing into speech. In their agitation, the men's explanations and excuses tumbled over each other's, colliding and crashing.

"We didn't...!"

"We would not...!"

"Our orders are to hold this *fem* in her cabin, but she will not remain within."

"Really, fellas, this is a *girl* you are talking about. Are you telling me two trained warriors can't find a way to subdue one female without getting physical with her?"

Both of the men stopped and turned comically dismayed faces toward Nnora. Almost in unison, the two warriors heaved a heavy sigh. They looked so pathetic, she found herself pitying them even as their reactions sparked barely controlled hilarity. She glanced at her sister's fierce scowl and had to cover her grin with a strategic hand.

"We are at a loss what to do." Guard number one shook his head.

"Our additional orders are to inflict no physical harm upon her," guard number two chimed in.

Nnora smiled. "I'm glad to hear that."

"But, *Chyya'va,* she will not obey our commands!" Guard number two's voice held a plaintive note. His consternation at having to deal with a *fem* like Dohsan was plainly obvious.

"I commiserate with you, guys, I really do. Trust me, I know *just* how much of a handful she can be." She cut a fulminating glare at Dohsan, who bared her teeth in an evil grin, flung back her riotous mane of hair and triumphantly flipped the double bird at her two erstwhile guards.

Another universal symbol, judging by the instant ire it produced in its targets. She sighed, muttered to herself and shook her head at the Dohsan's juvenile clowning. "Get over here. And stop that!" Nnora pointed to the deck by her feet. Her little sister responded obediently to her summons, coming to tower over her.

"As I said, gentlemen, I understand your dilemma, however, Dohsan *is* my sister *and* a royal princess." She narrowed her eyes in threat and warning. "You have to outweigh her by at least two hundred pounds between you. I'd better never see you lay rough hands on her again."

The guards fell over themselves offering their assurances.

She waved them away and while they didn't go far, just down the corridor, she figured they'd allowed enough space for private conversation. She took the opportunity to confront her hellion of a sister. "Dohsan, what the hell are you up to now? What are you *doing* here? Hell's bells, don't tell me they kidnapped you, too!"

"*Kidnapped*? Of course not, Nnora." Dohsan hugged her, having to lean down to do it. "But I am so glad you came. I bet Kardenez and Puorgkrow you would. Our brothers thought you would defy Father again. I told them, no way. I knew you had learned your lesson with that Grunt basketball player. I told them—"

"Dohsan!" She reached up to grab her young sister by the shoulders, emphasizing each word with a sharp jerk. "What. Are. You. Doing. On. This. Ship?"

Dohsan twisted her body in a supple move, easily slipping out of Nnora's hold. "I'm here for the same reason you are, sister dear. Oh, Nnora, I am so *glad* you decided to come. I don't mind making some lucky *Rb'qarmshi* a beautiful bride while cementing our father's political aspirations, but I didn't want to have to marry your prince—he is not my type. Besides, ruling is too much work and not enough fun!"

Nnora pressed a hand to her aching head. "What is your father thinking of? You can't be a bride. You aren't even old enough to vote!"

"*Our* father is thinking he can regain a kingdom through our marriages. He plans to take this opportunity to right the wrong done to our family a thousand years ago. Anyway, I don't intend to marry right away. I will choose my life-mate once we arrive on *Rb'qarm*."

"Just how long does it take to get *Rb'qarm*?" Reeling under all the new information, she cursed Dev anew for keeping her in the dark. "Where is it situated, in relationship to Earth?"

"You had better ask your prince that question if you want a decent answer. I suck at galactic geography. But with ships like this one, journeys between there and Earth shouldn't take more than a week. Look, let's go inside and get comfortable." Dohsan rolled her head on her neck. "I'm getting a crick in my neck looking down at you."

Nnora accompanied her sister a short way down the hall, quickening her steps to keep up with the younger girl's long-legged stride.

"Here is my home away from home." Dohsan opened her cabin door. "As the grown-ups say, 'Come in and be welcome.'"

Nnora stepped into the utilitarian cabin, peripherally noting the two guards exchanging relieved glances as they took up their assigned positions at the door.

"You are not far from being a 'grown-up', yourself. On Earth, they count you as an adult when you reach age eighteen. You only have one more year to go."

The door whooshed closed behind them, giving them some privacy from the listening guards.

"I wish!" Dohsan grimaced. "Traditionally, no unmated male or *fem* is an adult. I think that is one of the reasons your prince is only the Regent. His father wants to quit, but he can't hand off to a non-adult."

"But why come here looking for a mate, why not seek one among the *fem* on the home worlds?"

Dohsan looked at her sister. "He didn't tell you? All their women are neuter, poisoned by the enemy during the last days of the war. It backfired on the losers, because their women became neuter, too. If they can't find breeders, their race will die out."

Nnora gasped. No wonder the prince was so desperate...and her giant got hard so fast. *Poor Dev.* She understood some of his desperation, now. Hell, all the men had her sympathy. But...what about the poor women who were suffering through no fault of their own? Why hadn't he simply told her?

Nnora felt the beginning of tears as she said, "Dohsan, my heart bleeds for those women. Imagine *knowing* you can never have a child..."

She didn't understand the look that came over her sister's face. Dohsan shook her head, yellow-bright eyes glowing with the unaccustomed sheen of tears.

"It is worse than that, Nnora. Way worse. They don't flower, and they can't make their mates' *terat* soften. Can you imagine never being *seated* again, once you've experienced it, grown accustomed to it?"

Nnora's cunt pulsed at the memory of the intense pleasure she had experienced in the grip of Dev's *terat*. Just the thought of never having those wondrous muscles working her nipples brought sympathetic tears to her eyes. She could just imagine how devastated the *fem* were, how they suffered.

"All right, Dohsan." She made herself comfortable on the couch. "I obviously need bringing up to speed, so start talking. I want the truth, the whole truth and nothing but the truth, so-help-you-god. Begin with why father sent this prince to me, if indeed he did any such thing."

Dohsan threw herself down on the low couch, facing Nnora, arranging her lithe body in an instinctively sexy pose. "Oh, *Chyya* Glendevtorvas is an essential player in Father's game." She chuckled, tossing back her sunburst of curls. "Though I suppose you couldn't say Father sent him, per se. I'm sure the prince is capable of playing his own games as well as Father ever could.

"By the way, sis..." Dohsan winked at her, licking her lips suggestively. "Your future husband is quite a piece of work!"

Dohsan cocked her head at a considering angle, as if deliberating just how much she wanted her sister to know. "I had a long talk with your prospective beau when he first arrived..."

"And? Go on." She wanted to learn everything she could about him. The sex between them was volcanic and mind-blowing and just thinking about him could make her wet, yet, there were other things more important to her than sex. There were a few things she needed to find out about Devtorvas before she could make up her mind one way or the other.

"Now, don't take this wrong, Nnora, but personally, I found him way too formal, stiff and arrogant. For my tastes. But those same traits are the ones which makes him just what you need."

"Oh! I guess that means I'm formal, stiff and arrogant myself, huh, sis?" To resist strangling her aggravating sibling, she sat on her hands.

"See! I told you not to take me wrong. You make me wonder if I should tell you anything else."

"I'm sorry, hon, my nerves are on edge. Please, go on. Tell me why you think the prince is right for me because I desperately need convincing." She dared not tell Dohsan how her gut twisted with need whenever Dev walked into the room, or glanced at her with the glittering light of want shining in his eyes. Or how her heart melted when he stood towering over her, firm muscled body between her and the rest of the world, protecting her, guarding her, making her feel safe and wanted.

"Well, he's taller than you, for one. That means there's no need for you to dust off that age-old height anxiety of yours." Dohsan enumerated her points on the tips of her fingers. "In the second place, he is a first-born royal as are you, so you wouldn't be marrying down. Also, being equivalent in blood and rank means he cannot dictate the terms of your bonding. You stand on equal ground." Dohsan broke off with a laugh. "Too bad things have changed since the colony split off a thousand years ago. You'd be sitting pretty about now."

This was getting interesting. She sat forward. "Why?"

"*Rb'qarm* used to be a matriarchal society. When our ancestors left home a thousand years ago, the *fem* were in *charge*."

"Get out of here!" When she considered the benefits of being in charge of Devtorvas for a change, her lips kicked up into a wide smile. She chuckled. "I'd sure like the chance to turn the tables on a certain cocky Prince."

"I kid you not. You never had a chance to learn our history, but haven't you ever realized all us *fem* are bigger than the males?"

"You are not *that* big, Dohsan."

"I'm way bigger than you, Nnora, and I haven't even started my second growth spurt yet. You are the runt of our litter. Course, it isn't your fault. Our hydroponics team specially preserves and cultivates some of the food brought from the home planet. We got it added to our diets on a regular basis while you, being stranded on Earth, never got any."

"Okay." Nnora held up her hand. "And your point is…?"

"A thousand years ago, upon your marriage, you would have taken the throne with the prince as your consort—not the other way around."

"While I find this fascinating, it is way off the subject of Dev's suitability as a husband. Could we get back to that?" Before the words were totally out of her mouth, she regretted having used the diminutive of the prince's name. She just knew her audacious sib would pounce on her mistake. She could almost see Dohsan's teasing radar pop up.

"Dev?" Dohsan purred, coming to a state of alertness. She straightened out of her slouched position. "Have we gotten intimate enough to use short names?"

Her cheeks heated, but she refused to rise to Dohsan's teasing. "You were about to tell me your other reasons…?"

"All right, already. He is devoted to his subjects and he fights for causes. Which is right up your alley—you being such a sucker for lost causes."

She bristled, but before she could comment, Dohsan had already resumed. "No arguments. You really can't deny that only a crusader would be teaching in that low-income Grunt school of yours, Nnora.

"But my main reason for thinking you two made for each other is—and this one is a doozy—he is as bossy as you are. I predict a lot of fireworks between you two."

She gritted her teeth. "Those don't sound like marrying reasons to me!"

"I wasn't finished!" A stubborn expression hardened Dohsan's pretty face. "But I could be, if you want to keep interrupting…"

Nnora flung her hands up in surrender. Seemed her *little* sister had a touch of bossiness, herself. "My apologies to you, Miss Priss. Please, continue."

"I am very serious about this, Nnora." Dohsan had a hurt look in her eyes.

She rose and moved to sit next to Dohsan. "I can see you are and I'm very sorry, Dohsan. I realize you are trying to help me. This has been a hellacious day, but that's no excuse for me to take my bad humor out on you. Please, forgive me—and tell me what you feel about the prince."

"He believes the family unit is sacred and should never be broken. If the situation ever came up where you and your children were in danger, he would find ways to protect and cherish you and his children without having to send you away.

"No matter how much you and Father skirt the issues, we all know you don't want to come home because deep down, you have never forgiven him for losing you. All these years, you felt betrayed and abandoned. You need a man that will make you feel safe and loved. I believe the prince is that man and I think you should marry him." Dohsan's voice held a thoroughly adult firmness.

She sat speechless, stunned by Dohsan's insightful comments. She'd never wanted her little sister or brothers to learn of her lingering feelings of abandonment, of being an outcast, outside the family circle, the only one sent away to be raised among aliens, where her height and—to Human eyes—strangely colored eyes had set her further apart. Separated from her people, isolated, different from her foster family…*alone*.

"I like him, Nnora," Dohsan said quietly, oddly sincere with all her brashness discarded. "I told him he had my blessing."

A hysterical bubble of laughter rose in Nnora's throat. She ruthlessly suppressed it. "Then *you* marry him."

"Oh, I'm not queenly enough for him. Besides, I don't want to rule a planet or two. I just want to rule the man I mate with." With that, every ounce of Dohsan's set-aside sauciness returned. She stood to her feet, twirling a sexy jig about the room. Laughing out loud, she swung her hips and shook her shoulders, setting her breasts to swaying.

"You are incorrigible!" Nnora rolled her eyes, laughing along with her sister.

"Yes, I am. And I'm willing to teach you everything I know."

That caught her attention. Young as she was, Dohsan was a fount of knowledge concerning all things sexual. She'd probably forgotten more than Nnora would ever learn about *Rb'qarmshi* sexuality. "You are? I mean…you *will*?"

For once, Dohsan didn't tease her about the pitiful note of hope in her voice. "You betcha, big sis!"

"Then I have a few hundred questions for you."

Chapter Thirteen

Dev ran a finger through the red line marring his once pristine bulkhead, his anger gathering like thunderclouds before a storm. His brows creased as he traversed corridor after corridor, finding the garish demarcation on almost every partition. He rubbed his forefinger and thumb together, and the waxy, shiny stuff smeared and clung to his fingers. Without thinking, he wiped his hand on the leg of his flight suit, transferring the scarlet smudge to the light blue material. His eyes narrowed, anger and confusion warring within him.

"GanR'dari, what is this—this disgusting…*uzak*?" He glared at his second-in-command.

"I do not know, *Chyya,* but I believe the *Chyya'va* could tell you." 'Dari stood stiffly.

"You think *Nnora* did this?" He smothered an angry exclamation, thrusting his nose close to the smear and sniffing. "It does not smell of her. I would have thought this kind of juvenile prank more along the line of what Dohsan might think up. What possible reason could Nnora have to disfigure my ship like this?"

"Let's see…reasons to disfigure your ship… Well, there is the fact that you kidnapped her," his friend and closest companion drawled, ticking the items off on his fingers. "That you *seated* her, bringing her to loud, multiple climaxes. This occurred in a thin-walled room adjacent to the room where you had your keen-eared warriors stationed. You announced before a shuttle full of warriors your intent to mate her fully—in our presence—

should she dispute your claim on her…"'Dari paused and bit his lip.

Dev knew he was fighting the urge to burst into laughter. He trained his eyes on his second-in-command. Leaning against the bulkhead in a deceptively relaxed pose, he crossed his arms and ankles, waiting for his *ex*-friend to deliver the punch line.

"But you have done nothing to piss her off in the last hour, *Chyya,* so I would not dare to hazard a guess at what reason the *Chyya'va* could have to return an insult to you," 'Dari deadpanned.

"I will ignore those smart-assed remarks, my friend, as it would not do for the *Chyya'va* to be without a bodyguard in these unsettled times," Dev deadpanned right back.

"Thank you, Dev." 'Dari swept a low bow.

"Do you think the marking is meant to be permanent?" He returned to the problem of the oily markings, troubled by visions of his crew forever scrubbing at the never-fading stains.

"Judging from the ease with which you just transferred it from the bulkhead to your flight suit, I would say…not."

Dev glared at his second-in-command, sure 'Dari hid a smirk behind that bland look of his. He glanced down at his ruined uniform and sighed heavily. "Where has my Princess gotten to?"

GanR'dari shrugged his massive shoulders. "If I might make a suggestion…?"

Dev inclined his head. "By all means."

'Dari pointed down the brightly marked corridor. "Follow the *uzak.*"

Breathing a foul imprecation, Dev strode off in search of his life-mate.

* * * * *

In Dohsan's cabin at the end of the lipstick trail, the biology lesson continued. "So," Nnora asked, "even when I am not in *pava,* that fluid can still be secreted from my breasts?"

"Yes, though the 'gift' doesn't release every time you are *seated.* It happens only if your mate is skilled enough to make you come, much like a regular orgasm." Dohsan rested her arms back along the spine of the couch. "But isn't it a glorious feeling when it happens?"

"And what would you know about how being *seated* feels like, young woman? You are a little young to be playing at sexual games. Besides, aren't the males too young? Have some of them reached sexual maturity?" She was more than a little shocked Dohsan's apparently intimate knowledge of the highly erotic act.

Dohsan purred, stretching her body in a sensuous slither. "You really must lose that Earth-influenced small-town mentality, Nnora. Even boys who haven't grown their stones are capable of softening their *terat,* my innocent big sister. Just because I haven't entered first heat doesn't mean I'm not mature enough for *seating*-play."

"I wish you wouldn't call our *pava* by that horrid term. It makes us sound like animals—cats or dogs, unable to control our sexual urges." Nnora still had a struggle to accept that she had no power over her cycles. She would much rather she suffered the normal pangs and pains of a human woman's menstrual cycle. Bleeding monthly might be messy and inconvenient, but it sure beat the physical pain and horniness she'd suffer on a daily basis for the next year or so.

"We *are* animals, Nnora," Dohsan quipped insouciantly. "And why should we control our urges when giving in to them feels so much better?

"I feel sorry for you. I really do." Dohsan came to her feet to hug Nnora tightly. She reseated herself, flinging her body down in a typical teenager's loose sprawl. "Still, if you haven't already found out how hotly delicious foreplay can be, I'll wager the prince soon finds an excuse to tutor you on the subject."

"I don't need tutoring, I need explanations." Nnora's temper was fraying along with her patience. "I need to know what game Father is playing, what the prince is hiding from me..." She trailed off, rubbing at the back of her neck, trying to relieve the building tension. "This is all so hard to take in—"

Dohsan broke in, laughing suggestively. "Believe me, hard is the ooooonnnn-ly way to take it in."

The pun hit her and Nnora wrinkled her nose at her sister. "That's not what I meant and you know it. You've just told me I can only get pregnant once every three years. And that, although the prince's chemical makeup is now linked to mine through the enzyme we exchanged when he *seated* me I am only sexually predisposed to him, I can still choose another to mate with until we...uh...totally—"

"Fuck. Yep, and you know what that means..." Dohsan's grin was down right gleeful.

"Watch your language." There was no heat in the remark. She met Dohsan's encouraging grin with one of her own. She could use this information to turn the tables on Dev. At the least, she could make him sweat, worrying that she might choose one of his men as her marriage partner. "It means that I'm in the driver's seat!"

"Neat pun sis, but remember…" Dohsan's voice took on a cautioning tone, "That kind of pleasure is addictive. If you are thinking about using the prince's needs against him, you'd best be prepared to withstand your own."

Nnora waved the warning aside, her excitement rising. "This is wonderful, Dohsan. This means I have some control. I have choices in this situation."

Her sister frowned. "You always did, Nnora."

"That's not true, little sister, and you know it. Father signed those contracts without even talking with me. Do you have any idea how that made me feel?"

She didn't bother waiting for Dohsan to respond. "I felt like he was throw—sending me away again. I felt abandoned and alone, as if—" her words ended in a wail, and suddenly she was crying, sobbing her heart out. Horrified, she twisted in her chair, hiding from her sibling's pity.

Two slim arms encircled her, rocking her. After a few moments, Nnora looked up to find Dohsan's vivid lemon-lime eyes awash with sympathetic tears. Ducking her head, she turned into her younger sister's arms, holding on tightly.

For once, Dohsan did not tease her. Her arms tightened round Nnora in a convulsive hug.

Nnora rested her head on her sister's shoulder. It was the first time she had ever relinquished the 'elder sister' role. She felt closer to Dohsan than she ever had before.

"As if we would have let Father do such a thing again, *Chyya* or not! I was there for the formal signing, Nnora. While it is true Father signed the contracts, signifying his consent, there is a blank line on those papers where your name must go to make it all official."

"*What?*" Her head snapped up from Dohsan's shoulder. "You mean he *lied* to me?"

Dohsan chuckled. "Well, whaddya know? I didn't think the stiff-necked prince had it in him to pull a stunt like that!"

Anger, hot and furious, blazed through Nnora. She sat up, scrubbing at the tears that had spilled onto her cheeks. "He's going to have something knocked *out of him.*" She gritted her teeth. "That low-down, sap-sucking, snake-bellied *shark*! According to *him*, our marriage is a done deal, all but gift wrapped and delivered. I swear, Dohsan," she vowed darkly. "Glendevtorvas is not going to get away with this."

"Wow!" Dohsan breathed, eyes sparkling, probably in anticipation of the coming fight. "You really sound pissed."

She widened her eyes in feigned horror. "How could he do such an underhanded thing when he promised Dad to woo you in all honor? *Tsk! Tsk!* Are you telling me he brought you no flowers? Sang you no mating song?"

Nnora glumly shook her head at the thought of all the traditions she'd missed.

"You mean he didn't go down on bended knee and quote bonding poetry?"

"He didn't even propose!" Nnora remembered and fumed all over again. "He stormed into my bedroom like he owned it, told me I was going to belong to him, stuck my nipples in his chest, and before I could recover from that admittedly cataclysmic event, jerked off in front of me. Hell, he even demanded I help him…several times. To top that, he snatched me out of my apartment against my will, and then bragged about what I had done to him in front of his men!"

"No...*really?*" Dohsan bit her lip in an effort to conceal her hilarity at Nnora's innocence. She would have paid money to be a fly on the wall during that confrontation! The most hilarious element was that her elder sister lacked the slightest clue of just how telling the prince's actions were.

Dohsan might not have known Devtorvas long, but she had picked up enough information about him to know his emotional reaction to her sister must have knocked him for a loop. To screw up so...*royally*, he had to have been pole-axed by Nnora, which must have flabbergasted and angered him. He was, after all, a male used to being in command. Finding himself *out* of command had to be a little disconcerting for him...to say the least.

She wished, for the umpteenth time, there was some way she could open up her older sister's eyes, make her see her own radiant inner and outer beauty. Repeated telling didn't work—she'd been telling the stubborn woman how beautiful she was since the first day they'd met. No one—not her mother nor their father—had been able to make a dent in Nnora's human-conditioned, iron-cast mind.

Yet, even by human standards, Nnora was strikingly beautiful. She simply had no idea how many Earthling men tracked her with hungry eyes and lolling tongues, drawn by her queenly stance and enticing curves. Nnora persisted in seeing herself as a gawky, hulking ogress when Dohsan knew her to be the fairy princess in the story, the one who gets her man. Come hook or crook, she planned to see that Nnora got the man she wanted.

Somehow or other, I need to get Princey-boy to declare himself in the most romantic way possible. Dohsan tuned out Nnora's continued accounting of Devtorvas' many sins while she turned several scenarios over in her head.

Deep down, she knew, Nnora didn't believe the prince could be smitten with her. She didn't believe herself worthy of his love, because most of her life, with the exception of the Brewsters, people around her, like her ex-hubby—who should have been a dead ex-hubby in Dohsan's not-so-humble opinion—had treated Nnora like yesterday's trash. Humans had done almost irreparable damage to Nnora's self-esteem.

How can I get Nnora to see even a glimpse of what the prince finds so fascinating about her?

Princey-boy-toy wasn't her cup of tea, but since he seemed to float Nnora's boat, that was good enough for Dohsan to give her blessing. Meanwhile, on the QT, Dohsan would make damn sure big sis had a paddle...and a life jacket just in case her boat sank.

Chapter Fourteen

Dev's eyeballs felt gritty and hot with steadily building rage. The further he followed the brazen path of scarlet desecration, the angrier he became.

How dare she deface his beautiful ship, his *Blazing Star* in such a fashion? He'd be damned if he'd tolerate this statement about their relationship. While he had no wish to break Nnora's wild and wonderful spirit, he fully intended teaching her a thing or three about respect—and about keeping her feminine defiance within proper, *private* bounds!

The two guards at Dohsan's cabin door braced to attention at sight of him, saluting smartly. He nodded, noting the shocked looks on their faces. He did not often venture down into crew's territory, so he could understand their reactions to his unannounced presence.

Sighing inwardly, he thought of the future. His crew might as well adjust. He knew Nnora—if she had her way—would have him doing many unaccustomed things.

He was dismayed to find Nnora's trail ended at her sister's cabin. Dohsan's presence was one of the many things he had withheld from his princess. The thought of just how displeased she likely was had him hesitating at the door. *Rejas!* Nnora would have his *cherzda* and *sirat* in a vise if that precocious, vixenish little sister of hers had blabbed his other news.

Sending an awkward plea star-ward, he took a fortifying breath. Gesturing for the guards to step aside, he released the manual lock and opened the cabin door—

And stepped into chaos.

Sixteen high-born *Rb'qarmshi* colonial *fem* were crowded into Dohsan's tiny cabin. According to Devtorvas' tortured eardrums, they all seemed to be talking at once...at the top of their lungs.

Like any self-respecting male *Rb'qarmshi*, the prince had a healthy dread of being the center of attention for so many *fem*. Hoping to escape their notice, grab Nnora and run, he hugged the wall, sidling around the perimeters of the room.

He had almost reached his unsuspecting goal when a lanky *fem* whose towering height, white hair and pale tangerine eyes—closely resembling the norm on *Rb'quarm*—spotted him. The *fem* pointed towards him, her shrieks alerting the other women to his presence. The entire flock advanced on him, murder and mayhem in their eyes.

"Dog!"

"Deceiver!"

"Trickster!"

"Kidnapper!"

The epithets rang out and Devtorvas blinked, nonplused by the vehemence displayed by the *fem*. He spread his hands, calling on his usual diplomatic mien to subdue and calm this group—*gaggle?*—of *fem*. "If we might have a little quiet, please?" When the noise level dropped to a low-voiced buzzing of disapproval, he continued, "That's better! Now, gentle-*fem*, what seems to be the problem?"

The room erupted again. Dev gave up trying to make sense out of the commotion, turning instead to Nnora, who stood in the midst of her overly-vocal supporters, aloof and cool. "Have you any idea what this is all about?" he yelled to be heard over the ruckus.

"You have injured their pride by insulting their Crown Princess, kidnapped the lot of us and made yourself an enemy of our *Chyya*. They are not inclined to forgive that barbaric behavior and neither am I!"

"Insulted you how, Nnora? By loving you...by offering you the treasures of two worlds and access to a thousand more? What are you talking about?"

"I am talking about our marriage contracts, and the fact that I have yet to see them, let alone *sign* them, you bastard!" She was in high dudgeon, and the *fem* echoed her sentiments at the top of their lungs.

He groaned and tried to get closer to Nnora, only to find himself outflanked, cut off by three enormous *fem*-in-waiting determined to thwart his every move. After two abortive attempts to sidestep them, he gave up the useless endeavor. The wily *fem* didn't intend to let him pass without physical intervention.

Had to be Dohsan. How else could all his plans have gone awry so quickly and so completely? Shooting an "I'm-going-to-kill-you-the-first-chance-I-get" look towards Dohsan, he held out his hands in a conciliatory manner. "I can explain—"

"Oh, I'm sure you can." The love of his life sneered at him, eyes glinting coldly, and his heart sank. "You can explain why this ship is heading *away* from Mars with two royal princesses. If you put your mind to it, you could probably even convince us we are not all hostages to ensure my father's compliance to your will. However, I do not wish to hear your explanations."

He ran nervous fingers through his hair, pushing the damned unruly locks off his forehead, while sparing a quick thought to his missing hair-tie. *Oh, yes,* he recalled fondly, *Nnora's clutching fingers had ripped it off while he'd been lapping at her delicious pussy.* But all that was in jeopardy now.

What would be an acceptable approach? At a loss at how to deal with an angry *fem*, one he was desirous of pleasing in every way, he listened to her quiet, driven comments, his heart hurting in tandem with the pain he heard in her low words.

"You have manipulated my emotions, lying to me from the very beginning—" She broke off, shakily sinking her teeth into her plump bottom lip, battling to withhold the tears that hovered on the edge of her thick eyelashes. He might just cry with her. His emotional state was so entwined with hers that all his celebrated statesmanship flew out the door, reducing him to the lowly status of a hapless male pleading with his mate, ignorance his only argument.

"Nnora! Please, *Nippa*, if you would just listen to me—"

"I listened to you in my bedroom, and look what it got me." She had the misfortune to blush as she obviously remembered just what listening to him had gotten her...several times.

Dev worked at suppressing the smile that wanted to escape his lips at her tell-tale coloring. It broke loose as he tracked Nnora's blush. He recalled the incidents as well as she did. "You liked what it got you!" he retorted, taking the opportunity to move in closer.

"Can you honestly say you regret our interactions in the bedroom, Glennora?" He kept his voice low, not wanting the others privy to their intimate conversation.

She hesitated, then took a different tack. "Why didn't you tell me my sister and these others were also going back to *Rb'quarm* to be groomed as wives for your favorites?"

"I planned to tell you everything. I was waiting for the right time. If these crises hadn't cropped up—one of them helped along by your spoiled brat of a sister, I might add." He threw another disgruntled look at Dohsan, who retaliated with an evil, saccharin-sweet smile that chilled him to his bones.

He knew himself a brave man, but if *Chyya* Glenbrevchanka had only had the one daughter, he might have been returning home unmated. He did not envy the unsuspecting *Rb'qarmshi* who would eventually take that *Deth*-brat to wife. The poor male would end up her slave, or a raving lunatic.

He got back to the safer prospect of cajoling his fiancée. "I wanted to concentrate on our situation without all these added distractions." He indicated the others with a wave of his hand.

"Don't listen to him, Princess. He's lied before, and he's no doubt doing it again!"

"That's right!"

"I say dump him and find someone worthier!"

Dev growled low in his throat, seeing his hopes for a painless extraction going down the tubes. Nnora had managed to put the length of the room between them again, and he worried she was seriously considering taking the advice of the interfering *fem*. He had to do something fast, before the situation deteriorated beyond repair. Keying his wrist communicator and opening up his secured priority channel, he hailed GanR'dari.

"*Chyya*?" His second's voice came clear and undistorted through the powerful miniature speaker.

"The *uzak* has hit the *Riahc* generators. Scan my coordinates and translate the *mr'nok* squadron to me immediately."

For a split second, silence sounded loudly from the wrist unit. Then, "At once, Sire!" GanR'dari's voice betrayed his shock.

Dohsan's face screwed up into a disgusted frown. "Oh, *shit*!"

"Watch your language, young lady!" Nnora ordered sharply. "You're still an adolescent, regardless of how sexually advanced you are. There is a certain standard of behavior *I* demand of my younger sister. You better learn fast that a woman cheapens herself when she uses such gutter language."

Outside of the bedroom, that is.

Nnora blushed as she caught Dev's knowing gaze, raised eyebrows and quickly hidden smirk.

"We are not women, we are *fem*. I keep telling you behavior norms are different for us. And you'll be cussing in a minute," Dohsan warned, grimly. Pointing an accusing finger at Dev, she spat, "That...that *tyrant* has sent for the goon squad, his bully-boys...*reinforcements*."

"Yes, I have, Dohsan. You have instigated quite a mess here, little Princess, and now I am going to straighten it out." Dev widened his stance, crossing his arms. Intense satisfaction blossomed, as he watched Dohsan's face darken with anger.

"By placing us all under cabin arrest again?" Dohsan sneered, her anger at his earlier treatment of her plain on her face. "Pretty high-handed of you, Princey-boy-toy."

Princey-boy-toy? He was not amused.

"Yes, if I must, Princess-brat."

The thought of upsetting the little horror almost made up for having Nnora mad at him…*almost*.

"Those guards were not for her protection? You had a Royal Princess—*my sister*—placed under cabin arrest?" Nnora's disgruntled voice intruded upon his war with Dohsan. "Why?"

Dev pushed away from the wall, aware his hopes of fucking Nnora anytime soon were fast flying out the space dock. He'd better tailor his explanations so they placated her protective feelings for her sister.

He tried to gather his arguments, aware of heat building inside as he felt Nnora's eyes following his every movement. He hid his smile, hoping she recalled how she'd felt when he'd held her in his arms, lavished her with all the love he felt for her. He thrilled, heart pounding out a triumphant beat when he saw her tongue swipe her lips in a nervous gesture as she shifted her stance, releasing the sharp sweet scent of her aroused pussy.

His *cherzda* jerked and swelled, pushing boldly against the tight, form-fitting material of his ship suit and Dev turned so his condition was evident to Nnora's wide-eyed stare, while shielded from Dohsan's. It seemed a good idea to let Nnora know she affected him too. "Perhaps I did it because your sister delights in causing trouble. No sooner had she set foot aboard, than my second-in-command caught her urging on a fight between two of my most trusted warriors. The idiots were vying for her immature favors, totally forgetting she has yet to enter into her initial *pava. Rojas* and *Deth* help us when she does get her first flowering!"

"Surely you are not trying to blame Dohsan for the unruly actions of your own men." Nnora's delicate eyebrows rose in disdain. "Perhaps they simply followed your own sterling example of how to treat us Colony-born *fem*—"

"On top of that..." He paused, but chose to ignore, for the moment, Nnora's snide dig. If he succeeded in winning her back, there would be time to deal with it. "On top of that, we caught her spying in posted off-limit areas.

"Admit it, *fem*." Devtorvas growled at Dohsan from between gritted teeth. "Go on. Or will you lie to your sister?"

"Dohsan?" Under Nnora's disapproving, questioning gaze, the young princess hung her head and scuffed her feet, blushing. On an almost eight-foot tall being, that diffident stance should have been incongruous, yet even Dev was moved to pity by the predicament the youngling destined to become his "little" sister found herself in. Dev could see how much Dohsan worshipped her older sister, wanting Nnora's approval and love.

Nnora let loose a long-suffering sigh. "Why do I have a sinking feeling I really don't want to know what my rebellious sister has been up to?"

She tapped her foot when she received no response. "My *baby* sister's continued refusal to meet my eyes isn't doing much to alleviate my fears. Dohsan."

A stubborn expression turning her youthful face sullen, Dohsan glared at him before turning to meet Nnora's worried gaze. "Okay, already! I was having a bit of fun with his men—it was no big deal! As for spying, I was just exploring the area out of boredom. There was nothing of interest to see, anyway. Besides, according to the deal made with our father, we are supposed to be allies, so there was no reason for Mr. High-and-Mighty to throw me in his version of the clink."

"This is a military ship, young *fem*." He knew his voice was sharp, but Dohsan had a lesson coming. Best it came from him. From Nnora it would wound her badly. "It is *not* a playground for your childish pranks. Be thankful I only confined you to quarters. By rights, I can still have you stripped and lashed for insubordination, then dumped in a shuttle and returned to your father!"

The color fled from Dohsan's face. She bit her lip, focusing beseeching yellow-green eyes on her sister.

"May I speak with you alone?"

Nnora's voice sounded diffident, her tones softer than they had been. *Good.*

"You may speak with me anytime…anywhere. I will always be available to you, *cherzda'va*."

Offering his arm, he led her to an unoccupied section of the room. He relished the bright stain on her cheeks, which bloomed when he pulled her close and tucked her under his shoulder.

"For all her flamboyance and bravado, Dohsan is still an adolescent, with adolescent needs and little trust in the adults about her."

The warm weight of her curvy body summoned his desire for her. No matter how many times he tasted her, had her, he hungered and thirsted after her like a man dying in an arid desert.

"Here, light years away from our father, I am the only parent-figure she has. I know she has acted abominably, but...please...couldn't we just allow her to stew for a while, get good and scared? I will guarantee her behavior is appropriate from now on. If I tell her I am the one who will be punished for her future misdeeds, I don't believe she will let me down."

A smile welled up from the depths of his soul. Still swamped with lust and now growing respect for Nnora's compassionate heart, he could only marvel at how she lightened his world with her goodness.

The smile she awarded him in return brightened the entire room. It dimmed when he tightened his hold. "I will let your sister off the hook, but you taking her place and her punishment will be no mere verbal invention."

Nnora's gaze snapped to his. He caught a fleeting look of unease, quickly hidden in their tangerine depths.

He glared down at his fidgeting mate. He worked at keeping his expression fierce, finding he felt more hurt than anger. "Let us discuss spying and juvenile acts of rebellion, *Nippa.* I would dearly like to know why my bulkheads are stained with a bright smear of...*uzak*. I also want to know why I find you here when you gave me your word you would do no more adventuring without a guide?"

The silence was deafening.

"So...?"

He paused, giving her time to provide an answer. None was forthcoming. "I see. While you bargain for my leniency for your sister's misdeeds, recall that you have earned none for yourself. Dohsan's punishment is negotiable…yours is not." His voice hardened as his anger rekindled.

Why did she continue to resist him? How could he get through to her? Make her see how much she had grown to mean to him? When would she stop fighting him?

"You *lied* to me, *Nippa.* I will tolerate no dishonesty between us."

Nnora raised her stubborn chin in answer to his low-voiced challenge, her proud spine stiffening in battle readiness. Her stance declared that if he thought her cowed, he had a few surprises coming.

A fierce feeling of pride swelled through him as he realized Nnora would never allow him to see her fear.

"I didn't lie, exactly…" Nnora's voice was low and hesitant. Her words trailed off at his pointed glare. "Well, at least, I didn't mean to…and the lipstick will come off easily. See?" She held up her fistful of treated Kleenex. "I brought these along to wipe off the line on my way back to my cabin. I'm sorry, Dev. I just…I was so bored waiting for you to come back."

Her inner struggle showed on her lovely face. "I missed you, Dev. I needed something to take my mind off of what we'd shared."

Something tight eased in his chest at her words, at the evidence she offered, proving she had not been rebelling against their growing relationship.

"You have just earned my leniency," he whispered, lowering his head to take her lips. He never completed the move, distracted by the commotion at the front of the cabin.

When the panels of the cabin door retracted into the walls, revealing a squadron of ten muscular *Rb'qarmshi* males—GanR'dari at the fore, each warrior a prime specimen of virile maleness—Dev felt and heard Nnora's breath catch in her chest. Her throat worked, swallowing repeatedly; her pussy gushed wetness, scenting the air. He knew she had never seen so many mature, attractive males. Still, his brows snapped together at her involuntary feminine reaction.

With a growl of angry possessiveness, he caught her up and took her lips in a hard, driven kiss. One hand swept down her back, clutched the round swell of her ass and jerked her closer, silently but graphically staking his claim. Satisfied all had gotten his message, he lifted his head. In a fierce voice almost a snarl, he rapped out specific instructions to his second-in-command.

GanR'dari, stern-faced and grim, stepped forward and took reluctant charge of Dohsan.

With a final command for his men, Dev returned his attention to Nnora, none too gently propelling her down the corridor, away from her sister and the other *fem.*

Behind her, Dohsan cupped her hands to her mouth and hollered after her sister. "Don't let him bully you, Nnora. Remember you have the upper hand!"

"Keep up this talk of upper hands, *fem* and you'll soon feel one on your bottom!" GanR'dari hauled her along behind him as the rest of the warriors cleared the remaining *fem* from the room.

* * * * *

Dev grinned to himself while Nnora pretended to give her surroundings her full attention. True, there was a lot to peruse, since his quarters were twice as large as her assigned cabin. As the ruling *Rb'qarmshi* Prince, he was widely traveled and his travels showed in his eclectic collection of art and artifacts. His accommodations overflowed with the bounty of a hundred worlds, more than enough to occupy one jittery *fem*. Still…

He bit his cheek, reining in his humor. Nnora deliberately ignored his presence, seeking to put off what she thought of as her coming punishment. She moved about, touching everything, ooh-ing and ahh-ing over all his exotic items.

Arms crossed as he leaned against the door of his cabin, he patiently watched her flit nervously about, her graceful, almost airy movements calling to mind the flutterbies of Novus Ten. Yet her dainty looks belied his memory of her surprisingly powerful struggles and the equally strong grip of her hands in his hair. He replayed her eager, lusty response to the numerous explosive orgasms he'd given her and reminded himself she was sturdier than she looked.

His heart thudding with heightened awareness, full arousal only a beat away, he pondered how he would take her first. She was smaller than the normal *fem*…petite, actually. Their first joining might be so painful she would find no pleasure. He wanted to make it good for her, but he feared he would lack control. Much as he ached to fuck her, he didn't want her memory of their bonding to be one of pain and disappointment.

He wavered, desire, love and fear pulling him first one way, then another. Should he claim her now, make her his *cherzda'va* in reality or allow her request and wait the length of their journey to home-world?

His breath caught anew in his throat as he watched her, glorying in the simple fact that she existed. For twenty dry, barren years, he had worked and labored for his people…for what? For the opportunity that now lay within his grasp: the chance to claim his mate. A part of himself, joined with him, the only being who could send the life pulsing through his veins, pounding in his cock. Nnora was the culmination of his dreams, the realization of his hopes. She was the reason his heart beat. He loved her.

He wanted to lock her away and keep her totally to himself.

Dev's eyes narrowed, jealousy kindling flame hot in his chest as he recalled Nnora's instinctive reactions around his men.

She was his, by *Deth*! He would allow no one to come between them…not if he could help it!

That quickly, he made up his mind. The seesaw of indecisiveness slowed and stopped. He pushed away from the door and stalked over to Nnora, halting only when their bodies were almost touching.

"I'm sorry, *Nippa*, I should have told you the full truth about the marriage contracts." He caught and held his mate's gaze. "Perhaps we could have avoided this present situation."

"Why didn't you?" She maneuvered to widen the space between them without actually backing away.

He shrugged, moving a few steps forward to counteract her uneasy withdrawal. "I took one look at you, and any vestige of sense flew out my head. The only remaining thought dictated that I make you mine at any cost. I could not…" he closed his eyes, heaved a sigh "…*cannot* let you go."

She backed up again, lips lifting in a snarl. "You called me a liar, yet *you* lied to *me...repeatedly*. How am I supposed to trust you?"

He advanced. "I admit to withholding information, but I did not lie."

She retreated. "I consider it the same thing. You deceived me!"

He feinted. "I am now willing to tell you everything if you are willing to listen with an open mind. I'll even promise not to touch you while we talk."

She parried. "Again, I don't know that I can trust you to do as you say..."

He retreated. Verbally, anyway.

"You are wise not to trust me." He relaxed his facial muscles, letting her see his contriteness, his knowledge of just how guilty he appeared in her sight.

"Where you are concerned, I am not to be trusted. For when I am this close to you, all I can think of is burying your beautifully long nipples in my chest and milking you dry. This time, I won't stop with the *seating*." He dropped his voice to a deep rumble. "I promised to fuck you deeply enough to feel your heart beating, but I ache for the emotional closeness as well, *Nippa*. I want to *mate* you...finish the journey we started in your bedroom and built upon in your quarters—mentally as well as physically."

Nnora swallowed audibly, her pleasure at his frank words evident in the flushed color of her cheeks. "You're talking what I would call marriage."

"Yes. Bonding...marrying...mating...life-sharing... mutually exclusive rights... Whatever you call it, I want it with you."

"Sweet talk will get you nowhere."

He deliberately sniffed the air, and then met her eyes. "Your pussy says differently."

"My *pussy* responds as it wills." It was well that she did not deny what they both knew. "But it is my mind that controls my actions."

He half-raised his hand to cradle her cheek, stopped short of making the tender connection. Curling the hand into a fist, he lowered it to his side with a rueful shake of his head. "I promised not to touch you while we talked, and I will abide by my word, hard as it is. But…oh, *Nippa,* how can you doubt the depths of my desire for you? Do you recall how hard I became in your eager hands, how heavy I grew with arousal? Remember how my body surrendered when you stroked me to completion?"

Nnora's cheeks took on a darker hue as she searched his face. "I—I want to believe you."

"Then listen to what I have to say. It is all I ask."

Should she listen to him? Could anything possibly justify his actions? Nnora worried her top lip in indecision, debating. She closed her eyes against his potent appeal. In the dark space behind her closed lids, alone in her mind's quiet place, she realized she *wanted* him to have logical, honest reasons for the way he had behaved. *Drat!*

"All right, Dev," she heard herself say, inwardly praying her trust was not misplaced, "I'll listen." She had been silly enough to fall in love with him. She might as well be a total imbecile and let him have his say.

Chapter Fifteen

"I still cannot believe they would use chemical warfare against your females!" Even though Dohsan had explained, it seemed more horrifying hearing it from Dev's lips. "How could anyone deliberately plan to destroy a people—their *own* people?"

"The *Rb'nTraqshi* felt they had no choice." Dev heaved a despondent sounding sigh. "They no longer felt connected to us *Rb'qarmshi*. The war between us had dragged on for over two hundred years and they were losing badly, running out of replacement warriors to fuel their war-machine. Still, not all of the *Rb'nTraqshi* agreed to the plan. Unfortunately, the protesting Elders were either shouted down, voted out, or shut up…permanently. A few honorable Council members tried getting word out to us, but to no avail." Though Dev's voice was quiet, the air throbbed with his pain as he recalled those first, horrible days.

Nnora thought quietly, weighing the situation from all angles. "Is it true your doctors and scientists hold forth no hope? They have determined that *all* of your women were affected by the poisoning? None escaped?"

"None. As far as the scientists and doctors can tell, not one of our mature *fem* escaped the poison. They all suffer from the same symptom, namely, the inability to flower."

From her conversation with Dohsan, she knew that meant the *Rb'qarm* and *Rb'nTraq fem* could not produce the wetness necessary to lubricate their *pavas*, as well as trigger the male's olfactory system.

"Haven't your doctors been able to discover a cure, find some substitute to alleviate that problem?" It seemed a simple enough problem, just synthesize the fragrance and lubricate the *pavas*. "I find it hard to believe a race so technologically advanced as yours is stumped over a problem of this nature."

Dev nodded. "Our technological advances do not help with a biological problem such as this. All attempts at synthesis have failed." Well, perhaps it wasn't so simple. "Our *fem*—our mothers, sisters, aunts and cousins—are sterile, incapable of flowering. As they cannot stimulate us males, we cannot soften our *terat* to *seat* them. Without the *seating*, we are doomed."

He got up and began to pace, his agitation evident in his stiff posture, clenched fists and stern visage. "You wondered about the liquid you secreted into my *terat* each time you came whilst being *seated*..."

Nnora nodded, wordlessly urging him to continue, wishing there were some way she could alleviate his pain.

"There is good reason it is called 'the gift'. Without that fluid, our sperm is lifeless. It is essential to our sexuality. It will bond me to you and, once my body has transmuted the fluid, will in turn bond you to me through the injection of my sperm. As you found out, our sperm acts as an enhancer, an aphrodisiac to our women. In fact, over time, you will become addicted to my sperm, your body needing it to survive, as I will need your *gifting*."

She tensed, sitting up straight on the bunk. Dohsan had left this part out of her lesson. "Does this mean I will die without your sperm? If you decide not to fuck me, I'm doomed?" A slightly queasy feeling settled in her belly as she contemplated what her life might be like, so completely dependent upon another person. Then she thought of Mom and Pop Brewster, how both seemed to be extensions of other. She knew for certain that neither one would long outlast the death of their partner; they were that connected.

He stopped his agitated pacing to stare at her, his expression of mixed horror and bemusement almost comical. "No, you will not die. First, I will never refuse to fuck you. Secondly…well, let me just say…you would not be the only one affected in a situation such as that. But if I were to stop for some reason—though I am told it can be extremely painful, it doesn't end in death." Then he grinned wickedly. "So, little Dohsan doesn't know everything."

"Thank goodness." She drooped in relief. Being ready to commit is one thing. Facing the possibility of death from lack of fucking is another!

"As for Dohsan… She knows plenty about sex but nothing about mating. My foster parents taught me that true marriage involves the bonding of two people into one. Isn't it ironic that I had to leave Earth before I could experience that?"

Dev halted in his steps, his eyes lighting up. "Does that mean you—"

"Wait a moment!" She flung up a hand, cutting short his jubilation. "It means *nothing* until I hear the rest of the story." On that, she would brook no argument.

His eyes dimmed and his shoulders slumped. He nodded, resuming his explanations…and his pacing.

"Our healers offer a very dim view of our race's future. Thousands of our mated pairs have already died and our population has decreased to the point of negative birth rate. You see, they released the chemical through the nutrient chain. The poison targeted our *fem* by destroying one of their hormonal enzymes. It accomplished this by mutating the *Rb'kylla* plant, the food responsible for stimulating the growth of that enzyme. So far, our scientists have been as unable to duplicate the needed substance as they have the *flowering*. They fear there is no way to reverse the damage and we are facing a permanent, fatal situation."

Nnora's brow furrowed with the beginnings of a thought. An insistent, niggling, something familiar digging at her brain, trying to break through. It scattered at Dev's next words.

"With one fell stroke, the enemy assured our demise as a people. *Rb'qarmshi* males cannot become sexually aroused without the exchange of pheromones. If our *terat* do not soften, we cannot gather the liquid that bonds us to our *cherzda'va*."

She reached over and took Dev's hand, her heart aching with the echo of his pain, sickened by the horrendous results of an age-long war. "What of the young girls, the babies? Do you think any of them might have escaped the chemical?"

"What young girls?" His tone was so bitter she nearly wept. "There have been no babes born for almost twenty years. Every *fem* has proven to be affected.

"There were no tests that measure whether a *fem* will enter *pava* and flower upon reaching her maturity. We waited with bated breath to see whether the children would prove to be fertile. Not one escaped the effects of the poison. As it stands now, our mature *fem* might as well be neuter, and we males with them. We may have won the war, but unless we can find a way to reverse the effects of the biological poisoning, we face extinction." His voice was flat and dull, as though he had recited these same statistics too many times for the pain to bleed through.

"My people were desperate. The discovery of your colony has given us new hope, a way of realizing our dreams. To find *fem*—lots of mature, fertile *fem* willing to return to *Rb'qarm* as mates—has given us back our future. "

"We faced the same situation as you, only in the reverse." How strange that seemingly random elements that brought the home-world and its lost colony to the same straights. "War is to blame for both our situations... Do you think there is a fatal flaw in our makeup...a gene on our DNA strand that prompts us to destroy ourselves?"

"I pray not." Dev's eyes grew bleak. He lifted his hands and then let them fall as he shrugged his shoulders. "I hope with all my heart that we have learned our lessons. I am fighting to forge a lasting peace between our two planets...and now, with your colony."

"What happened to the perpetrators?" She hoped the retribution had been swift and painful.

Dev shook his head. A grimace, masquerading as a smile, marred his face as he came and sank down next to her. "Now that the results are known and it is too late for their sorrow to matter, our enemies—the few that are left—are appalled at the barbarism of their leaders' action. Their punishment is to share our fate. You see, the *Rb'kylla* plant grows only upon *Rb'qarm*. In times past, before the war broke out, we imported the food to *Rb'nTraq*. During the war, their store of *Rb'kylla* diminished until they were forced to pay an exorbitant price for the smuggled goods."

The ugly irony wasn't lost on her. "In other words, your people were denying the *Rb'nTraqi* people the same enzyme, using it as a lever in your war. Faced with the same outcome that you now endure, they decided to make sure you shared in their fate. 'Leveling the playing field' is how we say it on Earth."

Dev blinked. His face bore an arrested look. "I fear you are very much correct, *Nippa*." His words came slow and measured as if he tested each one before speaking. "Why is it I am only seeing this, now? Why did it take your words to open my eyes to our own guilt? Our actions towards the *Rb'nTraqi* make us just as responsible for this current disaster as they are. This puts a whole new light on the negotiations and reparations talks. We have been grossly unfair to *Rb'nTraqi*. I am a fool, and unworthy to lead my people. What will become of our worlds?"

"Hey, don't beat yourself up." She turned and ran her hands along Dev's shoulders, working the tightness out of the heavy muscles and tendons as she spoke. "Look, I happen to think you are the best man for the job. The fact that you are willing to admit you can make mistakes tells me you will do whatever you can to rectify the situation. Your people are lucky in having such a leader."

Dev turned to her, easing her hands off his shoulders and keeping hold of them. His grip was warm and encompassing, firm, as if he feared to let go.

She glanced down at their joined hands and then back up at Dev.

He quickly released her, scooting away until he had placed a foot between them, mumbling half under his breath, "Hands to yourself, Dev. Remember your word."

She smiled. He was a good man. "I'll forgive this instance, since I started it. Now, finish your report."

He took a deep breath, slapped his hands on his thighs and pushed up from the bed. Standing at attention, he clasped his hands behind his back, looking for all the world like a boy in the principal's office, awaiting punishment. "You will not like what I have to say next."

She raised an eyebrow. "Then you'd best just get it said." What could possibly be so bad he feared telling her? Leaning back on her hands, she waited for Dev to continue.

"When first we met, I told you of a planned attack…told you we discovered and captured the rebels before that attack took place—"

"Yes, go on." She came erect. A dark feeling of dread swamped her limbs, making her body heavy, her head light. She prepared herself for the worst.

"In obedience to your father's orders, I lied to you about that. Your father fell captive in that attack and the leader of the rebellion demanded we deliver you to him in order to save your father's life."

"Oh, my god," Nnora gasped, feeling the blood leave her head in a rush. She sagged against the pillows, glad she hadn't been standing when she received the unsettling news. "Is he…he's not…?" She couldn't force the word out her mouth.

Dev rushed back over to her, sweeping her into a tight embrace. "Nnora…*Nippa*," he crooned as he rocked her back and forth, soothing her. "Be calm and fear not. Your father lives.

"Before the attack, he and I met and made plans, determined to break the back of this rebellion, once and for all. The *Chyya* would allow none but himself into danger. Despite your stepmother's and my arguments, your father's stubbornness won the day. My part was to get to you before the rebels could find you, whisk you away out of danger and coordinate my men's counter-strike on the rebel base when I received the signal from your father. That signal met us when we arrived aboard ship."

He paused and she waited, breathless, to hear the rest of it. Her mind reeled. Her father had been in deadly danger, and she had been kept ignorant of his peril. Anger roiled through her, joining her fear in the pit of her stomach.

"I sent the men as agreed upon. They rescued your father and captured all the rebels not killed during the retrieval exercise. At that point, I had promised to return you to Mars. Then the message from home came with these new troubles. It was imperative that I head back immediately. Your father objected."

He stopped talking and met her gaze dead on. His eyes glowed iridescently golden orange, the mixture of colors a sure sign of inner agitation.

"Taking you from your apartment was no kidnapping, since I had your *Chyya's* permission and request to remove you from danger. The kidnapping occurred once we were underway. Your father had begun talking about mating you to the rebel leader to ensure a lasting peace. We came seeking *fem* for mates, yet I had found more than a mate. I had found my heart's home. How could I give you up?"

She blinked, speechless. She had no idea how to respond to the bombshells he was dropping.

Dev's crooked smile tugged at the corners of his mouth. "So your father had nothing to do with you being here, really, other than seeing to your safety. I am the sole culprit in this situation, *Nippa.*" He sighed heavily. "Know that I would do it all over again, even though this trip to Earth could not have come at a worst time."

Her insecurities rushed to the surface. "Damn you!"

Dev pinched the bridge of his nose between forefinger and thumb. "Do not be so quick to hear insults where none are intended, Nnora. I do not regret our coming together at this time. The Creator which crafted us for each other planned this in His infinite wisdom. My regrets are that you are short-changed by these current troubles. I resent the calls on my duty for your sake. I have not been fair to you, and for this I say this trip is inconvenient."

His words calmed her ruffled feathers. "Thank you for that. I feel much better."

"The situation facing my people is volatile. If I am to avert disaster between the two worlds, I must be in close contact with both *Rb'qarm* and *Rb'nTraq,* able to move quickly should the balance of peace suddenly change. Yet, here I am, trying to placate you—*kidnapping* you and starting another war—when I should be on the spacial-relator, coordinating the thousand and one details needed to maintain the fragile peace. A peace, I might add, that I've spent the last twenty years of my life drafting. I don't have the time for this."

"I'm sorry, Dev! It's just…*difficult* for me to get used to the idea that you would even consider delaying something so important for me. It blows my mind that you would consider starting a war to gain my hand in marriage." She shook her head. *How did I get lucky enough to be kidnapped by this guy?*

"I feel like my name should be Helen of Troy, or something."

"Helen of who?" Dev frowned in puzzlement. "You really don't know what finding you has meant to me, do you?"

A giddy feeling of happiness bubbled up inside her and she had difficulty constraining her laughter. "I'm beginning to get some inkling. Care to elaborate?"

"Even though I knew you would be angry with me, perhaps enough to reject me, I simply could not bring myself to let you leave me. I'm sorry. The two worlds are my duty, but you are my life. How could I leave you behind?"

He didn't wait for her to answer. "It was wrong, my choosing to take you with me against your will. I knew I should have returned you to your father. I could not do it.

"As far as *Chyya* Glenbrevchanka is concerned, I have stolen both his daughters, along with all the highborn court *fem*. He's been burning up the spaceways with his threats of war."

He smiled at her then, eyes twinkling brightly—whether with merriment or tears she was unsure. "To tell you the truth, Nnora, I am more worried about alienating my future Bond-father than I am about the threat his armada constitutes. My ship is faster and has more firepower than anything your father can launch after me."

"I cannot fault you for heading home." He had received a message requesting his intervention in a potentially troublesome situation brewing between the *Rb'qarmshi* high-caste Lords and the *Rb'nTraqshi* serving on the panel to oversee the joint prisoners of war.

"My objections always had to do with your methods. If only you had laid the truth before me, given me a choice—"

He met her gaze straight on. "Would you have come with me?"

"I—yes! *No!* Oh, who knows?" She raked her bangs off her forehead. "At this point, the question is moot. I'm second-guessing myself after the fact. I was strongly attracted to you. Would I have chosen to come with you? I just don't know! Thanks to your high-handed actions, I will never know."

"And for your sake, I am sorry. I have ruled two planets for most of my adult life. I am unaccustomed to any questioning my orders. It will be hard to change who I am, *Nippa*." Dev rose from the couch to stand over her, holding out one hand, beseeching her understanding and acceptance. "If I could undo the past, I would do things differently. All I can do to rectify my...*high-handed*...blunder is give you my solemn promise never to lie to you again...by word or deed."

"Never?"

"*Never*. Not even by omission. This I swear." His earnest gaze was openly vulnerable.

She laughed. *Right*.

She knew he believed he meant what he said. "I'd really like to believe that, yet I've never in my life known a male who could be completely honest."

"Not even your father?"

"*Especially* not my father, who is constantly plotting, hatching schemes to trap his enemies, or advance his own position. Brevchanka would be the first to tell me that some dissembling is always necessary."

"I love you, Nnora." His golden-orange pupils fathomless, he captured her heart in his gaze. "By fair means or foul, you are here now, and I beg you to stay."

He dropped to his knees before her, "Will you be my *Cherzda'va*? Love only me? Bear only my children? Rule beside me, and help me guide all our people through this pivotal point in our history? After all, your court *fem* will need a friend in high places when they try to deal with the desperate, arrogant males that will take them to mate."

She knew that forever after, she would remember the moment she entrusted her future to this lordly man. For in this moment, she ceased to be the unwanted, abandoned misfit who had tried so hard to fit in, to be accepted. Stepping forward into Dev's outstretched arms, she raised both hands to his cheeks. Cradling his dear face, she whispered, "Yes, my love. I'll stay with you."

He threw back his head, roaring his triumph to the ceiling. His happy shouts echoed off the metal walls of the cabin. His arms tightening about her in a crushing embrace, Dev stood and swept her off her feet.

His hands firmly clutched her rounded buttocks, he swung her around in an excess of joy. He sensually kneaded her ample curves, his fingers pressing into her flesh as he easily supported her weight. With a guttural sound of need, he buried his lips at her throat.

Grabbing his hair, she dragged his head from her neck and brought his mouth up to hers. She laved his full bottom lip, nipped his upper lip. She giggled when his mouth opened and settled over hers, preparing to take over the kiss and devour her in turn.

"Wait! We need witnesses!" Dev jerked his head away, set her down and lifted his wrist. He spoke rapidly into the tiny microphone attached to the thick, functional band he wore. Closing the channel when he finished, he turned back to Nnora and enfolded her in his arms, bending his head for the kiss she had demanded.

Their open lips met in a hungry, claiming kiss, and Nnora's universe spun around as she opened herself up to his masterful touch. He bent her backwards, his arm a bar of steely flesh easily supporting her large frame.

"I want you...so much, so badly." He swept his tongue into the crevice of her neck, nibbling her fragrant skin, and groaned heavily. "I want you with an ache, an intensity that has grown during this day until my control is frayed beyond repair.

"Then take me." She bowed her neck to afford him greater access. "I want to be yours...completely."

"By *Deth's* gate, you smell so sweet...taste divine." Dev rooted at the soft bend where her shoulder met her neck, his tongue laving the curve, and she shivered with pleasure. "What you do to me..." he praised her between licks and nibbles. "You have but to breathe to make me hard...throbbing."

She moaned, running her hands across his wide shoulders. "That's how I want you...hard..." Her hands encircled his head to clasp behind his neck. She laid a string of open-mouthed kisses over his chest. "...hot and long and throbbing between my thighs, in my pussy."

"I want that, too, *Nippa,* but we haven't time for a full loving, not unless you want our witnesses to witness more than our signing."

She shot him a disgruntled look of reproach. "As my mom would say, 'Why'd you stir the pot if you aren't gonna serve the soup?' Dev, please, don't tease me. I'm burning up for you."

She rested against his arm while she reached down and cupped his balls through his flight-suit, kneading the soft warm mass while keeping her eyes on Dev's face.

"Do we have time for a cocksicle?" She licked her lips, pouting them at him, letting him know of her hunger. "Cause I have an appetite for the kind of lollipop that doesn't melt in your mouth!"

"Time enough for that, aye."

She swiveled her hips and felt his cock swell and press against her belly.

"By the stars, *fem*, my balls are curled up and churning with seed. I want to see those lips wrapped around my cock, *Nippa*. I want to know just how hot that tight little mouth of yours is." His hands went to her shoulders, pressing suggestively.

"Hot enough to burn *you*." She licked her lips again, making them wet for him, then slipped to her knees before him, tabbing open his suit at cock level. She sighed happily when his shaft, hard and heavy fell into her waiting hands. "Oh, my god," she warbled, stunned anew at his beauty, his size and his readiness. She felt some churning in her own belly. A gush of wetness pulsed out of her, dampening her mound and thighs. She wiggled, squeezed her thighs together, trying to stimulate her clit as her tongue honed in on the drop of pre-come—his *zhi*—glistening at the tip of his broad cock head.

"Mmmmmmm! Tastes delicious..." Lapping at the just the head, she squeezed as much of his balls as she could grab one-handedly, milking his seed out of him. It came in dribbles, oozing from the dark red glans.

Above her head, Dev moaned like a man in pain. His large palms cradled her head and neck, the sides of her face. His voice rumbled around her, through her. "Your mouth feels like paradise...yyeess!" He flexed his hips, nudging his cock against her lips.

His width made it almost impossible for her to take more than the first three or four inches behind the meaty head.

He tasted like heaven, his licorice flavored come hitting her system like a dose of pure energy. She felt the tingles beginning deep in her cunt, felt her muscles cramping with lust, her heart beating in her chest with a hurried, heavy rhythm. Her nipples awoke and screamed in need, stretching and stabbing toward the twin temptations of his *terat*. She slipped one hand under the hem of her dress. Opening her thighs, she began to flick her clit, hips rocking forward in rising arousal. She cried out in protest when Dev's hand snatched hers away from her aching pussy.

"None of that, *Nippa*," he admonished. "I have plans for that clit."

She frowned up at him in protest. "But I'm not finished—"

"Well, I nearly am!"

Bending, he picked her up and placed her on the bed. Carefully easing her dress over her head he said, "I want you kneeling on the edge of the bed, sweet one."

She struggled to obey, so far gone in lust she could barely hear, let alone control her wayward limbs.

"Knees spread wide," he instructed, helping her into position. Bending her backwards, he lowered her until her head touched the cover, her thighs splayed widely, muscles pulled taut. In this position, her pussy gaped open to the cooled cabin air and her nipples stabbed straight up. Her breasts inclined toward her chin, their undersides available to Dev's tongue and *terat*.

She heard him muttering, "Hmmm, this is going to take some doing." Then his body was moving down hers, the ends of his hair prickly against her skin as he sank further along her torso.

"Nnnoo," she moaned, weakly tugging at his long locks as they flowed over her breasts. "No, Dev! I don't want my pussy licked, I want fucking."

Dev disentangled her fingers, hushing her. "Shhh, *Nippa*. You want this, trust me." His hands began to pluck at her tight nipples, stretching them, teasing them, pulling them into tighter and tighter points. His mouth covered her navel, dipping in and out of her shallow indentation. His fingers plucked at her clit, making it stand tall and erect.

Her toes curled and she felt like giggling at the tickling sensation, at the same time, howling at the arousing flicker of fire beneath her sensitized skin.

"Dev, please! Your cock?"

"Not yet."

Tears overflowed her eyes when he denied her the second time.

"Shh, my *Nippa*...this is something just for you."

He lowered his full weight over her lower torso.

Her first impression was of heat engulfing her clit as it slowly sank into a fleshy opening.

What the...?

She opened her eyes as the familiar tingling pain began—not in her nipples, this time, but in her clit.

Oh. My. God! He'd inserted her clit in one of his *terat*!

Her mouth opened on a silent wail as her body bucked, trying to dislodge Dev's grip on her clit. A pleasure so intense it registered as pain screamed through her a hundred times more fiercely as the enzyme coated then penetrated the skin covering the sensitive bundle of nerves. High octane bliss burned through the tissue, scorching her, negating the pain, whipping her into a mindless heap of orgasmic flesh.

She screamed when he began fucking her clit with his *terat*, his shoulder tucked hard into her thigh, holding her open for the erotic torture. Each tug, each tight caress spun her into oblivion and out again, the pleasure so intense it hurt, the pain so ecstatic it numbed the mind.

She pressed her clit deeper into his clinging, suckling *terat*, knowing her addiction to be complete. Tightly enclosed in the constricting cup, her clit throbbed and pulsated madly and she screamed her way through another gut-clenching orgasm.

Her body caught fire, skin giving off enough heat to dry her sweat as it formed. She writhed in a conflagration of passion, mouth open on endless wails of completion, lips dry, pulse pounding the cadence of love in the hollow of her neck and the narrow corridor of her cunt.

She lost herself. Lost her mind. Lost her heart to the man whose inventive loving took her beyond reality into a realm of dreams.

* * * * *

An eternity later, she opened her eyes, disoriented and drugged with pleasure. Dimly, she felt his hands soothing her, smoothing back her hair, brushing her cheeks. Heard his voice calling to her.

"*Nippa*, love, come back, come back…"

She tried to swallow. Her throat hurt. "Water..."

Almost instantly, she felt his hand under her neck supporting her head while he pressed a glass to her dry lips.

"Drink, *Nippa*."

She guzzled the water, spilling more than went into her mouth.

"Slow down, *Nippa*," Dev warned. "You'll make yourself sick."

"I thought *terat* were for tits," she croaked.

"For...? Oh, you mean for nipples." Dev cleared his throat, eyes sparkling. "*Nippa*, my *terat* are, first and foremost, for giving you pleasure."

"You're looking extraordinarily pleased with yourself."

"We aim to please, my own."

"Yeah? Well, A+—and that better not be laughter I hear in your voice," she rasped, throat raw from screaming her way through the hardest, most glorious orgasms she'd ever experienced.

With Dev, the sex just kept getting better and better.

Fucking him would kill her. She knew it.

She couldn't wait.

Chapter Sixteen

"Will you please put your dress back on?"

Her mate sounded frustrated. He should be. He still hadn't had an orgasm.

Lying on her side, chin propped on her palm, Nnora watched Dev rifle through the stack of papers littering his desk, ignoring the important-looking sheaves falling to the floor.

"Ah-*hah*! Here they are!" He held aloft a fistful of documents sealed with official tokens. Striding over to his desk, he beckoned her over.

She eased her legs over the side of the bed, careful of her sore clit. Dropping her dress over her head, she sauntered across the room to stand by her lover.

She had never hurt so good. Her clit twanged with every stride, reminding her of the unusual loving it had undergone.

"No more coercion, *Nippa*. Will you sign these willingly…without duress?"

"Nope, I can't do that." She leaned against Dev, brushing his hair off his forehead.

The smile slid off Dev's handsome face, leaving behind the harsh and craggy angles of cheekbones and jaws clenched in heart-deep pain. "But…I thought—"

Taking pity on him, Nnora smoothed his brow with soft strokes. Feathering her fingers across his sinfully thick lashes, she spread tactile adoration across the line of his full lips. "I cannot sign without duress. For love constrains me…always. I shall never be free. Nor do I desire to be. Or, as the Bard would say… How do I love thee, let me count the ways."

Dev's tongue darted out to lave her finger, nipping the tip before she could withdraw it. "Against your will?"

"You hold me against my better judgment. Against my nature, perhaps, yet never against my will."

"Then sign the damn things so we can inform your father that I hold you legally. Maybe then he'll stop threatening to send his war ships after me."

She pulled back to gaze at her mate in awe. "He did that…truly?"

Dev hugged her close. "His exact words were, 'I fought a war to preserve her inheritance, but I would give up her inheritance to preserve her right to choose.' "

She wept.

"Hey! I thought that would make you happy!"

"It did. I *am!*" she wailed, sniffing.

Dev gave a shrug. "I will probably never understand a *fem's* emotions, but for you I will try. If these tears represent your happiness, I shall endeavor to cause weeping every day. I suppose—"

She wiped her eyes and bestowed a radiant smile upon him. "Oh, shut up and kiss me. Happy as I am right now, I'd be happier if our witnesses were already come and gone. Once we get these papers signed, I'm locking the door. Your meetings will have to wait until after I get my fucking. I'm not taking another 'no' for an answer."

* * * * *

"Don't bruise the merchandise, honey," Dohsan spat. "You can take your scraggy hands off me, now, Bitch! Your keeper is not here so you don't have to show off how brutal you can be."

"*Fem*, you have the foulest mouth I have ever heard!" Dohsan's uncouth behavior finally goaded him out of his self-imposed silence. He picked up the pace, hurrying towards his Prince's cabin. The sooner he finished this assignment, witnessing the signing of the nuptial agreements and escorting this terrifying teen back to her quarters, the better.

"All the better to suck your giant cock with, darling captor," the unrepentant horror sang, sneering. "I saw that heat-seeking dong tenting your skirt when you were around my sister. Better keep the meat under wraps or your prince will cut it off, wanna-be-lover-boy."

"You'd best change your ways, or you will be left unchosen. Even with the present shortage of viable women, no *Rb'qarmshi* Warrior will consent to being saddled with a brazen brat who ignores his commands and belittles his dignity."

Dohsan stopped dead in the corridor, narrowing her eyes and leveling a baleful glare at him. "A thousand years ago, you would be obeying *my* commands and currying the favor of my mother. It is hard to believe your so-called civilization has sunk so low that *qarmshi* are bossing *fem* these days."

She favored him with an especially knowing glance, boldly allowing her eyes to rove over his crotch. "Once I flower, I will be able to pick and choose from an entire planet of males," she boasted. "I can have anyone I want…including *you!* Furthermore, I will tell you now, no *qarm* will ever order me about. I *will* be the head of my household, as the natural order demands."

He snarled, his pride pricked because he could not truthfully deny her accusations. "You are an undisciplined child to spout such ancient nonsense. The *Chyya* should have ordered you whipped. I would have seen to it, gladly."

"The *Chyya* is not the man for my sister if he could order such a thing." Dohsan suddenly sounded worried, and chewed at her generous bottom lip. "Nnora's self-esteem is very fragile. He was very angry… Do you think he will hit Nnora?"

GanR'dari gaped at the young *fem*, stunned at this insight to her true nature. All his snarls and threats had not fazed her, yet the faint—totally unrealistic—possibility of her sister being mistreated had her anxious and worried. "Our *Chyya* would never hurt his *cherzda'va*, and you know this. You only seek to malign my ruler."

"I do not. I supported his claim to both Nnora and our father. I would hate to be found wrong in my assessment of him."

"Any fool can see he is stars over comets in love with the *Chyya'va*. The prince will do nothing to harm her."

"I hope so." She worried her lip again. "I will not allow him to harm my sister and live."

His eyes drawn to the *fem's* swollen, abused flesh, he felt his cock swelling under his tunic. He swallowed a sick lump of dread. 'Dari cringed at the thought of what his mother and sisters would say should he bring this uncouth *fem* home as his *cherzda'va*. Not even her status as royal princess could redeem her behavior.

By Deth *and His minions, do not let me be attracted to this one,* he pleaded to the gods of old. As usual, they proved unresponsive to his cries.

"There speaks your ignorance and your disrespect. You are a disgrace to the royal family. You would have to flower with the scent of a hundred *pavas,* and we would have to be much longer deprived than we are now, before a *traq* or *qarm* chose you!" He tossed her arm away and let her flounce along in front of him.

She skipped backwards to confront him.

"Is that your warrior's resolve talking?" she mocked, snapping her fingers. "*That's* for your resolve, GanR'dari. One day, I'll make you eat those words."

"I'd rather eat them than you," he returned crudely, allowing his eyes to rove over the scanty cloth covering her young cunt. "You'd probably give me indigestion."

"One day you'll beg me to do both," Dohsan whispered, a chilling smile curving her generous lips. "And I plan on giving you a lot more than indigestion, soldier. I plan on rocking your world."

* * * * *

"GanR'dari will be here shortly." Dev's voice hardened. "Along with Dohsan. We're not that far from her new quarters." He reluctantly released Nnora to search for a pen.

"You'd better learn how to get along with my sister." She came up behind him and slipped her arms about his waist, snuggling against his back, tucking her hands around his balls. Her confident trust in the unconditional love Dev held for her made her bold.

"I couldn't stand it if you two didn't get along." The happy sparkle within her dimmed at the thought of her family members being divided.

"Anything for you," Dev promised, catching her hands and crossing them over his *terat*, pulling her forward so her breasts flattened against his back and her belly nestled against the rounded curve of his muscular buttocks.

"At the moment, I would be satisfied with just…this!" She sent her hands groping down his front, smiling when she found what she was looking for. She sighed, stroking his long staff through his hastily-donned uniform, grinning at the instant results her touch netted. She rubbed her still aching mound against the back of his hard thigh, trying to assuage her growing need.

Dev flexed his hips, thrusting his cock into her cupped hands. "A flight suit is not very concealing. I don't think it would be wise for Dohsan to see me in this condition."

She had only to think about what her uninhibited sister might say, before she grimaced and reluctantly applied the brakes. "I see your point." With a last lingering squeeze, she released Dev's thickening cock. Giggling, she added, "I felt your point as well as saw it."

"And so will Dohsan, if you do not stop tempting me!" Dev turned her in his arms and crashed his mouth into hers for a brief, passionate kiss. His lips were moist from the silky nectar of her mouth when he lifted his head to examine her swollen and bee-stung flesh. Intrigued, he ran his thumbs back and forth over her bottom lip.

"Once we get all the official proceedings finished, I'll let you lock everything and everybody out. You can have free rein of my body."

"As for me," he continued, "I'm going to take a very long time exploring and learning every inch of your delectable body before I push you beyond every limit you think you have. I plan to claim every inch of that delectable body and make it mine." He catalogued her charms with callused palms.

Unable to resist the temptation to taste her unique flavor yet again, he nibbled the curve of her full bottom lip before delving once more into the lush sweetness of her mouth.

"Well, Princey! I see reason didn't work, so you decided to resort to seduction." Dohsan's sarcasm disrupted the intimate heated silence.

Dev's kiss having transported her to another world, Nnora jerked in startled surprise, turning in the circle of his arms. She had trouble focusing on her sister's angry face. "Dohsan, it is not what you think! Dev is—"

"A damn smooth operator!" the lanky teen snarled, starting towards the embracing duo with eyes blazing, only to find herself jerked back by GanR'dari's steely grip. Her tugs proved ineffectual against his implacable hold, so she haughtily chose to ignore him in favor of hurling insults at Dev, who remained uncharacteristically stoic in the face of her spitting rage. "Tell me, Your Highness! What did you do to make her forget your lies and schemes against our father?"

"I simply told her the truth, little one." Though he knew it was wrong, he could not resist taunting his future Bond-sister, and looped his arms about Nnora's middle, letting his hands brush the underside of her lush breasts.

Nnora pinched him, and then rested her cheek against one muscular forearm and swayed lazily, rubbing her body against the rigid bulge straining his body-hugging outfit.

Her actions made him dizzy with lust.

He leaned forward and whispered in her ear, "Dohsan's eyes are glowing iridescent with ire." He chuckled. "She'll go all the way ballistic if she learns her sister is using my log-sized hard-on as a prop to lean against."

Another, harder pinch to his waist reminded him of his earlier promise to attempt to get along with his new sister.

He sighed. Giving Nnora a quick squeeze, he acknowledged receipt of her message.

"Dohsan, regardless of what you might think, I planned no treachery against your father. In fact, you and GanR'dari are here to witness your sister's signature to seal the ratification of our marriage agreements and treaties."

His heart lurched and his breath caught as he announced, "Crown Princess Glennora Brewster 'abret Glenbrevchanka has, of her own will, decided to sign our marriage contracts, at once becoming my bride, the Queen of *Rb'qarm,* the Queen of *Rb'nTraq* and…queen of my heart."

Dohsan's jaw dropped. Her brows drew together in a suspicious frown. "Wha—? How?"

GanR'dari dropped Dohsan's wrist and shouldered her out of his way. He grasped his leader by the hand. The two friends exchanged a warrior's handclasp while they laughed and pounded each other on the back.

"Congratulations, *Chyya*! This is a cause for great celebration!"

Dev saw the brief flash of jealousy 'Dari had not quite managed to suppress in his sincere wish for his prince's happiness. "'Dari, my heart aches for your loneliness, but rejoice with me, for I have won my heart's desire," Dev admitted freely, unashamed to show his love and respect for the *fem* at his side. "Have patience, my friend. Have faith that a *fem* awaits your finding. Your turn is soon to come."

"Now, both of you please witness Nnora's signature so I can relax. Until they are sealed, she can change her mind!"

Dohsan sidled over to Nnora while the Dev and 'Dari talked. She frowned now, speaking under her breath, "I have to admit I am stunned and still not ready to believe your quick turn about. Nnora, are you the same uncertain sister who questioned me so earnestly just an hour ago? What has the Prince done to you to bring about this change? Has he forced you in any way?"

Nnora almost choked with laughter at the thought of the orgasms Dev had "forced" upon her. No way would she share that with her suddenly prune-faced sister. "You were the one trying to convince me Devtorvas was right for me. Now you seem to have changed your tune."

"Well, yes, because I left you spouting vengeance and find you cooing and billing like love birds."

"He has simply managed to convince me that he loves me, Dohsan. Dev has given me what I lacked all these lonely years. Please be glad for me. Please, Dohsan," Nnora murmured, pleading for peace. She so wanted her sister and her new husband—both of whom she loved dearly—to coexist in peace. "Do not spoil this special day for me!"

"All right, I won't," Dohsan relented. "But you better be happy." She turned to the Prince. "You better not hurt her."

"My word to you, youngling." He gave Dohsan a deep, respectful bow. Then he took Nnora in his arms, and gave her a deep, tongue-tangling kiss, embarrassing his aroused deputy commander, and further disconcerting the adolescent princess.

He dragged his mouth away and handed Nnora a writing utensil vaguely resembling a pen. "Your signature goes here, here…and here. Now, *sign*!"

Nnora glanced over the contracts, noting the concessions her bridegroom had made in exchange for her hand in marriage. She also noted, with raised eyebrows, her privileges and rights within the union. She met Dev's loving gaze, then bent to add her signatures beside his slashing marks. The pressure-sensitive point touched the surface of the paper, burning the line of fluid script into the specially prepared medium.

"*TA-DA*!" With a flourish, Nnora finished signing and slapped the contracts and writing tool onto her mate's outstretched palm, smiling when he captured her hand and held it against his chest.

"At last, you are my own, *Nippa!*"

His risqué play on words to his unsuspecting princess did not get past GanR'dari, who hastily covered his shocked laugh with a poorly executed cough.

Dohsan blushed scarlet.

* * * * *

Dev sighed as Nnora lightly rubbed her hands all over his cock, touched her tongue to the tip, tasting the slippery fluid seeping from the small aperture in the head. Tilting her head, she licked along the underside of his stiff rod, her darting tongue growing bolder as he responded to her touch with a helpless spurt of growth.

"Tell me if I do something wrong," she said before nibbling her way back to the top of the jutting organ.

Was she joking?

A harsh cry of need rose in his throat as she engulfed the bulbous head of his cock in her mouth. He was so hard, he ached with it. So full and swollen that just the broad head of his *cherzda* filled the cavern of her mouth, stretching the edges of her lips.

"Mhm—mmh...uhmm...mh—hmm..." she mumbled, her words distorted by a mouth full of throbbing male sex.

"What—what...did you say?" He had a difficult time getting the words out, his whole attention directed to the erotic display Nnora put on for him. There was something profoundly star-shaking about seeing his erection half-buried in his woman's mouth, her lips pouty around his swollen thickness.

She released his member, and it exited her mouth with a slurrupy plop. She fondled the saliva-slick tip. "I said you taste like summer rain and autumn winds...with a touch of licorice."

"My stars and comets!" Dev groaned, hips bucking. He fought a feeling of vertigo as she reinserted his straining length, sucking up as much as she could, her cheeks bulging, lips clinging around his cock. She squeezed him firmly, milking him in the dark, tight cavern of her mouth. As she drew strongly on him, his legs trembled with approaching orgasm and he grasped the sides of her head as he tried to orchestrate their lusty dance, not wanting to feed her greedy, loving mouth more than she could take of his stiff erection.

Nnora resisted his takeover bid. She drew on his organ, sucking the tip like it was a huge sweetmeat, the loud, wet, sloppy, carnal sounds mysteriously, erotically exciting to him. Her lips curving in a smile, she used her teeth inventively, lightly scoring his tight flesh as she worked her way along his rod.

"I need your nipples. Right now!"

He growled, anxious to get to her pert, jutting tips. Impatient with her slow movements, he began ripping her flimsy clothes off.

"Let me help you." She shrugged her slim shoulders, letting the flimsy remains of her dress slip down her arms. Cupping her breasts, one in each hand, she offered them up to him, the high-standing, berry-hued crests already stiff with desire.

"Such long, hungry nipples..." He fondled her tightening buds, stroking and pinching them into greater prominence.

"Such lush, plump, tasty nipples!" He thrilled as he ran his flattened tongue around the pebbled aureoles and across the beaded peaks, preparing her for his *terat*. "You like being *seated*...don't you, my love?"

"I—I...ooh! Yes! Yes, I love it!" Desire stole her breath.

"I'm going to milk them dry and drain all your lovely cum right out of these full, aching nipples."

Nnora moaned at his dark promises. She pressed her legs together to stem the flood from her pussy.

"Clenching your thighs will not assuage the pounding ache welling in your juicing pussy," Dev taunted sexily.

"This time, it won't be just my tongue and fingers filling that hungry little mouth." He brushed his fingers through her oozing juices to play her clitoris. "This time we meld mouth-to-mouth, *terat*-to-nipple, *cherzda*-to-cunt."

She shuddered, her passion bathing his fingers.

"You know what your sexy words do to me...?"

"Tell me..." He ran a possessive hand down her flank.

"They excite me...make me hot. Make me shiver..."

"You make me shiver, too, *Nippa*." Dev's eyes glowed with impatient lust. "I want you in me."

She pursed her lips. "Funny, that's what I want, too...you in me!"

His body mantled hers, and she lifted her torso, brushing her breasts against his chest.

Slowly, eyes locked with hers, he inserted her nipples into his *terat*.

The powerful genital muscles clamped down on her captured flesh and immediately began to pull on her engorged tips. As his chest rose and fell over her, his *cherzda* and balls thudded against the sensitized outer lips of her pussy and Nnora groaned, arching. Her muscles locked up as she tumbled into the first orgasm. She came with racking convulsions, her *seated* nipples spilling her liquid, her 'gift' into the greedy mouths of Dev's suctioning *terat*.

Chapter Seventeen

"You know…I would have sworn Dohsan had lost the ability to blush! Dev?"

Splayed across Dev's—now hers—double bunk, her long black hair her only covering, Nnora lifted her head, searching for her husband.

"Dev…?"

"I'm here, *Nippa.*" He strode around the corner from the direction of the cleansing room, draped in a towel and nothing else. Tossing aside his towel, he came over to her, settling his big body between her widespread legs.

She loved looking at his beautiful body. He was all hers; miles and miles of sexy man to drape over her, dwarfing her. Her magnificent mate's height and bulk made her feel petite…wanted…needed…*cherished*—all the things she had thought never to experience. His naked body was a delight and a wonder to her. She no longer had to constantly fight the urge to run her fingertips over his tightly stretched flesh, probing the ropy muscles that flexed and shifted smoothly below the surface of his teak-brown skin.

"What could possibly make her color up like that, when I have tried and failed for years to embarrass her?"

His large hands brushed her from ankle to thigh in caressing sweeps. Every now and then, he dropped open-mouthed kisses into the arch of her feet or behind her bent knees.

She squirmed beneath him, wordlessly asking for more, and growled when he shook his head, a pirate's grin curving his brazen lips.

"I'm going to take a long time with you," he promised, stringing a line of kisses across her breasts and down to her quivering navel.

"Mmmmhhhhh! Long is good." She propped herself on her elbows, watching him duck between her thighs, his broad shoulders holding her legs open. For her, the visual stimulus added to the arousal factor.

"You didn't answer my question about Dohsan."

"How can you think about your sister at a time like this?"

She narrowed her eyes at him. "Because something is going on and I will not be distracted seeking the answers I feel you have, Dev!"

"Good." His fingers parted her weeping folds, opening and preparing her, his touch possessive and bold. "I want you to pay close attention to this..." He drew his rasping tongue along the quivering length of her petals, dipping his tongue into her. When she quaked beneath his bold ministrations, laughter rumbled in his chest, echoed in her body.

Her neck felt boneless. Her head fell back and her spine tightened, lifting her pelvis up to her husband's creative mouth. In answer, he delved deeper, plunging his facile tongue in and out with a provocative rhythm that had her hips writhing to his soundless music. In desperation, she grasped his hair, mashing his face against her mound and moaned, "More...Harder...*Please!*"

He looked up at her. "Are you distracted yet?" he teased, eyes dancing.

"Hell, yeah! Left distracted behind at the last bus stop. I'm…getting *there*." When his mouth resumed eating at the tender petals of her pussy, she let out a gasp. "For God's sake, when are you going to *take* me, Dev? I swear I can't stand much more."

"*Nippa…*" he said between leisurely tongue lappings, ignoring her present pleas, "is another name for…your *pava*. A less polite, more graphic name…"

She tensed in disbelief, her ardor grown cold as his words penetrated her reasoning. "You've been calling me a *cunt?*"

Sitting up, she pushed at him. He didn't budge. "No wonder even Dohsan blushed! Where I come from, Buster, that word is not suitable to use in public." Horror washed over her. "You called me a cunt…*in front of your men!*"

As her tone was not exactly one of pleased discovery, Dev hastened to explain. "On *Rb'qarm,* it is an acceptable endearment between bonded pairs—"

"I can't believe you've been calling me a *cunt*." Uncertain whether to laugh or beat him repeatedly about the head, she yanked his hair, forcibly drawing his face up to meet her glare.

He sat up and captured her hands. "I've been calling you *mine*," he corrected her sternly, hands firmly cupping and fondling that part of her under discussion. "*My* pussy. *My* cunt. *Mine!*"

His finger took over where his tongue had been, sinking in to the middle knuckle. She lost the thread of their argument. Spreading her knees as wide apart as they would go, she offered herself to him in helpless abandon.

Who the hell cared what he called her, as long as he called her "his"?

Working another thick finger inside her opening, he pistoned it in and out of her, stretching her clasping passage. He touched every one of her secret places and awakened them.

She arched her back, seeking a deeper penetration, empty and aching to be filled with his cock. Her fingers roamed, grabbing at him. When they brushed past his swaying erection, she grasped the massive cock, squeezing the bulbous head in her fisted hand, marveling that she had once held this luscious object in dread. It had quickly become the object of all her desires.

"I'm not afraid, anymore, Dev." She twisted under his relentless fingers. "I want your cock…your *cherzda*, deep inside me. Deep and hard and *now*. I'm going out of my mind with wanting you."

"And I want you, my wife, my *cherzda'va*," Dev panted, easing his fingers from her pussy. He dabbed her fragrant cream on each nipple and smeared it over her lips. "I also want a taste of your honey-coated candies."

Kissing his way up her body, he assiduously licked the perfumed dampness from her skin. Her nipples came to stiff attention, wet from his worshiping mouth. The air caressed the little points, furling them into tight buds.

"I love it when you suck my nipples."

Her hands cupped her mounds, offered them up as twin sacrifices. Her head lolled on her neck as he bent his head to accept her offering.

"No one has ever suckled me like you do, my love."

Happiness welled up inside him. He felt a thrill of satisfaction at her praise.

"No one ever will, my *Nippa*."

Shackling her ankles in his big hands, he lifted her legs, bent them, held them wide. Kneeling between her thighs, he stared down at the beautiful sight of her wet *pava* lips fluttering in helpless arousal.

"Come in me…fuck me."

"Yes…now." Carefully positioning his straining sex at the damp mouth of her pussy, he edged forward. He breached her petite portal with difficulty. Working the broad head of his penis past her small petals, he popped through the outer ring of muscles. The width of his crest stretched the dainty opening painfully wide.

She felt incredibly hot and tight surrounding him. Her delicate *fem* muscles tightened involuntarily, trying to force him out. Instead, their rippling contractions caressed his bulbous tip, causing a growth spurt that made it difficult for him to ease his cock deeper into her cunt. Moaning, wanting to thrust, he forced himself to hold stationary just inside her.

"Oh, it hurts!"

Her cry wounded him. He would die before injuring her, but how could he stop *now*? *Damn*. He *was* hurting her. And it would only get worse before it got better…

"Oooh, Dev!" She hissed through her teeth, shifting.

Trying to get away?

"Shhh! I love you. I'll make it better, *Nippa…*" Touching his forehead to hers, he broke out in a sweat as he battled to do the honorable thing. He had feared her small size would make it difficult if not impossible to mate her without medical assistance. It seemed his fears were realized.

Heartsick, he started to pull back, pull out of her. "We will postpone our full joining until the healers of *Rb'qarm* can examine you, my *Nippa*."

"No!" She clutched his shoulders. Her legs lifted, encased him. Ankles crossed, locking about his waist. "You're already in. We can do this..." She panted, inhaling short quick breaths to avoid the pain.

He used his hands, taking a long time to reawaken her arousal, plucking at her clit, rubbing round it with fingers soaked in her wetness. Smoothing his fingers down the crease between her buttocks, he palmed her plump cheeks and smearing her slick fluid into the secret puckered hole nestled behind her pussy. He rimmed the tight aperture, dipping in, wanting only her pleasure.

When she again began writhing beneath him, whimpering and crying out for his possession, he sighed with relief, knowing she was as ready as he could make her. He inserted her nipples into his softened *terat* and sealed her mouth with his own.

"Mouth...terat...cherzda...

"I'm sorry...sorry to hurt...don't want to..." Amid murmured apologies, he drove his cock up into her pulsing *pava*. Hating that he hurt her, he burst through her barrier. Taking her mouth, he smothered her scream of pain with a devouring kiss.

Tears ran down her cheeks. He licked them away. He lay frozen within her, his marble-hard cock throbbing, anxious to sink even deeper. His balls ached. He had never felt anything like the incredible tightness of her sheath. His cock stretched her newly tried portal, and from her whimpering he knew it remained uncomfortable.

"Nippa?"

"I'm…okay… Are you…in?"

Creator of all, grant me the skill to ensure my mate's pleasure outweighs the pain.

"Not quite yet, my dearling."

He luxuriated in the blissful heat and tightness of her wonderful pussy. With her breasts buried in his chest, her mouth filled with his tongue, her feminine passage crammed full of his cock—he felt powerful and humbled all at once. *This is my home! My mate. My* fem. *My hope for the future.*

Nnora shuddered beneath Dev, her muscles squeezing and rocking his cock. He grew within her, expanding to an even greater length and width. She fought the instinct telling her to struggle, to eject the hurtful intruder. This was Devtorvas…her Dev, filling her and soothing her, waiting for her pain to subside before riding her like a wild bronco. She only needed to hold on…it definitely couldn't get any worse, and she couldn't wait for it to get better.

One thing about it, she thought, *Dev is certainly not swimming around in there!* A laugh ghosted through her as she recalled her ex-husband's petulant complaints.

"Dev, I can feel your cock filling my pussy to overflowing." She pulled him closer with arms and legs. "My ex-husband used to cry, 'Grip me tighter, I'm swimming around in here!' He made me feel large and ungainly. I never enjoyed sex until you came along."

Dev chuckled. "Whatever made you think a puny human male could satisfy a woman of your stature, *Nippa?* You were simply faced with the dilemma of too much woman and not enough man! Just let me know and I will supply all your needs." Pushing his hips against hers, he sank another two inches into her clasping depths. "There's plenty more where that came from."

With their laughter came easing. Her feminine muscles relaxed, allowing her mate's huge cock to sink even further in. She let out a yelp of orgasmic surprise when his cock head moved beyond where she thought she ended.

"It excites me when you cry out with pleasure," Dev rasped in a husky whisper, flexing his hips, circling them, barely moving in her. "I love it when you tell me what you want, what you need." He pressed his thumb against her ultra-sensitive clit. "I want to hear you scream with pleasure, not pain. Scream for me, *Nippa*."

Her hips lifted off the bed, and her pussy engulfed more of his hard, distended length. When the surging head thudded against the mouth of her shuddering womb, she screamed her pleasure again, her legs locking around his rough-hewn thighs.

She gazed up into Dev's eyes which had gone incandescent with desire. "Please. Harder…I need you!"

Dev looked down at her. "I'm glad to see you are enjoying your new toy." His laughter sounded of masculine triumph. "So, are you all right now? Can I move?"

He'd been holding himself in check trying to minimize her discomfort!

Oh Dev.

She fell in love with him all over again.

"Oh yes, love. Take me, Dev. Fuck me! Fill me up with your huge cock." She hugged him close. "Show me how to please you."

"In these last two hours, alone, you've given me more pleasure than I've had my entire life," he gasped, entering and re-entering her with a series of smooth, metered strokes, pulling on her turgid nipples as he drove past her clinging labia. And in reverse, bearing down on her peaking nipples while his pumping rod abraded her clit, surging along the honeyed corridors of her pussy.

Grown frantic with lust, she caressed and kissed Dev, letting her hands wander his muscular, rangy body. She brushed the high curve of his buttocks, followed the deep crevice bisecting his manly cheeks, sinking her fingers into the tight, elastic flesh and teasing his anus. He rewarded her with faster and deeper strokes, pounding into her, riding her hard and fierce.

His masculine groan of need rumbled deep in her mouth, where his tongue flicked against hers. He drew her tongue into his mouth, suckling on it as if he would suck it out by the root.

Drowning in an ocean-swell of sensation, she bucked as her culmination drew near. Her nipples twanged, swelling in the suctioning grasp of her mate's *terat*. His thick cock fucked her deep, forcing her inner muscles to part, widening the corridor of her cunt to thud against the door of her womb. The exciting friction triggered a need for more of the same.

And *more…*

"I'm coming!" she warned him, sensing her approaching orgasm, her spiraling ascent. Her buried nipples burned and tingled, fucked raw by his clinging *terat*. She flung her hips up at him, meeting every heavy thrust as he loosed his constraints and rode her hard. His fevered, jackhammer strokes slammed into her hot, fiery pussy, stoking the flames. Their force moved her body up the bed, his cock sinking to new depths with each relentless blow. He pounded into her forcefully, his full *sirat* slapping against her ass.

Helpless before his stormy assault, she grasped the metallic bar that served as a headboard, trying to anchor herself in this galaxy. Joyfully surrendering herself to the conquering thrusts of her mate, she realized that she and Dev—connected mouth-to-mouth, breast-to-chest, and pussy-to-cock—were two souls joined. Forever bonded, their union forged in the fiery heat of their passionate love.

As her body and mind spun away into dazzling star-shine, the knowledge that she would never be lonely again washed over her, completing her ecstasy. Her nipples convulsed, giving up their nectar as streams of glory flowed over her, flinging her to the far side of the universe. Radiant ribbons of unfurling splendor spilled through her as she convulsed under her bond-mate's pistoning body.

"Yessss!" She chanted, her voice breaking hoarsely on the age-old cry, "Fuck me hard, Dev. Come in me…flood me with your cum…fill my belly with your love. Give me your child…"

Warm liquid splashed onto her face, startling her. She opened her eyes to see Dev's face above hers, his eyes flooded with tears. Moved beyond words, she opened her mouth, welcoming him as he swooped down, delved into her mouth. They shared a series of tongue-deep kisses, each wordlessly reassuring the other that they were loved.

Withdrawing until only the head of his *cherzda* rested within her drenched cunt, he gathered himself for one final climactic thrust. His muscles tensed in preparation. Holding her gaze, he slammed back into her. He pierced her welcoming cleft with a power that left her moaning and bucking under him.

Penetrated to the depths of her womb, she felt Dev's embedded *cherzda* swell to immense proportions, remolding itself to the contours of her *pava* channel until every creaming crevice, cranny and fissure was filled with his pulsating sex. His cock-plug formed, Dev held high in her cunt as his *cherzda* pulsed, swelling and contracting as the apertures all along the head of his penis oozed the thick, viscous fluid called *zhi*.

The liquid sparkled inside her, lighting every dark crevice with life, with sizzling brightness. A fireball ignited in her belly and roared outward, sparks catching in the tinder of her flesh until the surface of her skin joined the nova of her body. Arms falling limp at her side, she flung back her head and gave herself up to the starlight streaming through her.

Time dissolved and ran down in shimmering strings of light as Dev's primal roar rang out. His fingers sank deep into the plump hills of her ass when he lifted her hips in his hands, bringing her flush against him. Her cunt clamped down on his cock, gripping and holding his straining flesh.

Letting out a guttural cry, he pumped furiously between her widespread thighs. His seed shot from him in hot, spuming jets. Her husband came hard and deep inside her, filling her with his foaming ejaculate, returning her 'gift' in the form of his living sperm.

Endlessly.

Timelessly.

* * * * *

Sometime during that long night of repeated loving, he gave her his baby, fulfilling the hope of his people and beginning the slow rebirth of his race.

He prayed for a girl.

Chapter Eighteen

On Rb'qarm, Thirteen Fael Later (Earth equivalent: 16 Months)

The Welcoming Ceremony of Crown Princess Glenvdevtoria 'abret Glendevtorvas took place on the second *Fael* anniversary of her birth. Hundreds of Royal Heads of State traveled from their home worlds. Over a thousand Ambassadors, dignitaries representing the fifty Allied Worlds and the Four Hundred Kingdoms—each with their aides and attachés accompanied by their requisite support staffs—also attended.

Both royal grandfathers had joined in a rare show of mutual support for this auspicious occasion. The two former kings had much in common—mainly their predilection for arguing with their children—but they knew how to present a united front when policy dictated. Both agreed the Welcoming of their first grandchild warranted a state of truce.

Nnora's father and his band of exiles had come suing for repatriation and reintegration into their home planet society six months ago. He claimed his decision had to do with the Humans launching a program of aggressive solar system exploration. His mate claimed he missed both his daughters.

Acting upon his mate's wise suggestion, Dev had bestowed a high *Rb'nTraqshi* title upon the former *Chyya,* along with enough land to make his bond-father marginally happy. It also located the former king on another planet...far enough away to maintain peaceful relations between the father and daughter.

Dev's father had fared no better than Nnora's father.

Now that Dev's bonding with Nnora had accorded him adulthood status, he had sternly demanded his father's abdication as had been agreed upon in the nuptial contracts.

Like Glenbrevchanka, *Chyya* Quasharel found himself given a lesser title and "put out to graze"—his favorite term adopted from the Earth colonists.

* * * * *

Chyya Glendevtorvas surveyed the banquet hall. A wave of ribald hilarity caught his attention. Of course, his nemesis stood in the center of the commotion.

Dohsan and her younger brothers were under foot, as usual, getting into, or being the cause of trouble. No one paid much attention to the trio of siblings anymore, having gotten used to the constant upheaval that followed the fiery princess and her brothers.

Dev grimaced. He took a fortifying gulp of his drink. Thank *Deth*, the dour presence of GanR'dari, the Commander of the *Chyya'va's* personal bodyguards, kept anyone from lodging more than verbal complaints. He'd heard the high society *fem* matrons awaited Dohsan's flowering with bated breath, praying his friend would claim her for his mate, as none of them wanted her in *their* family...royal princess or not. He felt sorry for 'Dari if the wind blew that way. He wouldn't wish that hellion on friend or foe.

He scanned the hall, restless until his eye fell on the stately figure of his mate and co-ruler. A heady mix of love, lust and pride filled his heart, constricted his breathing and heated his loins as he watched Nnora's easy interactions with the assembled dignitaries and visiting royalty. None of their guests carried themselves with a more dignified mien than she, though many of their guests and subjects towered over her.

He smiled, gaze glued to his wife as she tossed back her head, her light, infectious laughter spilling out of her beautiful mouth. Her joy was evident in her twinkling eyes, the iridescent orange swirling in excitement, and Dev compared this lively, queenly *fem* to the diffident, nervous mate that had first ascended the throne beside him.

She'd grown in maturity and assurance over the last sixteen *Fael*, taking up her duties and accepting her responsibilities with the same fervor she seemed to bring to every aspect of her life. His balls tightened as he recalled how eagerly she had taken to being *seated* and then well-fucked, aggressively demanding his attentions at times. He loved that she didn't wait on him to initiate their lovemaking all the time, but took an active part in their intimate relationship. He had never felt more appreciated, more loved.

By Deth's *ballocks, I am a lucky bastard*! Dev grinned, thinking of some of the ploys his *fem* had used to drag him away from his sometimes-dry duty, tempting and teasing him until his control shredded and he pounded into her tight, wet pussy, driven to claim and master her again and again.

A greeting from the king of Polramis brought his wandering attention back to the present. He muttered some inane return to his powerful ally, ignoring the laughing taunt that, being in thrall to his very luscious bride, he obviously no longer ruled the two worlds of *Rb'qarm* and *Rb'nTraq*.

"So speaks the man who gave away a kingdom to gain his own bride," Dev teased in return, slapping his friend on the back. "See how I ignore your loutish behavior? I recall mouthing much the same sentiments at the recent welcoming ceremony for your new son."

"So you did, Dev. And glad, I am that you now find yourself in the same circumstances. Better luck has no man." The Polramisian king lifted his full glass in honor of his friend's mate. "She is lovely beyond compare…as long as you do not compare her to my own queen!"

Dev laughed, letting his gaze linger on his wife, his lips widening in a quick smile when she caught his eye and winked, reminding him of their rendezvous planned for later that evening.

"I forgive you for saying such, since I know Loreena would kill you should word of your praises for another come to her ear."

King Talvin threw back his head and laughed. "Your mind is not on our usual exchange of insults if that is the best you can come up with. Go. Mingle and spread yourself around. You have a few hours more before you can honorably sneak away to fuck your queen."

Dev's sharp bark of laughter caused him to inhale his drink up his windpipe. His friend roared with merriment at his dilemma. Waving away a hovering servitor, Talvin pounded on his host's back, eyes and teeth gleaming as he administered the crude treatment. "*Hel* and *Deth*, Devtorvas, how could you think I would miss that torrid shared glance? It almost burned me to cinders. You truly have a bad case of *pava* fever."

"Call it what you will, Talvin." Dev gratefully tossed off the remainder of his drink and sat it down with a solid thunk. "I only know I would far rather be in my queen's arms than performing a political dance with these power-mad representatives and their entourages."

"I commiserate with you, Dev. However, you will need their support if your two worlds are to be admitted as an equal participant in our trade consortium."

"You are correct, as usual, my friend." Dev sighed, resigned to the performance of some of his own diplomatic maneuverings. He would not wait a moment past the appointed time to snatch his *fem* away. He clapped his friend on the back. "I'd better get back to my royal pandering. Stay beyond the Welcoming. I'd like to talk more with you."

Talvin smiled. "I will, unless circumstances dictate otherwise."

Devtorvas worked the crowd, mingling amongst the different factions with outward good will and inward impatience. He always knew the location of his *Chyya'va*. Conscious of his mate circulating at the far end of the hall, surrounded by dames and warriors, young *fem* and scholars, politicians and kings, he took pride in her popularity.

His queen seemed to draw all the strata of society into her orbit by her calm, friendly manner. She ignored no one, didn't care about the social status of the person seeking audience. Devtorvas knew Nnora loved her new subjects, as he knew his people returned the love of their new *Chyya'va*.

Tonight marked the third and last day of the welcoming party, which looked to continue unabated far into the night. The lively entertainment and lavish food riveted the attention of the guests, so that few noticed when the *Chyya* gave the *Chyya'va* a high sign and both quietly slipped away.

Hand-in-hand, they escaped the noisy crowd of revelers, intent on taking advantage of their freedom.

As they exited the ballroom, Dev noticed Lori Brewster hugging the far wall. "We need to do something about your sister, *Nippa*. She is still not happy here."

Nnora's hand tightened in his grip, signaling her tension. "I know. I plan to talk with her tomorrow. Much as I dislike the thought, we may have to send her home to Earth. I just don't believe that is the answer. I don't feel returning Lori to Earth would be in her best interests."

He drew his love closer to his side. "We will help her all we can. For now, don't worry over it. This night is ours. We will deal with Lori and all our other problems on the glowrise."

"Our other problems? What has Dohsan done now?"

He threw back his head and laughed. "I shudder to think!"

Still chuckling, he drew her down the garden path to their private section of the palace.

They stopped off at their daughter's nursery, the Queen insisting on her nightly visit. The room echoed with the sound of the departing battalion of royal nurses who had early on learned to vacate the room whenever the royal parents visited. Dev stood by as Nnora leaned over her little princess, glad to see their babe soundly sleeping.

Not even for his daughter would he give up this hard-won time with his consort.

"Look at our little slob!" Dev teased. "That's a thousand-credit *sirrilian* sheet she's drooling on."

The child lay on her stomach, bottom in the air, small fist stuffed in her mouth. Nnora leaned over, brushing a feather-light kiss on her downy cheek. "*Sirrilian* sheets can bear up under a lot more than baby spit, Dev. Don't act like they came out of your Reconstruction Budget. This set is a gift from the Regent of Barodan, so our daughter may drool to her heart's content," she huffed in hushed tones.

Dev smothered a laugh, hustling his wife out of the nursery and into their royal suite. A quick backward glance saw the nanny horde resuming their positions, descending upon the sleeping princess in full force. "I refuse to argue with you. I have something much more important planned for us."

"Oh, yeah?" She looped her arm about his neck, smiling up at him as he backed her into their private quarters. "What did you have in mind, mister?"

"This!" Supporting her knees with one strong forearm, he swept his startled mate up and hurried across the room, plopping her down on their wide bed. His heavy body came down hard on top of hers, crushing her into the mattress, one impatient thigh wedging between her legs.

Nnora laughed up at him, her eyes alight with love. "You certainly seem to like this position. We end up in it so often."

"I believe I once told you I intended to be inside you at every opportunity, every minute I could steal away from the grueling job of ruling two planets."

"And you are a *Rb'qarmshi* of your word," Nnora crooned, shifting under him, canting her hips up at him and rubbing her mound against the growing bulge of his arousal.

He lowered his mouth, engaging her in a series of wet, deep tongue-entangling kisses while he removed both their ceremonial trappings with a considerable lack of adroitness that revealed the intensity of his need. He stroked his naked chest against her full, luscious breasts, sighing in relief as he felt her nipples poking into his chest. "I need you inside my *terat*, *Nippa*. I need to be inside you…*now*."

"I need that, too," Nnora panted, helping Dev remove her torn top. She inserted her breasts into his dilated *terat*, one nipple at a time. Reaching between them, she took hold of his *cherzda* and squeezed, causing his cock to spurt out in another inch of growth.

Growling in need, he covered her hand with his broader one. Together, they aimed his jutting cock at the mouth of her pussy. He inserted a finger to test her readiness. Her cunt dripped with her fragrant juices, ready for fucking.

He entered her on a smooth, gliding slide, sinking the outthrust length of his *cherzda* into her welcoming heat. Inch by slow, thick inch, his blunt tip forged past her tight entrance, pressing apart her slick pink lips.

He shuddered as he halted halfway in, refusing to seat himself to the hilt. The bulbous head of his staff throbbed, wedged tightly in her narrow pussy. The heat and pressure against the head of his cock and along the shaft was tremendous. The molten glove of her cunt gripped his swollen sex deliciously.

He wanted to thrust hard and fast into her until his sensitive head thudded against the mouth of her womb. Instead, unwilling to risk hurting her, he contented himself with miniscule movements. He fucked into her with little bumps and grinds that had him shaking, his buttocks tightening. Yet he resisted the growing urge to rut mindlessly, mindful of his mate's delicate build.

Beneath him, Nnora let out a husky groan, a pleasure sound he recognized as signaling the beginning of an orgasm. He ran a hand down her torso, latching onto her little warrior. Dampening his finger in her essence, he circled the puffy clit round and round until it swelled and firmed, poking through the soaked lips of her pussy.

He pushed his cock another inch into her steamy depths and she came apart in his arms. Her pleasure sounds increased, and he drank them in, his muscles tightening, nerves jumping, balls rising in response. He surged in deeper, pulled back only to return, sliding smoothly through her slick depths until he butted against her womb.

Stretched out beneath him, his long thick cock rested in her, finally seated to the hilt, she didn't want Dev's caution and care. She wanted him driving into her cunt, reaming her pussy with the strong, deep strokes she needed to attain the world-shaking orgasms she could feel building within her quivering flesh.

"Oh, gods, yes!" she cried, flinging back her head and locking her legs about his hips as she came a second time. "Fuck me, Dev! Fuck me deep. Fuck me *hard!*"

Instead of giving her what she demanded, he pinched Nnora's nipples in the spasming grip of his *terat*, drawing strongly on the meaty little tips. He felt her shivers, heard her gasps and moans as he milked her breasts. He shivered as well, groaning aloud when his balls drew up to nestle under his cock. *Not yet! Not yet!*

"Are you all right, *Nippa*? Tell me when I can move." Two long *Fael* had passed since they'd been able to fuck, and his control threatened to unravel any moment.

"By the stars—*now.*" She ground her hips up into his pelvis, trying to entice him into thrusting.

Relieved to hear her frantic command, reassured of her need for him, he rocked his body into hers. He devoured her lips, his tongue mimicking the thrusting of his *cherzda*.

It had been two whole *Fael* since their child's birth, and Nnora wasn't going to allow her cautious mate to ride her tamely. Grabbing a fistful of his long silky locks, she tugged his head up, forcing him to meet her eyes. She sensed Dev had reached the outer limits of his control and she helped it erode.

"I'm not in the mood for a session of gentle lovemaking," she gritted through clenched teeth. "I want to be taken hard and deep." She grasped the base of his cock, ran her fingers up to where they were connected. "Don't hold back! I want a fast and furious fuck. I need to be filled with every last inch of this glorious cock."

She knew she had to arouse him beyond his celebrated, vaunted restraint, before he would break down and give her the forceful, pounding fuck she longed for. It took a lot for Dev to relinquish control, but once he did, he was magnificent.

"C'mon, lover," she moaned, thrusting her nipples deeper into his *terat,* raking her nails through the curtain of his black hair, then on down his back where she gripped his waist, feeling the muscles shift and roll beneath her hands. "Shaft me good. Pound that thick, wonderful cock into my hot, hungry pussy."

"If I hurt you..." Dev moaned, his hips flexing, cock sinking impossibly deeper into her drenched cunt. She loved the deliciously erotic sense of being impaled on his mammoth pole of marble-hard flesh, loved having her pussy overfilled, stretched to capacity by her husband's huge erection. A sinuous ribbon of carnal joy wound throughout her body, binding her nerves with prickling ropes of sensation, causing her clit to pulse and fill with hot blood.

"You won't. You never have!"

"You're so small, *Nippa*—"

"I hate to tell you this, love, but Devtoria is bigger than your cock. And she came out the same way you are going in."

Dev hung over her, an arrested expression of comical proportions washing over his face, a sheepish grin widening his mobile lips.

"Have I been holding myself back for nothing?"

"Well..." Nnora considered, "maybe you should continue to take it slow initially, but once the preliminaries are taken care of, there is no reason you cannot unleash your full passion. I hate it when I feel you are holding back...holding out on me. I want all you have to give, I want your surrender, just like I surrender to you, always. C'mon, babe...give it the old gusto!"

Dev laughed. "I love your quaint turns of phrase, *Nippa*. All right, let's try it your way." He carefully released her nipples from his *terat*, applying mouth and teeth to the reddened points, coaxing both into a tighter, harder erection.

"Turn over on your belly. I want to take you—how did you tell me once? Oh, yes—doggy-style."

Grabbing her about the waist with one hand, Dev pulled Nnora's plump cheeks apart with the other, opening her, preparing to sink deep into her hot sex. His heart beat hard and fast, ripping out a frenzied cadence as he gazed down on the lush curves of his *Nippa's* ass cheeks, her tight little back hole winking at him, her sweet cunt oozing her honeyed juices. Many of his darkest fantasies had featured taking his *fem* in just this position, knowing his cock could achieve a greater penetration, but he'd always denied himself, never indulged his deepest held desires, too fearful his lust would get the better of him and he would end up hurting his beloved mate.

"Spread your legs and raise your bottom for me."

"Doggy style, huh?" Nnora said breathlessly, settling her knees wide apart and lifting her bottom. "In your case, I'd say you're more equine than canine."

Dev nudged the heavy tip of his sex through the portal of her dripping sex, his knees going weak with pleasure. Love and lust swamped him as he slowly entered his *cherzda'va*. With a lusty groan, he surged forward and she rocked back. He sank to the depth of her quivering, flexing cunt with a loud groaning sigh.

Freed from worry, Dev pumped his cock in and out of *his* pussy—his *Nippa*—his strong thrusts causing her full breasts to sway back and forth. He held her close to his chest, nuzzling the fragrant skin in the bend of her neck, using one hand to brace himself so he could fondle her breasts with the other. He tugged on the hanging tips, keeping them hard while he sank into her repeatedly, reveling in her groans of pleasure.

"Oh, Dev…oh-h-h, Dev…*Yesssss!*"

"Lean forward, *Nippa.*" Dev alternated slow, easy thrusts with short, hard jabs of his cock. Her upper body slid to the bed as she folded her arms, her new position lifting her buttocks high. The rhythmic contractions of her wet pussy kneading his swelling length drove him wild. He licked dry lips, reaching down to rim her stretched opening and flick her clit before surging forward into her.

He impaled her over and over, banging his cock up to pound the opening of her womb, thudding into her quivering cunt. Sliding an arm under her armpit, he lifted her torso, still slamming into her.

Her moans rose in volume as his tempo increased and he responded with animal-like fervor to the raw sounds of her carnal joy. Still he struggled to restrain his powerful motions, lust-driven but unable to completely relinquish his habitual care for his loved one. Gasping for breath, he employed the last of his resolve and pulled out of her, the rampant length of his cock glistening with their mingled juices and so hard it hurt, throbbing and pulsing with his roiling seed.

Rolling her over, he positioned her crossways at the edge of their high bed. Grabbing her beneath the knees, he spread her legs wide and went back in, this time with a series of forceful lunges that arrowed straight to the heart of her cunt.

She clamped her legs about his flanks and she screamed, "I'm coming!"

"Then come for me, *Nippa.*" He ground against her, sinking heart deep into her milking pussy, deeper and harder and stronger than he had ever dared go before.

"I'm going to make you come all night long," he promised, pulling out until the broad head of his cock popped through the contracting lips of her pussy. He lurched forward; surging back through the pink slit again, and then again, until he finally embedded his mushroomed head in the mouth of her womb, holding the chamber open for the swiftly rising tide of his seed.

His *zhi* flowed out slowly at first, slicking the walls of her pussy, relaxing them, enabling them to expand enough to contain his burgeoning growth. The muscles in his belly fluttered as he felt her inner cunt muscles contracting around his growing cock plug, her body doing its part to weld them both together. His cock began to pulse, each vibration echoing up and down the length of his swollen shaft, the rubbing friction of her tight channel constricting about his buried length driving him mad with *almost there* lust.

A few more flexes of his hips had Dev's back bowing as his spine stiffened under the flashpoint heat of his approaching orgasm. With a hoarse cry, he threw himself against Nnora, jack-knifing into her welcoming heat. Canting his body so each outward surge scraped her up-thrust clit, he furiously fucked her pussy, hands clasping her thighs, holding her wide for his taking.

His cock plug formed, slowing then halting his frenzied movements. Emptying himself into his mate's spasming pussy, he managed enough control to *seat* her nipples, locking his upper body tightly around hers.

With love, need and passion ripping through him, remaking him, Dev fucked her nipples as his *cherzda* throbbed in her cunt, coaxing forth another orgasm. Head flung back in ecstatic triumph, his *terat* received her precious gift, taking from her even as he shouted, coming so hard he flooded and overflowed Nnora's womb with hot blasts of seed, her transformed "gift" returned to her on a surf-pounding wave of love.

* * * * *

"Devtoria is bigger than my *cherzda.*"

"Yes, love." She snuggled tiredly against Dev, almost asleep.

"Can we try another position?" His voice rose on a hopeful note.

She opened one eye and stared at her mate, exhausted. He was disgustingly energetic for someone who had come to completion four times already. "*Now*?"

"Yes!" He bounced up. "Look, put your legs like this…and…bend this way. Okay, now brace yourself against the headboard like this—"

"You satyr!" She shook her head at his antics, playfully batting away his hands. Laughing, feeling renewed by their love play, she launched herself off the edge of the bed's wide mattress and darted across the room, throwing her sex-crazed lover a teasing, over-the-shoulder come-hither glance.

Behind her, Nnora heard Dev scramble off their bed in pursuit, his bare feet thudding firmly on the carpeted floor. She sped up, racing away, luring her mate in the direction she wanted him to go.

"What a luscious, juicy sight you are giving me, *Nippa.* Your swaying hips and bouncing breasts has my *cherzda* hard as stone. So run, search out some supposed safety. When I catch you," he called out to her, voice sounding thick with excited lust, "I'm going to fuck you until your cunt is raw."

"Promises, promises!" Nnora taunted as she skirted their private parlor and increased her speed. The sound of Dev's laughter grew louder as his longer legs inexorably closed the distance between them.

She made it through the bathroom door before Dev ran her to ground. She evaded his first grab for her, fetching up against the ornate *utankli* tiled sink just as his arms came about her, capturing her in a crushing embrace. She winced in fake fear as Dev flung his head back, letting out a roar of triumph.

Crowding her against the sink, he proceeded to press ardent, open-mouthed kisses all over her face and neck. He lifted her up on the vanity, pushing her knees apart and wedging his torso between her legs, his hands going to her nipples to pull and tug the still-sensitive points, making them poke out in red defiance.

Far from complaining, she rolled her shoulders, pushing her breasts into Dev's warm palms. She licked suddenly dry lips, her breasts heaving under her agitated breaths. Her belly felt hollow, muscles fluttering wildly as Dev sank to his knees, electric-orange eyes fixed on her mound. Slowly, he bent his head, making a production of sniffing at her cunt, causing a rush of hot liquid to overflow her heated channel in response.

"Unveil yourself to me!"

His husky command caused a second spurt of juices to slick her labia and clit. Her entire body went slack as she felt the first heated touch of his lips against her weeping pussy. She hardly felt the impact of her head smacking against the decorated tile, too busy eagerly reaching down to unveil and offer herself to Dev.

Whimpering in need, she watched, tugging and pulling on her own nipples as he spread her swollen folds to lap at her. He ran his broad hot tongue up her slit and flicked it against her clit. His masterful mouth ate at her, sucking at her entry, his tongue stabbing inside her, poking at that maddening spot that caused her nerve endings to tingle and spark. He soon had her sobbing with ecstatic joy, quivering and jerking in a muscle-clenching orgasm, screaming in abandon.

Dev relentlessly continued to lap at her clit until she collapsed against the mirror in a boneless puddle of spent desire.

Regaining his feet, Dev bent solicitously over his wife. "Remember that promise I made you?" He licked the taste of her essence from his lips as he gathered her up and started back to their bedroom.

"The one about being in me whenever possible?"

"That one, too." He stopped walking long enough to sample her irresistible nipples.

"You mean the one where you promised to fuck my cunt raw?"

His tongue laved one breast with rough broad strokes. He gave the engorged crest a sharp bite. "I forgot that one," he admitted. "Is "my" cunt raw? Let me see…"

He detoured to the living room and stretched his queen out on the divan. Easing her legs apart, he opened her cunt lips with his thumbs and closely examined the lush pink folds. He couldn't resist leaning down to give her fluttering pussy a couple of hard tongue swipes.

"*Hhmmmm*...delicious! Remind me to have the chef add this dish to the menu of my personal favorites." He dipped his head and burrowed back into her wet folds.

Nnora took a mock swing at his head, her light blow glancing off without effect. "You are such a comedian."

A moment later, she gathered a handful of his hair in both fists and dragging his head away from her aching pussy. "Darling, stop for a while, okay? I'm a little sore right now."

Dev immediately sat up away from her, a frown marring his handsome visage. "You should have said something earlier, *Nippa*. By *Deth's* gate, I never meant my teasing words to become truth. I'm so sorry—"

"Dev, when a man routinely gives his wife multiple orgasms, the *last* thing he has to be is sorry." She sat up and ran her hands up her husband's arms, catching his hands before he could drag them through his disordered locks. "It's been almost three Earth months since we last fucked, Dev, so of course, I'm a little sore. I wish you would stop fretting over it."

"I vowed never to hurt you!" The mulish expression on her mate's face did not change.

Nnora heaved an exasperated sigh. "Dev, trust me, you didn't hurt me one bit and I know my tenderness won't last for long because I'm already creaming, wanting you inside me again. I just need a few moments between sessions...and I have the perfect activity to keep you happily occupied until we're ready for you to feed that delicious hunk of meat to my hungry pussy."

Dev blinked, looking at her with anticipation. "What are you speaking of, *Nippa*?"

She swung her legs off the divan and sat up, smothering a smile at Dev's obvious eagerness. "You know I had Lori bring me a lot of items from Earth, some of my favorite things I've been without for a long time?"

Dev nodded his head. She could almost see the question marks in his eyes.

"Well, I asked her to bring me a specific item, just for your enjoyment, and now that it has arrived, I get to live out one of my favorite fantasies!"

She rose from the divan, gesturing Dev to stay put. "I'll be right back. While I'm gone, I want you to go to our room and stretch out on the *Metari* rug." She shivered sensuously, recalling the play of flickering light from a crackling fire and the decadent feel of thick, dense fur caressing her naked flesh the times Dev took her in front of the fireplace. She swallowed remembering the weight of his body pressing hers into the furs as he plunged between her legs, fucking in and out of her, driving her mad with passion. She wanted to invoke the same sensations in her beloved husband.

She took out a small jar from the bag Lori had delivered and placed it aside as she gathered a shallow bowl, a small soft painter's brush, and a plush towel.

Nnora turned on the water and let it run. When the water reached the temperature she desired, Nnora filled the shallow bowl and tucked everything else between her side and elbow and returned to her waiting husband.

She froze in the doorway, breath knocked out of her in sudden awe. *My God, this man is beautiful enough to stop my heart.*

Dev lay at his ease on the *Metari* rug, the dense black fur a vibrant frame for the dark maple tone of his skin…and what skin it was. Tight and taut in all the right places, stretched over well-defined muscles that rippled underneath with life and vitality. His long, lustrous night-black locks lay about his head and shoulders, blending with the fibers of the animal fur. His eyes were wide open, staring at her, lust and love plainly stamped on his handsome face. His cock, distended and full, lay on his belly, swaying with his shifting movements, his *zhi* already glistening at the tip of the bulbous head.

All this is mine!

Nnora swallowed thickly, heart thumping, clit swelling and throbbing with excitement. Her breasts grew tight, nipples engorged as she slowly walked towards her lover, her hips shifting seductively under his hot gaze. She went to her knees beside him, carefully placing the bowl and other items on the floor within easy reach.

Keeping her eyes focused on his face, Nnora began lightly running her fingertips over Dev's brow, soothing and arousing him in soft, languorous sweeps. "I want you to relax and enjoy this." She pressed against his broad shoulders, holding him down. "Promise me you will remain still and accept whatever I do or I will have to bind you to our bed."

A raspy laugh answered her. "Bind *me*? I do the binding in our bed, *Nippa*. Never forget that!"

"Then show me you have the will power to remain still without restraints, my love."

Her challenge given, she resumed her slow, drawn-out pleasuring of her husband. Her focus on his face, she dropped soft, open-mouthed kisses on his brow, his eyes, his cheeks and chin. Avoiding his lips, she nuzzled into the warm flesh between shoulder and neck, recalling how his lips and teeth at her corresponding spot always sent shivers of arousal dancing through her, causing her toes to curl.

A groaned protest made her laugh. Coming back to his firm mouth, she nipped at his lower lip, tugging until he relented and let her in. Her tongue swept in tangling with his, dueling for supremacy. Dev raised his head, forcing his tongue into her mouth, sucking at her lips. She pulled back.

"Uh, uh, love. I am in control here."

"*Arrgghhh,* you are killing me!" Dev's head fell backward. His eyes twinkled, and he stuck his tongue out at her, wiggling it a bit before batting his eyelashes and giving her a simpering smile.

She battled the grin tugging at the corners of her mouth and proceeded down his body, her lips brushing the strong column of his neck and shoulders. She swirled her tongue about each masculine nipple, tugging and nipping on them until they stood erect and tight. She blew on both peaks. Her cool breath wafting over the damp flesh caused his skin to pucker into goose bumps. His breath caught then started again, faster.

Chuckling, she stuck her tongue into one of his *terat*, poking it in and out and playing catch with the chest muscle that tried to trap her tongue inside.

She loved having Dev spread out beneath her, open to her advances. And she thoroughly enjoyed being in charge. Thoughts of the contents of her jar—and her plans for their use—actually caused her to tremble.

No longer willing to wait, she reached for the towel and began running the soft, absorbent cloth all over her husband's body.

"What are you doing, my *Nippa*?"

"Drying you, my love. You recall Lori is a biochemist…"

"Yes. And…?"

"And I told her what I needed…" Nnora finished with the towel and laid it aside. Reached for the jar and unscrewed the cap. "She designed this especially for us. Well, for you."

"What is it?"

Nnora lifted the jar to the light. "At first glance, it looks like plain water, but it is something you will appreciate far more than H-2-0, my dear." Dipping the brush into the liquid, she painted an invisible circle around the flat buttons of Dev's nipples, then brushed the fluid over the raised flesh. She even dipped it into the shallow mouths of both *terat*.

"Do you remember when you asked me what my nipples felt like when they are immersed in your *terat*, when your enzyme releases and coats my nipples?"

Dev nodded.

"Well, I couldn't explain. I didn't have the words. This fluid acts like my favorite hair conditioner. In fact, it was using my conditioner that gave me the idea. See, I love my hot oil hair conditioner. It heats up when water is applied."

Dev raised his eyebrows and flashed a speculating look from the jar to the glistening brush. "I don't feel any heat."

"You will!" Nnora chuckled. "There is a difference between the hair conditioner and this concoction Lori dreamed up for me. The fluid activates with the application of my saliva. Let me show you—" She dipped her head and licked the tip of one flat, round nipple.

"Aaahhh!"

"Like that, do you?"

"Yesss," Dev hissed from between his teeth. "By *Deth's* ballocks...yes!"

"I tried this on myself first, to make sure it wouldn't harm you. This is how your *terat* make my nipples feel." She told him between delicately wet licks around the base of the erect, engorged nubs of male flesh. When she laved the inside of his *terat*, Dev's torso came up off the rug.

The sound of his harsh breathing echoed in the spacious room. She smiled and pressed him back. "Down, boy, it's still my turn. I haven't even made it to the main event, yet."

"Get on with it, *fem*!" Her husband's growled command almost convulsed her in laughter. She had no intention of hurrying this session.

Taking her time, she painted and licked, brushed and laved...all the way down to his bellybutton. She had to hold Dev's jutting cock out of the way while she painted the little dip of flesh. He was so erect, so hard, his cock bounced and bobbled, making its presence felt, refusing to lie down tamely.

After thoroughly licking and nuzzling Dev's inverted button, she turned her full attention to the impudent shaft. From root to tip, she brushed the invisible fire over, around, and under it, covering every spot. She made sure to lavish his balls with the clear coating. Then she proceeded to swipe a wet path over each highlighted area with her mouth and tongue.

"Holy *uzak*!" His hips jerked up from the rug. "You have painted my *cherzda* with *acid!* You are burning me alive, *Nippa!*" His hands caught her head between his palms, trying to wrest her away from his cock and balls.

With her lips she clung to his rampant cock, while her hands kneaded the mound of his ball sac. Its tightness signaled he rode the rising edge of orgasm. She gave him a few more swipes before she addressing him. "Calm down, Dev, this is my gift to you. Lori guarantees this liquid will not harm you. I love this monster too much to allow harm to come to it or you." She tightened her palm around the thick shaft of his cock. "Lie back down and let me finish you. *Please*?"

The low, desperate sounds bursting from his lips and the rippling convulsions of his stomach muscles were her only warning of Dev's eruption. Spine stiffening, back bowing, hips snapping up, he exploded beneath her hands and mouth.

Groaning and shaking, Dev thrust his cock deeply into her mouth, crying out as he came. Fingers clenched in her hair, he fucked her face while his seed gushed from him in torrents.

She swallowed and swallowed again, trying to catch every drop but he ejaculated in such copious spurts, his *zhi* overflowed her mouth. Saliva and cum dribbled from her lips.

Dev breathed harshly, air rasping in his throat, his lungs laboring to keep up with his gasping demand for oxygen. Rising to his knees, he took command of their loving.

Lifting Nnora up, he flipped her over onto her back and eased her to the furs then simply sat and watched for a few moments, waiting for her to begin exhibiting the effects of swallowing his aphorismatic sperm.

Her breasts took on a rosy hue and her thick nipples engorged with blood. He grinned. Kneeling high between her thighs, the bulk of his body held her open to his lustful gaze. Her little clit thrust from between the deep pink folds of her pussy. He breathed in deeply, inhaling her delightful aroma, his gut clenching as he imagined how she would respond when he painted her clit with her own brand of liquid fire, but first…

He leaned over Nnora and took a jutting nipple between his lips, letting her feel his teeth as he tugged and suckled on her engorged flesh. He gave the other nubbin equal attention until both were red and hot to his touch. Gathering saliva in his mouth, he laved her tips until they were swimming in moisture and then he took the brush and dipped it into the jar. Locking his gaze on hers, he swabbed his *terat* with the dripping brush, applying a liberal coating. His mouth turned up in a wide smile as he set brush and jar aside and lowered himself over Nnora, preparing to *seat* her nipples. He took her mouth in a deep, lush, tongue-tangling kiss before drawing back to whisper, "Let's burn together, *Nippa!*"

* * * * *

An eternity later, Dev leaned back to watch Nnora as she convulsed in another bone-jarring climax. Filled with lust and love and above all, pride in his choice of life-mate, he helped her rise from the rug, supporting her as she leaned on shaky legs, wobbly from the many ecstasies he'd forced upon her.

He hefted his mate up in his arms and strode to the bathroom and the sonic shower where he gently cleansed them both, preparing for another bout of lovemaking. His heart stuttered anew as he realized that every time they fucked they truly made love. Nnora was the queen of his heart…and of his cock—his *cherzda'va* in all verity.

"I am not through delivering on my promise to make you cum all dark long," he said, conversationally resuming their earlier conversation as if there had been no break.

"What?"

"I figure it is still four or more hours till glowrise. Between my imagination and your magic liquid, we should be able to mange another eight or nine more orgasms for you."

Nnora's gulp was audible.

"Yeah," Dev drawled, "I am a *Rb'qarmshi* of my word." He swept Nnora off her feet and carried her back to their bed.

* * * * *

The *Chyya* and *Chyya'va* were unavailable for audience the next day.

The End

Glossary of Words and Phrases

Words

'abret – Daughter of…

'abri – Son of…

Cherzda – Male sexual organ; cock.

Cherzda'va – Literally: Cock-riser or "my cock's possession"; colloquially: life-mate.

Chyya – Ruler (king/queen) interchangeable between sexes.

Chyya'va-Literally: "my ruler's possession"; colloquially: co-ruler.

Cycle-Rb'qarmshi/Rb'nTraqi year = 1.538 Earth years.

Deth – A mythical figure of *Rb'qarmshi* prehistory. He was a trickster who challenged the gods and as punishment was given several impossible tasks to achieve. He was allowed to command the assistance only of those he had succeeded in tricking. Another famous character in *Rb'qarmshi* mythology was *Hel*, commander of *Pythin's* armies. While mighty in battle, Hel was gullible in the extreme. Deth constantly deceived him to the point they became almost constant companions. Common curses include: By *Deth's* ballocks; By *Deth*'s gate; By *Deth* and His minions; By *Deth's* pillars; *Deth*-brat; *Hel* and *Deth*.

Fael – measurement of time. Closely resembles a month. 1 *Fael*=1.230 Earth months.

Fem – Female.

Flower – A physical sign of feminine arousal. The female gives off a scent that attracts the male, causing his *terat* to soften.

Gifting – the act of the female's secreting the catalyst that activates the male sperm, rendering it viable.

Glen – The syllable at the beginning of the name that denotes a first-born child and heir.

Glowrise – Daybreak.

Hurdles of Pythin – *Pythin* is the *Rb'qarmsh*i god of war. The hurdles of *Pythin* refer to a task the god set the trickster *Deth* for stealing the Commander of his Armies.

Lorme – shuttle craft that seats 20. Powered by *Riahc* generators.

Metari – densely furred wild and ferocious animal that ranges the high mountainous area of southern *Rb'qarm.*

mr'nok – disaster.

Nanofyle – the interactive biological computer programming of a nanobyte.

Nippa – Course, crass term for a female's sex. Permissible as an endearment among mated pairs.

Pava – the *Rb'qarmshi /Rb'nTraqi version* of ovulation. A female undergoes this fertile cycle every three Earth years. Last for a duration of 1.5 Earth years.

Qarm – male from Rb'qarm.

Rb'kylla plant – Plant that grows only on *Rb'qarm.* Only source of the feminine enzyme necessary to induce male potency.

Rb'qarm – Planet of Glendevtorvas' birth. Home planet of the colonists on Mars.

Rb'qarmli – Language spoken by all Rb'qarmshi and Rb'nTraqi.

Rb'qarmshi – Belonging to or coming from the planet *Rb'qarm.*

Rb'nTraq – Planet colonized by *Rb'qarm* in the distant past. The inhabitants revolted against their parent planet and a civil war ensued that lasted over 200 years. The *Rb'nTraqi* lost the war.

Rb'nTraqi – Native of Rb'nTraq.

Rejas – Technically, the name of the evil, hateful, demonic god of *Rb'qarmshi* theology. Loosely used as Hell! Damn! I'll be damned!

Riahc – clean power source created by harnessing sub-atomic particles. Used to power generators and vessels.

Rojas – Technically, the name of the pure, loving, supportive god of *Rb'qarmshi* theology. Loosely used as: good lord! Heavens! Will you look at that!

Seating – the insertion of female breasts (or other body part) into the male *terat.*

Sirat – testicles.

Sirrilian – Having to do with the planet *Sirrilic. Sirrilic* is a member world of the Trade Consortium.

Terat – Male sexual organs situated below the nipples. These mouths are filled with muscles which milk the breasts of their mate or lover. The *terat* soften when aroused, and secrete an enzyme that causes the production of the female's gift (the activated fluid that triggers male fertility).

Tlinis – female breasts.

Traq – male from Rb'n*Traq.*

Uzak – loosely translated: shit.

Zhi – male pre-cum that carries an enzyme that causes the interior walls of the female sex to become more elastic to accommodate the increased swelling of the male organ during orgasm.

Phrases

"Chyya! Hoden bra'qu…? Malau ne macinee?" Literally: "Ruler! Are you attacked? Is there need for my service?"

"Sh'tai, craal i nohtan'ka!" Loosely: "Warriors, a moment alone, please!"

About the author:

Camille Anthony welcomes mail from readers. You can write to her c/o Ellora's Cave Publishing at P.O. Box 787, Hudson, Ohio 44236-0787.

Why an electronic book?

We live in the Information Age—an exciting time in the history of human civilization in which technology rules supreme and continues to progress in leaps and bounds every minute of every hour of every day. For a multitude of reasons, more and more avid literary fans are opting to purchase e-books instead of paperbacks. The question to those not yet initiated to the world of electronic reading is simply: *why?*

1. *Price.* An electronic title at Ellora's Cave Publishing runs anywhere from 40-75% less than the cover price of the exact same title in paperback format. Why? Cold mathematics. It is less expensive to publish an e-book than it is to publish a paperback, so the savings are passed along to the consumer.
2. *Space.* Running out of room to house your paperback books? That is one worry you will never have with electronic novels. For a low one-time cost, you can purchase a handheld computer designed specifically for e-reading purposes. Many e-readers are larger than the average handheld, giving you plenty of screen room. Better yet, hundreds of titles can be stored within your new library—a single microchip. (Please note that Ellora's Cave does not endorse any specific brands. You can check our website at www.ellorascave.com for customer recommendations we make available to new consumers.)

3. *Mobility.* Because your new library now consists of only a microchip, your entire cache of books can be taken with you wherever you go.
4. *Personal preferences are accounted for.* Are the words you are currently reading too small? Too large? Too...**ANNOYING**? Paperback books cannot be modified according to personal preferences, but e-books can.
5. *Innovation.* The way you read a book is not the only advancement the Information Age has gifted the literary community with. There is also the factor of what you can read. Ellora's Cave Publishing will be introducing a new line of interactive titles that are available in e-book format only.
6. *Instant gratification.* Is it the middle of the night and all the bookstores are closed? Are you tired of waiting days—sometimes weeks—for online and offline bookstores to ship the novels you bought? Ellora's Cave Publishing sells instantaneous downloads 24 hours a day, 7 days a week, 365 days a year. Our e-book delivery system is 100% automated, meaning your order is filled as soon as you pay for it.

Those are a few of the top reasons why electronic novels are displacing paperbacks for many an avid reader. As always, Ellora's Cave Publishing welcomes your questions and comments. We invite you to email us at service@ellorascave.com or write to us directly at: P.O. Box 787, Hudson, Ohio 44236-0787.

Printed in the United States
24646LVS00001B/55-708

9 781843 605591